The Boy on the Porch

DEE HOLMES

BERKLEY BOOKS, NEW YORK

THE BOY ON THE PORCH

A Berkley Book / published by arrangement with
the author

PRINTING HISTORY
Berkley edition / January 2003

Visit our website at
www.penguinputnam.com

ISBN: 0-425-18815-9

BERKLEY®
Berkley Books are published by The Berkley Publishing Group,
a division of Penguin Putnam Inc.,
375 Hudson Street, New York, New York 10014.
BERKLEY and the "B" design
are trademarks belonging to Penguin Putnam Inc.

PRINTED IN THE UNITED STATES OF AMERICA

10 9 8 7 6 5 4 3 2 1

Chapter One

The house was bigger than he'd expected, and for a few seconds he stood on the sidewalk just staring. The last place he'd lived had been low and square and brown with prickly bushes that always scratched his arms when he was told to cut them.

He ventured a few steps closer, his eyes wide, trying to take it all in. Lots of windows, and big enough to walk through if they'd been doors. They didn't just lay on the house like they were pasted there, they seemed to push the house back in some places and pull it forward in others. It must be like a maze inside with all those curves and angles.

He walked carefully up the walk that was made with crooked flat stones that fit together like a puzzle. He'd never seen a stone puzzle. On either side, a lawn swept toward the house, sprouting flowers at the edges and some even in the middle. And trees. Not scrawny, limp, naked sticks stuck in wire jails, but tall and fat and kingly, dressed with leaves so thick and heavy they made noise even in the slight summer breeze.

The front steps seemed to pour down to his feet from a porch with cushioned furniture, shiny tables, and baskets of flowers. It looked like an outdoor living room.

All of this to thirteen-year-old Cullen Gallagher was a mind blower. He'd thought nothing would ever scare him after that night in the last foster home, but this place did.

Not scary in a bad way; this was a good scare. A heart-pounding, can't-wait scare, a Christmas morning scare when, to his surprise, there really had been presents with his name on them.

He stood up a little straighter, walked up the steps, grinning like Linc told him. "You're happy about this, so start with a smile. Don't cringe like some trespasser." He was happy; he was psyched.

Cullen rang the doorbell and wished he'd done a better job scrubbing his hands. Women get pissed about dirty hands. Linc had told him that, too.

He rang the bell again and waited. Guess they didn't have a maid or an official door-opener like he'd seen in movies about rich people. He liked that. He wanted them all to himself.

Finally, when there was still no answer, he walked around the yard to the back. More flowers and a garage for two cars and another porch.

And a dog.

Uh oh.

Cullen skidded to a halt as the large black, brown, and white animal came forward, then suddenly stopped. He didn't look fierce as much as he looked curious. Cullen pushed his hand into his pocket and came up with a dog biscuit. His mom had always carried cookies when she walked in case she encountered a dog. Weird how he'd thought of that when he'd been getting ready to go a few hours before. But like other things his mom had said, he remembered them when he needed to.

Linc had laughed, but not in a funny way; he told him if some industrial-strength dog came at him, he'd be the one getting eaten and no biscuit would save him. To Cullen's relief, this one didn't growl or bark or charge him, he just looked.

Cullen extended his hand, palm up, like his mother had told him. "Hey, boy, you the guard around here? Sure is a nice place. You like cookies?" At this, the ears came up and the animal sat, tilting his head slightly. Cullen tossed a biscuit toward the dog, who managed to snag it before it hit the ground.

"Nice catch." The dog munched it down in two bites. Cullen threw another one and again the dog caught it, chewing and looking for more.

Cullen eased his way toward the back porch, tossing biscuits like a trail of crumbs. "Hope they didn't get you to scare away robbers, boy. If they did, they got suckered." But he couldn't wait to tell Linc that the biscuit trick worked.

On the porch, he knocked on the door and peeked in a side window to the kitchen. Jeez, he could throw a football in there and hardly ever hit a wall. The room had two sinks, pots hanging from the ceiling, and he could see a leather couch at the far end. No answer to his knock.

Then, just because he wanted to, he searched around for a door key, but found none. And then he knew why none was needed. The door wasn't locked.

No one home and the house unlocked? Were they nuts? Or maybe they depended on that fake guard dog. Too bad he hadn't planned to be a house tosser when he grew up—this place would be a great beginning.

But he didn't go inside. Linc would fry his ass if he found out.

Then his attention was caught by a porch glider. Like a wooden couch, it was big enough for three, had a yellow-and-white-striped mattress and pillows with flowers. And it moved back and forth when he pushed it. He looked at the seat of his jeans to make sure they weren't dirty, then eased himself down like he was about to bust eggs, then carefully pushed off like he used to do on that old tree swing at home. It slid back and forth, back and forth, back and forth. . . .

Nearby was a small refrigerator. Not a cooler, but a real refrigerator. Inside was a full unopened milk bottle, a carton of orange juice, cream, and a box of butter. He wondered why they were there instead of inside. There were a couple of cans of Pepsi and a bottle of beer.

A whole bottle of cold beer. His throat worked thirstily. He hadn't had any since . . . but as he reached for it, the memory roared back.

Hey, Cullen, don't be a baby.

I'm not a baby!

So have some beer.

I don't want any.

Chicken . . . 'fraid his old man will throw him out. Cluck cluck, chicken Cullen . . .

I'm not.

Yeah, well prove it.

Then, later . . .

You've been drinking, young man.

No . . . no . . .

Don't lie to me. No son of mine would drink and lie.

You're not my father. I hate you.

Get out. Get out of my sight.

Then his eyes had gone dark and he'd moved closer, smelling like old books and stuffy attics. Cullen had turned and run, his eyes bleary from tears. Why had his mother died? Why hadn't it been his old man?

Cullen squeezed his eyes closed, grabbed the Pepsi, and slammed the door on the refrigerator as if he could lock away the chain of rejection and pain. He sat again in the glider, pushing back and forth while he swigged down the soda and pretended this was his house and his glider and he couldn't wait to tell Linc everything. He closed his eyes, sinking back into the pillows, thinking he'd never felt anything so soft. Maybe this time it will work. Maybe finally someone will want to know him.

And just as he drifted off, he thought he saw the dog on the porch laying down at the edge of the steps. *He wants me to stay,* Cullen thought. *He wants me to stay.*

Annie Hunter put the top down on her BMW when she came out of the office. She was at the peak of her career as an interior decorator, and while she relished the challenge plus the enjoyment of working with a family wanting to redecorate their home, or even just a room, today had not been pleasant. Fabrics delayed, furniture backordered, and the cream-colored hot tub had turned out to be round when it was supposed to be angled. And then to top off the day, she had to meet her mother.

It was July and no sane person with a convertible would have the top down on such a sweltering day. Sunburn, windburn, and road grit. Enclosed in an AC climate was smarter. But it was Friday and she didn't have to worry about being poised and perfect and professional until Monday.

She glanced at her wristwatch, knowing she was going to hear it because she was late, but it couldn't be helped. Then again, her mother would have something to say even if she arrived early. Annie wouldn't call it a love-hate relationship, more of one where her mother insisted on either treating her as a child or chastising her for any behavior her mother assumed needed pointing out. Annie simply ignored most of it, but she wearied of the constant criticism, the inevitable attempt to let Annie know her disapproval.

She took off her jacket, and opened the top buttons of her blouse. In the car, she backed out of her parking space and headed in the direction of the cemetery.

Today was the first anniversary of the death of her

husband, Richard. His parents were in Italy, but Annie's mother had called her before she'd left for work that morning asking what she planned to do.

"Do?"

"Like as in flowers for the headstone? Surely you didn't forget."

"I didn't forget," she muttered. Annie sighed, irritation bubbling, but what would be the point? Forget? Not a chance. In fact, she'd awakened that morning immediately recalling that terrible phone call of a year before.

"Roses, then," her mother continued. "He loved roses. And oh how his rose bushes thrived when he was taking care of them. The last time I was at your house, Annie Jean, they looked sad and scraggly."

Annie gritted her teeth. "I'll buy some roses."

"Why yes, that would be lovely. A dozen or two, don't you think? Red ones. He did love red roses."

Actually, he didn't. But Annie wasn't in the mood to argue. And so she'd called May over at Silvia's Greenhouse and ordered the roses. She picked them up on the way, arriving at the cemetery and parking behind her mother's Honda. Richard had bought it for her two years before, when her Tercel had given out.

Marge Dawson had always adored Richard, and when at forty-two he'd died of a massive heart attack while working on a restoration project in Connecticut, Annie's mother had appointed herself as the queen mourner. Annie, who'd loved her husband beyond her ability to express, had been devastated by his sudden passing, but she neither put her sadness on public display nor did she expect others to continue to offer condolences long beyond a time when it became maudlin rather than empathetic.

Her mother's overdone wretchedness, Annie guessed, was due more to her own limited social life than to true grief. She had only a few friends, none of them male, and she suffered mightily the absence of Richard to flatter her and coddle her and spoil her. He did so with abundant charm and never with impatience because, well, because he was a kind and generous man.

Annie wasn't inclined to be so solicitous of her mother; she'd always believed Richard had tried to make up for her own failings in the devoted-daughter role. Issues with her mother that mostly surrounded the disappearance of Annie's father years before were made more frustrating by her mother's refusal to talk about it, ever. That stubborn silence, when Annie desperately wanted information, had left a gulf between the two women that Annie was in no hurry to bridge.

Now, as she approached the granite headstone, her mother was busy deadheading a rose bush that Annie had planted beside the plot, the previous fall. She dropped the discarded flowers into a basket she'd brought with her. "I was wondering if you were coming, Annie Jean. And look at your hair. My goodness, I had no idea it was that windy." Then she scowled. "I thought we'd decided on red roses."

Annie put on her best face. "Richard preferred yellow. I brought red ones for you to take home. You know he always gave you red roses on your birthday."

Her mother seemed jolted by the gesture, and Annie thought for just a moment that she really should try harder to get things settled between them.

"Why yes, he did. But it's not my birthday."

"I know, but I think Richard would want you to have them."

Her eyes welled up. "Oh, Annie Jean, he was such a wonderful man. If only he hadn't died so young. If only you'd had children . . ."

"Mom, don't . . . please."

"Annie Jean, you should have started much sooner."

"Yes," she said softly. "We should have, although I doubt it would have made a difference."

Annie turned away. No children was one regret she couldn't dismiss. She and Richard had figured it all out as if it were the master plan for the perfect life. Get their careers established, then Annie would ease into working from home so that when the babies started coming, it would all run smoothly. They planned on a nanny for those first months, but Annie intended to take care of her children. The nanny would just be there to help in a pinch. They could afford it, and Richard wanted only the best for his wife and family.

Except no babies came. Her periods came late a few times, and her joy soared, only to be sunk when her cycle resumed. Each barren month had been more wrenching for Annie than the one before. What was wrong with her? Why could her friends produce babies as if they were mother bunnies, and she couldn't get pregnant with one? Richard suggested adoption, and after that last failed year of doctor visits, infertility failures, and frustration, she'd agreed, but only if it was an infant.

They'd just begun meetings with a private adoption attorney when all the plans and hopes came to an end with Richard's sudden death.

Months later Annie thought about trying to adopt on her own, but the attorney didn't give her much encouragement, since she wanted an infant. Most birth mothers involved in private adoptions wanted two-parent families, and frankly she couldn't blame them. A child needed a mother and a father. The attorney suggested that if she would reconsider an older child . . .

But she wouldn't. And yes, that made her feel selfish, but realistically she thought it more selfish to take a child because of guilt than because of love and a real desire.

Now she placed the fanned bouquet of yellow roses in front of the headstone, her mother fiddled with it to get it just right, and they bowed their heads for a few moments of silence. Annie made sure the flowers had plenty of

water before mother and daughter returned to their re-
spective cars.

She retrieved the long white box of red roses from the
back seat. She'd parked in the shade to keep the sun at
bay.

Her mother cradled the box in a way she would never
have held an arranged vase. "You remembered that I like
to fix them myself."

"Yes."

"I'm sure they are lovely, but never as beautiful as the
ones Richard grew."

Annie sighed. Why did she put herself through these
never-able-to-please moments? She turned away and
climbed into her car.

"You really should put the top up, Annie Jean. Now I
know why you looked so mussed up."

*Actually, I just climbed out of bed with a sexy stranger
who made me come three times in ten minutes.*

But even given the irritation she felt toward her
mother, she couldn't be that flip. Although God knew she
wanted to be. She started the car, but she didn't put the
top up.

"Goody-bye, mother."

"Yes, yes, good-bye, dear." But her mother had already
forgotten the chide; her attention was on peeking inside
the box at the roses. "Now, I could put these in the living
room on that pie-crust table. Right near that picture of
Richard."

Annie drove away, as her mother's mutterings trailed
off behind her. She drove home with the wind making an
even more tangled mess of her hair. As she turned into
the drive, she anticipated a quiet Friday afternoon and
evening. She wanted a cool shower, an icy glass of char-
donnay, and no phone calls.

She started toward the back porch, coming to a stop
when she saw Rocky sprawled across the top step. Just

beyond the husky, she saw someone . . . a teenage boy, a very ragged-looking teenage boy, asleep . . . asleep? A ragged teenager asleep on her glider?

She drew closer, setting her briefcase on a wrought-iron garden bench. She shoved her hair back, tucking it behind her ears. Rocky, from the porch, simply looked up at her.

"You're supposed to scare them away, not invite them in for a nap. And what have I told you about strange biscuits?" Rocky seemed to grin, and Annie reached into her bag for her cell, took a few steps away, and called the police.

"It's a young boy, poorly dressed, obviously exhausted since he appears to be sound asleep. No, I have no idea. I've never seen him before. Maybe he's a runaway, or he's lost. It's forty-five Morning Glory Drive. Yes, I'll be waiting. Hurry."

And within a few minutes, as promised, a patrol car followed by another pulled into her drive.

"He's still asleep," she whispered, as if she might wake him.

The officer wasn't as gracious. He glanced at his partner and the two officers following behind. Annie hadn't intended for this to look like police overkill, but a poorly dressed teenager in this neighborhood did tend to make the police take notice. It struck her as a bit elitist, but she also knew that her neighbors had become rabid about teenage troublemakers ever since a spate of robberies had taken place the spring before.

"Kid out from booze? Drugs?" one officer asked another.

"Or both."

Annie hadn't thought of either. She just thought he was asleep.

"Sure don't look like he belongs around here."

The first officer started toward the porch, and Rocky

rose. Annie hurried forward, soothing the dog, who looked none too happy about his biscuit source being disturbed.

"This dog must be his," the officer said warily.

"No, he's mine."

"Got a leash?"

"Well, yes, but he won't—"

"Sorry, ma'am. The animal needs to be restrained. He appears to want to guard the kid."

"Don't be ridiculous. He doesn't even know who the boy is."

Rocky growled at that point, and Annie, wondering what kind of biscuits had made the usually placid Rocky suddenly aggressive, said, "I'll get the leash."

But even with the leash Rocky wouldn't budge. The eighty-pound husky resisted as if he'd been glued to the step. Annie pleaded and coaxed, and chided the dog about keeping the police at bay when he should have kept the kid at bay.

Finally, she distracted the dog enough so that the first officer was able to get onto the porch. The boy had awakened with all the commotion and sat there blinking as if he hadn't a clue where he was or what was going on.

"What's your name?"

"Jeez, what's goin' on? I didn't do nothin'." Even from where Annie stood, she could see his eyes dart fearfully from one uniformed figure to the next.

"What's your name, kid?"

"Cullen. Cullen Gallagher."

"Where do you live?"

"Uh, right now?"

The cop scowled. "No, tomorrow. Don't be a wiseass. Yes, right now."

"Seventeen thirty-two Central Street. Look, I didn't come here to toss the place."

"Central is miles from here. What are you doing in this neighborhood?"

"I have some business here."

Annie almost smiled. It wasn't cockiness, but a sureness of tone that had her thinking that whatever the business was, he was very serious about it.

"You don't say," one of the men mocked. "And what might that be?"

He peered around the two officers, looked at Annie and then pointed.

"I think she's my mother."

Chapter Two

Annie blinked in astonishment, too taken aback to even respond. Rocky sat placidly beside her as the officers turned to one another. Their expressions ranged from curious to a kind of "now, there's a new excuse" look. The boy, however, leaned sideways so he could see her ... waiting, waiting. . . .

Waiting for what? she wanted to ask. For her to rush forward and embrace him? She resisted saying *This is a joke, right?* But no one was smiling, and the boy certainly wasn't guffawing. In fact, he looked so earnest and serious despite his obvious mistake, she felt sorry for him.

Admittedly, she was less than fascinated by teenage boys. Her experience was limited to the opinions of friends, who mostly complained that they mumbled, dressed as if looking nice were akin to drinking poison, and all wore attitude like a designer label. But this boy— perhaps it was the presence of the cops, or his misguided belief and out-of-nowhere appearance on her porch— seemed different.

"Mrs. Hunter? What about what the boy said?"

"He's obviously gotten some bad information. I have no idea what he's talking about."

"You have no idea what he's talking about?"

She stared, irritation making her defensive. She wanted to ask him whether he was deaf. "Why don't you ask him the questions? He's the one who came here; he's the one making this stuff up. Absolutely, I don't know what he's talking about. I don't have any children. I couldn't possibly . . . uh . . ." then she stopped, horrified that she'd been about to toss out personal details to a scruffy kid and a bunch of cops she didn't know. Get a grip, here. What was it Richard always said? In a verbal showdown, the one who remains silent the longest gets the benefit. She just wished her silence was due to some brilliant strategy rather than total befuddlement.

To her relief, one officer scowled, approached the boy, and hauled him to his feet. "Okay, kid, whatever you're up to, you're coming with us."

"Nothin'. Lemme go. I didn't make no mistake. I know what I'm doin'. I had his name."

Annie scowled. "His name? Whose name?"

"You can ask Linc. He helped me, and Linc wouldn't of said it was okay if it wasn't."

"Linc who?"

"McCoy."

Which meant nothing to her, either.

"Richard Hunter," the boy said. "I had his name."

"Well, it must be another Richard Hunter. My husband didn't know anyone named Linc McCoy. Where did you or this McCoy person get the idea to come here?"

"I just got it, that's all," he said wavering as if suddenly realizing he might be in some serious trouble.

Annie's earlier flirtation with empathy for the boy vanished. "Look, you come here with a preposterous accusation about me, and when that didn't work, you throw out my husband's name and then refuse to say how you got it?"

"What? You think I just made it up? I ain't sayin'

nothin more 'til I talk to Linc. He'll make it all right. Linc makes everything okay."

"So where is this Linc?"

"At Noah House."

Far back in the reaches of Annie's memory, some recognition stirred. The police all began to look restless and bored, making Annie wonder if Linc McCoy either walked on water or ate teenage boys with disciplinary relish.

She'd heard of Noah House, but not beyond a passing knowledge that it was a place that housed kids with problems, and was always listed as a needy charity during the Christmas season. But Annie suddenly recalled why recognition stirred.

Richard and his partner had given a check to Noah House as part of a local town-wide business fund-raising project a few months before Richard had died.

It's a good cause, Annie, and sorely underfunded, Richard had told her. *Evan and I thought our yearly donation would not only be appreciated, but put to better use if given directly.*

Annie knew Richard had always been a softie when it came to helping kids. She'd always known that their childless marriage had been difficult for him. He'd born the brunt of his family's disappointment, who undoubtedly blamed her because when adoption was mentioned, she'd wanted an infant. "Beggars can't be choosers," Vera Hunter had informed her, making it quite clear who she thought was responsible for Richard not being a father. Richard's father had always been kind and never vocal like Vera, but Annie knew that he, too, had wanted grandchildren from Richard.

Richard had never accused Annie, and in fact had fiercely taken Annie's side, going so far as stating to his mother that their childlessness was not a topic that either of them would discuss, defend, or explain. And that had ended it.

Since Richard's death, Annie, with some surprise, had enjoyed a cordial and even warm relationship with Richard's mother. A bit of a puzzle, she admitted, but nevertheless she'd embraced the family ties.

"How long has it been since we dealt with Linc McCoy?" one of the officers whispered.

"Not long enough. Last time was when that fifteen-year-old kid was picked up for drug dealing near Bedford Elementary and he accused McCoy of beating the shit out of him. The boy's PD filed charges."

"That were dropped."

"And no one knows why."

"Kid was probably lyin'."

"Or McCoy pulled some strings."

"There's that, too."

Annie listened with a mixture of disbelief and horror, conjuring up an image of Linc McCoy that was both curious and frightening.

Apparently his reputation had some resonance with the police. She wouldn't have said that the air hushed at the mention of his name, but it definitely changed.

"Okay, kid, you're coming with us."

"What for? I didn't do nothin'."

"Wait a minute," Annie said.

"Ma'am, the kid is from a halfway house that takes kids who get dumped from the foster-parent program. He ain't no choir boy."

"I didn't get dumped!"

"Yeah? You were a model kid, huh? Never gave none of those families no problems?"

Cullen glared at them. "I ain't saying nothin' til I talk to Linc."

Annie said, "I'd like to talk to Mr. McCoy, too."

Cullen was put in one of the patrol cars. It backed out

of the drive, and before the other one followed, the officer driving said, "Mrs. Hunter, I should warn you. McCoy isn't your garden-variety counselor for troubled kids. He has a lot of maverick ideas, and looking at you, ma'am, well, you're probably not gonna like him much."

"I already don't like him. What could he have been thinking sending that boy here with his outrageous claims? I want to know why he was told I'm his mother, and I intend to make sure Mr. McCoy answers that question. I'll follow you to the station."

After the second police car left, Annie unleashed Rocky, who immediately found some stray biscuit crumbs. In the house, she set her briefcase in her office and gave up any idea of a nice relaxing evening of wine and silence.

In the bathroom she looked in the mirror and pulled a brush out of the vanity drawer. Using some pins, she arranged her hair, then washed her hands, repaired her makeup and rebuttoned her blouse. Whoever this Linc McCoy was, she had no intention of looking as rattled in her appearance as she felt inside.

Maverick ideas usually intrigued her, for in the business she was in, it was the maverick ideas—those unexpected concepts—that kept her interior decoration skills fresh and in demand.

But she wasn't at all sure how maverick ideas worked when dealing with troubled kids. She would have thought consistency and nothing too "out there" would be the way to help kids who'd probably had very inconsistent lives and been subjected to way too much experimenting. But then how would she know? She had no kids, and the only teenagers she ever ran into were the untroubled kind like her two nephews.

But truthfully, how Linc McCoy ran Noah House didn't interest her nearly as much as how her husband's name got into the hands of Cullen Gallagher.

* * *

Linc McCoy stood in the middle of a bedroom that had enough broken furniture, graffiti-trashed walls, and shit-smeared windows to more than warrant the call he'd gotten just twenty minutes earlier.

"Linc, I don't know what to do with him." Penny Brewer, a foster parent for the past five years as well as the wife of an ex-marine buddy of his, looked more distressed and disappointed than shocked. "We knew he'd been doing some drinking, and we tried to deal with that. I don't like to whine and complain, since Nick and I both know these kids aren't ideal teenagers, but this behavior is beyond even my patience."

Linc moved deeper into the room, finding a cache of small liquor bottles among the Archie Comics and dirty socks.

"Linc?" Penny stood some distance away.

"Yeah." Linc wondered if he trashed then got drunk, or trashed because he was drunk. The order of things always made a difference to him, and especially so when it involved ever-evolving teenage motives.

"Say something. You're always so cool and laid back about this stuff that I wonder if anything ever shocks you."

Shocked. Ah yes, he should be, or at least pissed off or maybe disappointed, but instead he was only tired. Tired of innovative destruction and weary of the sure-to-appear vocal do-gooders who always assume that beneath the destruction lay a potential saint.

You must be more understanding, Mr. McCoy.

We cannot be so quick to judge the motives of others, Mr. McCoy.

Remember your own past, Mr. McCoy.

And listen. You must listen to the other side. Don't you

*believe in redemption, Mr. McCoy? In fairness? In help-
ing others?*

The problem he had with all of these observations,
comments, and criticisms wasn't that they had no elements of truth. They probably did. His uncertainty came
because the commentary was mostly delivered by those
who spoke not from experience but from the pages of the
most recent pop-psychobabble how-to book or from a
self-appointed expert whose closest ties with messed-up
kids came from a pristine office filled with case studies
instead of real life.

In real life, Linc knew, kids with altruistic motives for
being assholes were painfully scarce. One long glance at
Penny told a truer story of where the best of intentions
often landed. She honestly believed in redemption and
second chances and sinners into saints, but even a cursory
glance at her pale cheeks told him she wasn't so sure of
those beliefs right now. And that made Linc angry. For
the Pennys of the world didn't just talk and scold, they
jumped in with their hearts and their time; they were the
ones who kept the nasties at bay. And what had she gotten
for those efforts and hard work? A very unpotential saint
in one Eddie Montrosia.

The sixteen-year-old, who at the moment was curled
into a drunken blob amongst a litter of tangled clothes,
had severely tarnished Penny's usually unflappable ideals.

Linc stood over the teenager; he was so still he almost
looked dead, but he wasn't, as evidenced by a sudden
snort and a grab at his crotch. One thing could be said
about Eddie—no purple hair or nose rings or tattoos;
nope, all of those cost money Eddie would rather have
spent on booze or a buffet of drugs.

"Eddie? Come on, kid. You gotta move." But the boy
only curled up tighter. Linc kicked some of the debris out
of the way and crouched down, debating whether to just
carry the kid or make him walk. Glancing in Penny's di-

rection, he said, "Honey, I want you to call Max. He'll come in here and clean the place."

"I can't afford that."

"I'll pay for it."

"No. You can't afford it either."

Linc reached for his cell. "It's chump change, Penny." He punched out Max's beeper number, then another number the two men used to signal one another when they needed to get in touch quickly. Max returned the call within forty-five seconds. Linc explained, and hearing what he wanted to hear, he hung up.

"He'll have his crew here by six."

"Linc, this isn't right that you pay . . ." She twisted her hands together, but Linc knew that despite her objection, she didn't want to wade through Eddie's mess.

"Hey, a lot of things aren't right, including your efforts getting tossed in the Dumpster. Mind if I put him in the shower?" he asked, and she shook her head. He hauled Eddie to his feet while trying to not smell the stink and booze.

"Hey, whassa up . . . what you doin' man? Leave me alone."

"Shut up."

"Go fu—" But before Eddie got it out, Linc yanked his hair. "Ow!"

"Some soap for your mouth, too."

"You don't scare me."

"Oh, good. I was really worried about that."

Penny stepped gingerly through the mess to the dresser, where she pulled out some clean clothes. Linc dragged and walked the wiry, stumbling teenager into the bathroom. There he shoved the naked Eddie into the shower, turned on the cold water, and ignored the howls.

Penny came in, laying the clothes on the counter by the sink. "I can't thank you enough."

"Do me a favor, okay?"

"Anything."

"Call Nick and tell him you'll meet him for dinner. By the time you two get home, Max should have things cleaned up."

"I can't just leave you with all this. What are you going to do with him?"

"Get him sober and clean for starters."

"I don't want him just tossed into the street."

Linc raised his eyebrows. "What's this? Newly revised concern? When you called me you were so furious, I figured I'd find the kid hanging from his thumbs. Now, you're worried about me tossing him in the streets? Believe me, Eddie would like nothing better. Booze in abundance. Nope, the street would be too kind to him."

"Maybe I'm being too knee-jerk about this. Maybe I should give him another chance."

Linc spread his hands in compliance. "Say the word and I'm gone."

Then from the shower came a spray of obscenities.

"Our potential saint is sobering up," he said, undisturbed by the ruckus.

"Oh God, I don't know what to do."

"Honey, you need to discuss all of this with Nick. Go have dinner and in the meantime I'll call Social Services, tell them the story and that a clean-and-sober Eddie is at Noah House."

She cast a furtive glance at the closed shower door, jumping back when Eddie pounded on the Plexi. "How will that make us look?" she asked anxiously.

Linc sighed. "Smart."

She managed a small smile, then kissed his cheek. "If I didn't adore my husband, I'd marry you."

"Promises, promises."

She backed out of the bathroom and Linc sat back on the commode, stretching his legs out, bracing one boot on the closed shower door so Eddie couldn't open it.

More obscenities.

"Eddie, tone down the screeching, and make use of the soap. We both know you're not comin' out till I can't smell you anymore."

His cell rang.

"Yeah."

It was Vesco, a former drug addict turned good citizen thanks to the patience of Noah House. Now he was one of the many volunteers that Linc depended on. "Got a call from the cops. They got Cullen."

"For what?"

"Best I could figure, he fell asleep on some porch at that Morning Glory house and when the lady called the cops, kid made a big deal about wanting to talk to you."

"A high crime for sure."

"Cops say you gotta come down before they release him."

"Cullen okay?"

"He sounded more bewildered than upset. How you like that word, Linc?"

"Excellent." Vesco had only learned to read in the past year and had enthusiastically adopted a new-word-a-day regimen. "And Cullen is bewildered about . . . ?"

"Why he's being jerked around."

"I warned him this wouldn't be a cakewalk."

"Guess they weren't glad to see him like he wanted them to be. The cop said the Hunter woman is big-time pissed."

"And don't you just hate it when women like her get pissed? Safe in her big house—such a rough life." Linc could hear his own cynicism backed up with a heavy plate full of irritation and disgust.

"Linc, she's probably okay. You don't even know her."

"I have a feeling I'm about to."

But Vesco continued to defend her. "So she's got some

bucks. . . . Doesn't mean she shouldn't get some answers."

"I believe Cullen is the one looking for answers."

A long sigh was all the response he got.

"What about Richard Hunter?"

"Don't know. Cullen said he wasn't there. Kid said he'd been a no-show at the police station so far."

"Okay, I'll figure it out when I talk to Cullen. I'm bringing Eddie Montrosia to the house."

Vesco swore. "We're maxed out."

"We're always maxed out. I gotta go. Call the cops and tell them I'll be there within the hour."

The Bedford Police Station was a squat brick building with more angles than a trapezoid, thanks to renovations and additions in recent years to accommodate a larger force. The fast-growing population in Bedford had exceeded even the most generous out-year projections. The town, located in the northern section of Rhode Island, didn't have the cachet of Newport with her mansions and beaches, or the recent renaissance in Providence. But the medium-sized town, with its quiet meandering streets, its independent businesses and family-friendly neighborhoods, had been discovered in the late eighties, and the population had exploded. And with growth came a Wal-Mart to anchor a mid-sized shopping center and yet another superstore, Maguires, similar to Home Depot, was in the planning stages. These changes in Bedford also brought the inevitable rise in crime, hence Noah House.

When first proposed, the Noah House project had more than its share of not-in-my-backyard objections, but the folks in favor of the experimental endeavor eventually prevailed. The home for troubled boys wasn't a dismal building with institutional starkness; it was a real house, a renovated Victorian. If not for the abundance of boys playing basketball or hanging on the front steps, it might have been mistaken for the weathered grandeur of a shabby estate. It was a huge structure with fascinating architecture and numerous rooflines. Located on the south end of town, the house had been purchased by a now-deceased benefactor who had been inspired by a similar home in southern Massachusetts. Here there would be no warehousing of kids as if they were dogs in a kennel, there would be bedrooms, a real kitchen, and as true a sense of family as could be provided in such an environment.

At any one time as many as twenty-five boys were living there, and because over the years so many of the kids had turned their lives around, Noah House had been a source of pride for Rhode Island. It was privately funded, with some compensation from the state; the workers were mostly volunteers, and those who were paid weren't getting rich.

Linc McCoy had been the director at Noah House for almost three years. His own past included a mother who never gave up on her marriage or her oldest son despite enough reasons to walk away from both and never look back. To Linc, Evelyn McCoy personified sainthood, a realization that came to him late in life when all he deserved from her was disgust and banishment. Thanks to her determined belief in him, he had managed to get an education at a local community college between drug stupors and boozy hazes. He still remembered her at his graduation, standing tall with tears in her eyes, hands clutched tightly around a straw bag where she carried what money she hadn't hidden in her house—no banks for Evelyn McCoy—and a diamond bracelet. The piece of jewelry was all that remained of a necklace-and-earring set given to her by her husband in the heyday of Artie McCoy—a local hustler who moved up from the shady to the illegal to murder.

Then there was Michael, his kid brother, who had been

killed on Father's Day when Artie and Evelyn McCoy and
their two sons were on a picnic in a nearby park. The
gunshot, fired by a small-time hood who thought Artie
had ratted on him, had been intended for Artie, but it had
been Linc who'd seen the shooter, and in a wild attempt
to save his father, didn't know that ten-year-old Michael
was in direct range of the bullet.

His instinct to save his father had kicked in, but the
consequences of that heroic act had resulted in disaster
when it was Michael who had gotten shot. The shooter
had fled when other picnickers came running, but Linc
remembered little beyond his baby brother still and dead
on the grass. Michael's instant death had become a defin-
ing and devastating moment that twisted inside of Linc
like knots of rusted barbed wire. He couldn't get away
from it, he couldn't bury it, and he couldn't talk about it.
Those who knew the details never mentioned them in
front of Linc.

He'd been seventeen at the time, a little wild, a little
too cocky with his fast car and bevy of girls who were
all hot for Linc McCoy. After Michael's death, Linc's
teenage fascination for driving at sound-barrier-breaking
speed and getting laid as often as he opened a new beer,
had lost their attraction.

But Linc vowed to never forget, to envelope his brother
as a symbol of a life cut short, potential lost, a family
irrevocably changed and damaged forever. And because
he'd framed the tragedy in a bigger way than blanketed
guilt or self-pity, that broader truth nearly destroyed Linc.

He moved into drugs—anything he could find, for
when he was high enough he could almost forget Michael's body in the grass.

While Linc had been soaked in drugs, it had been his
father, flush with revenge, who'd gone after Michael's
killer. And for that Artie McCoy had gone to prison.

"Get your life fixed, Lincoln," was what his father told

him the day he was sentenced. "Nothing more can be done for Michael. Your mother is making me crazy with her blaming me about how I killed her two sons. One dead and one good as dead. She can't take much more. You already saved my life, now I want you to save your own."

"I can't."

"Don't have time for your self-pity, boy."

"You think this is about me? It's about Michael and all that he might have been."

"Then it's self-pity bullshit. Too late for Michael. This is about you. And it's about your mother finding a reason to be proud of some member of this family. Your future don't look too grand and glorious, boy. You're a mess and I don't take no pride in messes. Clean yourself up or I'll get it done for you."

A promise that Linc ignored to his peril, for Artie Mc-Coy never issued demands that didn't have consequences. The old man delivered, and none of it was prettied up in sensitivity and understanding, nor was there worry about Linc's self-esteem or pretty stuff like positive reenforcement. There was no rehab with counselors who brought food for the body and spiritual nourishment for the soul; no handy legal supplements to ease him off the drugs. His old man had his own cure. He had a buddy of his lock Linc in a one-room windowless cabin a long way from anywhere. Food was provided once a day and a bucket for pee and shit. Primitive, barbaric, and probably illegal, but the old man couldn't have cared less. He was out to save his oldest son in the best way he knew how.

Linc howled and cursed and begged and cried, but there was no release. His father had positioned a watcher nearby to check on him, but Linc never knew that until years later. He thought he was alone and on his own, and he hated his father. At the end of a week, he was let out, still cursing and howling, but he was clean.

"Next time, it's two weeks," the old man warned.

"Wise up, boy. My reach is farther than your most creative hunt for the next fix."

A tough lesson, but one learned by action and not a lecture. His old man never gave a second warning when the first one was ignored.

And while Linc was restrained by the rules of Noah House from implementing similar creative measures, that didn't mean he didn't consider them.

Now, parking his Harley in front of the Bedford Police Station and behind a BMW convertible, he looked over the cream-colored car. He'd known a few of those intimately a long time ago, and while that memory wasn't drug related, it sure hadn't been healthy. He'd learned that those with the most toys have too much money and too little sense.

He climbed off the motorcycle and pocketed his keys, walking past the expensive car with barely a backward glance.

Inside the station, the desk sergeant nodded and pointed down the hall. "They're waitin' for ya."

He passed an empty interrogation room and the lounge where two detectives were drinking coffee. At the door to the room where Cullen was, Linc knocked.

And as soon as he entered, he looked for the boy.

Scruffy, still too thin despite the Noah House cook's determination to fatten him up, but there was no mistaking his relief at the arrival of Linc.

Also in the room were two officers and, he presumed, Mrs. Richard Hunter.

"Good afternoon," Linc said easily, his voice even and polite.

"It's about time, Linc."

"Had another problem that had to be taken care of."

Cullen came forward. "I didn't do nothin' wrong, Linc. Honest to God. I didn't touch nothin' and I didn't go in

the house. I did just what you said and look at the shit
I'm in."

Linc squeezed his shoulder. "You did fine. We'll get
it straightened out."

"You told me what to do and I did it," he repeated, as
if Linc might have missed the terror in his eyes. "They
ain't gonna make me go some other place, are they?"

"No. And what have I told you about gettin' up a head
of steam before anyone lights a fire?"

"I wasn't scared until I saw all the cops." His tone of
voice was more disappointment than malice.

"I'm sure Mrs. Hunter didn't intend to scare you."
Then he looked directly at the woman across the room.
Physically, she was what he'd expected—attractive, expensively dressed, and here in the gray plainness of the
police station she stood out colorfully in her yellow suit.
She stood erect and poised, trying not to touch anything,
holding herself as if to project a dignity-in-distress aloof-
ness. But to Linc, who'd known too many women like
her, she looked a bit mussed and more than a little frazzled, a state he figured was due to the heavy stress of
cooling her heels at the Bedford Police Station.

"Mr. McCoy, I'd like an explanation," she said.

"Mrs. Hunter, I came down here because Cullen is
here. And he's here because of you, so I would suggest
that the explanation come from you."

"From me? It was my house and my property and he
was the trespasser. What was I supposed to do when I
came home and found a boy I never saw before asleep on
my porch?"

"We know what you did," Linc said, but she continued
as though justifying her actions.

"He was a stranger. Strangers in my neighborhood who
are on private property aren't politely quizzed. I'm sure
that calling the police wouldn't have occurred to you. You
would have just sent him on his way."

"Actually, I would have asked what he was doing there. Did he tell you that?"

"He thinks I'm his mother. It's the most ridiculous thing I've ever heard."

"It's not ridiculous when you believe it's true."

She sighed, exasperation evident. "Believing something doesn't *make* it true. Cullen trying to find his mother is understandable, but he has made a mistake believing it's me."

"Where's your husband?"

She seemed genuinely taken aback by the question. Then she lowered her head and squeezed her hands together. "He passed away a year ago."

Linc scowled. He hadn't known that, and the drain of color in Cullen's face indicated this was the first he'd heard, too. Or was it? Perhaps he had known and had simply refused to believe it. Denial, if embraced long enough, can make facts a lie and lies the truth. As bizarre as denial of a death might appear to an adult, to a kid whose relationship with adults had systematically resulted in abandonment . . .

"I'm sorry," he said softly, knowing his words were for Cullen as much as they were for Hunter's widow.

"So am I. He was a wonderful man and I miss him very much."

And for just a few seconds they stared at one another as if sharing some depth of understanding on how it feels to lose someone cherished.

Linc was the first to look away. Then she adjusted her shoulder purse and walked toward the door.

To the police, she said, "I'm not going to press any trespassing charges."

"All right, ma'am. See the desk sergeant on your way out."

She nodded, turning to Linc. "Mr. McCoy, I do think I'm owed some details about how such a mistake could happen. Perhaps we could meet—the three of us . . . sometime . . . in the next few days." She fumbled in her handbag, took out a business card, and scribbling a number on the back, handed it to him.

The white card was for a business on Locklyn Avenue called DESIGN AND DETAILS. Linc had never heard of it.

"That's where you can get in touch with me."

And with those words, spoken with a detached, almost superior tone, Linc's earlier sympathy disappeared like early morning mist. For a few moments he'd almost believed she wasn't one of those pampered, rich and haughty women so adept at presenting a practiced appearance of understanding and patience, and oh yes, generosity. Don't forget the all-important generosity. Linc knew the type; he encountered them at fund-raisers where he had to patiently listen to their ideas on how to deal with "boys at risk" so as not to jeopardize a potentially large check. Women like Brooke Varner. Linc shuddered even now at how stupid and blind he'd been about Brooke. But if Linc knew anything when it came to women, he didn't have to learn the ropes twice.

And here with Annie Hunter were a few signs, admittedly not all, of another Brooke. Her cool voice, an edge of impatience, but at the same time he couldn't imagine Brooke even stepping foot in a police station, never mind staying around waiting for the arrival of a guy she wasn't going to like. Yet the Hunter woman had waited. He had no clue what significance that had, and quickly decided it didn't have any.

"This your home phone number?" he asked abruptly.

"It's my private line. I own the business."

"Why am I not surprised?" he muttered.

"I'm sure little surprises you, Mr. McCoy," she snapped. "My purpose is neither to impress you nor to annoy you. I work hard and my hours are erratic, therefore you'd be more likely to get ahold of me at the office than at home."

But instead of simply nodding and saying something benign such as "I'll call you," Linc pushed a bit more. "Why don't you come to Noah House? I'm not real good on making phone calls." He gave her the address. "Sorry, I'm fresh out of business cards."

That last comment was flip and rude and he knew it. And it didn't get past her. Her eyes sparked with obvious irritation. "I'm not a big fan of sarcasm, Mr. McCoy."

"No, I don't imagine that your are." He had to give her credit; she gave as good as she got. "I'll tell you what, let's give us both some time and get together at your house, tonight."

"At my house? Tonight?"

And for the first time she looked very unsure.

"Other plans?"

"Well, yes, uh, actually no, but . . . I just thought . . . I thought if we met somewhere else . . ."

"You'd be more comfortable."

She looked directly at him and never flinched. "Yes."

She was scared. But of what? Of him? Possible. After all, he was a stranger and Cullen was a stranger making an assumption that she'd fiercely denied. But tossing aside letting strangers into her house, he realized something else was at work here—where all of this could go and what it had to do with her. Linc had little doubt that a meeting would have very little to do with Cullen and a whole hell of a lot to do with her.

A boy comes out of nowhere, claims she's his mother which in turn forces her to prove she's not; hardly a strong position for her, given the fact that should this get around, she'd be viewed with some suspicion. If Cullen is right, then she's a liar and deserves to be called such. But should Cullen turn out to be wrong, the damage would be done— to her reputation, perhaps her business . . . and how would she get any of that back? Perception, he knew too well, often obliterated reality.

Suddenly Linc just wanted it over. He didn't want to argue or reassure or even hope that in the end this would all work out for Cullen.

"Name the place," he said and didn't miss her relief at his compliance.

"There's a coffee house in the Locklyn Plaza."

He did know where that was. He glanced at the clock on the wall. "Say about seven?"

She looked more resigned than pleased; he wondered if she was really as mystified as she looked. Linc watched her leave before turning to one of the officers. "Any details on what happened to Richard Hunter? How he died?"

One of the cops scowled. "Nothing out of the ordinary that I recall. It wasn't a huge funeral like those that get big write-ups on the obit page. I had the detail directing traffic from the funeral home so I could tell by the number of cars. Hunter was part owner of a house restoration business over on Compton. Other owner is still there as far as I know."

"You happen to know the other owner's name?"

"Nah. Sorry."

Linc nodded, figuring that finding out a name shouldn't be too tough.

The cop looked at Cullen. "You got some proof about them being your parents? It seems strange that a married couple would give a kid up. She said they didn't have any kids."

"I know what I know," Cullen said defensively.

"Hey kid, what you think you know don't mean nothing. I asked about proof. The lady don't look screwy like she'd forget she had a kid."

Cullen lifted his chin in defiance. "I got the proof. I got it—"

Linc interrupted. "Take it easy, Cullen. The officer has a point. We need to do a little research before we go and talk to Mrs. Hunter."

Chapter Three

Annie's insides were still hammering five minutes after she'd driven away from the police station. What an odious man. And talk about a chip on his shoulder. For him to look at her and judge her as some rich bitchy snob who was clueless as to how the "real" world worked . . . Just recalling it made her furious all over again. Who the hell did he think he was?

She glanced at the dash clock. She had to meet him in an hour, and although she'd agreed, walking on broken glass had more appeal. In fact, never seeing or talking to him again would suit her just fine. Then she shuddered; she was thinking just like her mother.

Don't know what I'm gonna do with you, Annie Jean. You just won't see him as he really is. He ain't here. He left me. Don't see how the details change any of that. I don't want to talk about it no more, and I ain't going to.

Annie had wanted answers about her absent father, and her mother had viewed that as a personal intrusion, so Annie had had to go searching on her own. But this was different, she reassured herself. This was an accusation that had no basis, no facts, not even some vague suspicion. This was just there like some odor she couldn't get away from.

However, more was involved than her own pride and outrage; she wanted to put to rest, once and for all, their ridiculous speculation.

She absolutely knew she wasn't Cullen's mother, but there'd been a number of references to Richard—which, in Annie's opinion, were the real travesty. She would deal with this, but first she needed to get her emotions under control and debunk whatever asinine theories McCoy presented.

Richard couldn't defend himself—and she fully expected to be told that her late husband was Cullen's father. If it wasn't so outrageous, it would be amusing. Annie, however, wasn't laughing, nor did she intend to just ignore it. She wasn't about to allow her husband's memory and reputation to be sullied by some jerk who let a boy in his charge fling their names around like confetti.

She was particularly wary of accusations that were difficult to *disprove*. Allegations that harvested a bonanza of gossip that made even the innocent look guilty. Ask the teacher accused of molesting students, or the politician accused of doing drugs, or her own father, accused of abandoning his family when the truth was he'd simply chosen not to live with her mother anymore. She'd grown up with whispers of pity because of "that awful Nathan Dawson."

When she'd defended her father, she'd gotten patient smiles, but no one believed her. *Prove* he didn't walk out on his wife, his kid, and his responsibilities. *Prove* he wasn't some deadbeat more worried about money for his next paintbrush than money for food. *All he cares about is nourishing his art, whatever that means* . . . one helpful neighbor had told ten-year-old Annie. *Prove* the stories are false—that was the mantra, and of course she couldn't, because her mother refused to talk about it and when Annie finally located her father, he had died.

And now Richard was gone and Annie was once again trying to puncture false charges. But this was different. She'd been married to Richard; she knew him better than she'd known anyone. Yet here was a charge coming out of nowhere that Annie had to disprove.

Too many of their friends knew of Annie's desire for a baby, too many knew of the visits to the fertility clinic and her sadness and frustration at finally having to reconcile herself to a very hard reality—she would never give birth to a child. She could hear it now: *All this time you were miserable because you couldn't have kids, and now we learn you had one and gave it away? Seems strange that a boy would come out of nowhere and make such a wild accusation. Why? What's the real story, Annie?*

She could hear Richard's mother asking those questions in horrified tones. *You had a baby, you just wouldn't have one with Richard? Haven't you put us through enough? Now this?* She'd never forget her in-laws' devastation at the unexpected death of their only son; it would be horrible if they heard some outrageous story about a child from Richard's past.

The boy was thirteen, which meant he'd been conceived and born around the time Annie had been totally immersed in doing temperatures, scheduled sex, and getting injections. Getting pregnant had become her life.

She and Richard had argued a lot that year—Richard had insisted they should adopt and Annie had rejected that idea, wanting her own child. Neither, of course, had happened, but it was years before Annie finally and forever accepted that the only way she would have a baby was to adopt. And even that had been thwarted with Richard's untimely death.

And now out of nowhere comes this.

Damn you, McCoy! Where do you come off wrecking

other peoples lives? And she was sure this was his doing. Cullen was a kid who probably had some fantasy about finding his parents, and McCoy was egging him on. Annie could sympathize with Cullen, but McCoy? No way.

Fueled by a new burst of fury, she made a wheel-screeching left turn, then braked and stopped. Her hands were sweaty and her throat ached. She took some deep breaths. *Get a grip. Killing yourself isn't going to be helpful, nor is getting angry—that only makes it appear as if you have something to hide.*

She knew she was being far too reactive, instead of quietly determined to get to the bottom of this mess. Annie, the defender of those who couldn't defend themselves. She almost smiled. How ironic that she would think of that—it was in her high school yearbook just below her photo. She'd come up with it because all the kids were adding something pithy or philosophical about themselves. Now she wondered if her fanciful description had been uncanny in its accuracy. First her father and now Richard.

She needed some perspective on this, and she needed to be cool and objective when she met with McCoy. But most of all she needed some advice.

She drove slowly, turning into the driveway of a sage-colored garrison in the process of having an addition added and parked behind a red Yukon XL. A basketball net hung from the garage, and two bikes sprawled on the lawn between the walkway and the front door. Annie stepped around it all, and went to the door, pulling open the screen and calling, "Betsy, it's me."

Betsy Kearns came around the corner, her youngest riding her hip. When she saw Annie's troubled expression, she shifted fourteen-month-old Lydia to the other hip and sighed.

"I know what you're thinking."

Annie almost smiled. Most of the time, Betsy did indeed know what she was thinking. "Not this time. You'll never even guess this one."

Without missing a beat, she said, "That guy who washed your windows made a pass and you sacked out with him."

It was so preposterous and so very Betsy that Annie would have giggled if she weren't so upset. "I'm saving that possibility for my birthday."

"I think I'm jealous."

"No, you're not, you're happily married."

"Oh yeah, I forgot about that." Betsy repositioned Lydia, then sighed wistfully. "Guess those glory days of bad boys and good sex really are gone forever. Can't even relive them vicariously through you."

Annie and Richard's sister had been close friends since they had been teenagers and dating guys that horrified their mothers. Going out with bad boys had a risky cachet and a hipness that nice girls like Annie and Betsy viewed as fun and daring. But when it came to marriage, fun, daring, and risky weren't elements Annie sought. Marriage was serious commitment, not reckless experimentation; Annie wanted safe and secure and dependable. She'd found all of those in Richard, plus a deep and abiding love.

Looking at Betsy, the differences between the two women were the exact things that made their friendship work. Betsy was disorganized and blunt with an innate ability to start something on a whim and find success. Annie was more cautious, more aware of pitfalls and failure. She expected to get it right the first time; Betsy wasn't so rigid. Annie planned her career in interior decorating with research and inventive skills as well as a focused education. Betsy shuddered at the sameness of a nine-to-five job, and when she'd gotten pregnant, she'd sought a way to make money at home. What began as an occasional writing submission to the local newspaper on the ups and downs of motherhood garnered a flood of mail. Her practical and often funny observations were such a hit that the women's-page editor invited her to do a weekly column.

Betsy, who hadn't really planned a career, ended up with one that became accidentally successful.

Annie had planned and hoped and dreamed; while she'd found bountiful success in her chosen field, she would have traded it in a heartbeat for children.

Betsy said, "Okay, if it's not bad boys and birthday sex then what?" She scowled. "Uh oh, something is wrong. What is it?"

"I was just thinking how different we've always been and yet remained such good friends."

"That's because I tell you when you're too anal and you tell me when I'm an idiot."

"This time, I don't know what I am. I think I need some advice."

"Then this isn't because I didn't make it to the cemetery?" She looked relieved, but still explained. "I tried, really I did, but Lydia has been coughing and feverish, so I hated leaving her with a sitter, and both boys were off God knows where, and Ron is useless when Lydia is sick. I meant to call you at work and tell you I couldn't make it, but by the time I got to the phone you'd already left. I phoned the house just a little while ago. . . ." Her voice trailed off as her expression changed from apologetic to concern. "Oh, Annie, something really is wrong, isn't it? Here I am babbling——" She looked closely at her sister-in-law. "You look awful."

"I feel awful." Annie sat down in one of the kitchen chairs. The kitchen could have been featured in an ad for chaos, mess, and disorganization. Dirty dishes, crumbs, spills, toys helter-skelter—in other words, a kitchen where a family functioned. Annie thought of her own immaculate house, and while too much chaos made her cranky, the calm, the daily and nightly silence, was at times too empty. Perhaps loneliness, more than a love of her career, was the reason she worked so much.

"I wish I was pissed at you. It would be a lot easier to resolve."

"Your mother?"

"Well, I was, but compared to the past couple of hours, Mom is up there with Glenda the Good Witch."

"So tell me—no, wait. Let me get us some wine and we'll go out on the porch."

"I'll get the wine. You've got your hands full." Annie stroked the baby's cheek and got a smile from her niece. She was at such an adorable age, an age she'd once thought she would see her own child experience. It had been awhile since she'd felt that lurch of sadness around babies, but it was back now with a twisting vengeance. Damn that Linc McCoy, and maybe she should damn Cullen, too, for his ridiculous claim.

Betsy got Lydia's bottle, while Annie got glasses and took the Pinot Grigio from the fridge. Out on the screened porch, Lydia climbed into her mother's lap and settled down, content with her bottle. Annie poured the wine.

Betsy took her glass, taking a sip, while all the time watching Annie. "Okay, let's have it."

It was the "let's get it done" attitude that Annie loved about Betsy. Where other friends would have been soft and cushiony with concern and sweet empathy, Betsy just got to the point. And for reasons that baffled even Annie, she covered her mouth and began to cry.

"Honey, I know today was hard. It was for me, too. I kept thinking how Richard loved July because so many of his roses were in full bloom, and how he used to come over and shoot baskets with the boys and then slip me money to buy them some insane video game they told him they wanted." Betsy blinked at the sudden moistness in her own eyes. "My brother. . . . For a guy who never got taken in business, he sure was a sucker when it came to Jimmy and Ronnie. They could wrangle anything out of him."

"He did indulge them, just like he indulged my mother. He was a kind and considerate man who made others feel important. And it's so unfair that now this has happened."

"What has happened? You're scaring me," she said, and Annie watched her eyes widen with concern.

"Well, I'm scared, too." And she told Betsy the whole story from the moment of finding Cullen asleep on the glider, to going to the police station, to dealing with McCoy, and finally to the upcoming meeting in less than an hour.

When she finished, Betsy looked as stunned as Annie knew she must have appeared in that initial encounter with Cullen.

"But you couldn't have kids." Betsy stared at her.

"Obviously."

"Then why are you upset at this? I mean this is a nobrainer. The kid has you mixed up with someone else. Tell him that and forget about it."

"It's not that easy. He specifically mentioned Richard's name, and that's what worries me."

"You think this is Richard's secret son that he kept hidden away in some faraway state? Come on, Annie. I never heard of anything so preposterous."

"Of course it's ridiculous, but proving it with Richard gone . . ."

"Why should you have to prove anything? Richard Hunter and Annie Hunter aren't unusual names. The kid got mixed up. Tell him so. Case closed."

"I already did that, but I don't think Cullen believed me."

"Just because he believes it, doesn't make it true."

"That's what I said, but it didn't work," she muttered.

"Okay, how about this. He wants to think he's found

his parents. And it's probably easier to believe this and deny the truth than face the fact that he's got to look somewhere else."

Annie sipped her wine. "What worries me is that I got the sense that there is more coming, something more substantial than a name and accusation."

"Like what? If there's no truth, what could he possibly have? You've denied it. You know it's not true. To meet with them undercuts that."

"I felt trapped. I mean with the police there, and McCoy practically daring me to meet him—"

"In other words, he intimidated you, put you on the defensive so you'd look guilty if you refused."

"Yes."

Betsy got up and gently put the sleeping Lydia down on a cushioned mat away from the sun. She motioned to Annie and they picked up their wine glasses and moved to the far end of the porch and sat at a small table where a game of solitaire had been abandoned.

"Annie, don't you see?" Betsy said softly. "By meeting with them, you're only adding credence to their charge."

"But I want to know why and how they got Richard's name."

"Have you considered they might be hustling you? Richard left you a lot of money. Guys trying to bilk a widow by throwing out some bogus charge that catches you unaware and has the potential to hurt you and Richard—and to then offer to drop the accusation for some cash—well, that's not unheard of."

"But nothing about money has been mentioned."

"Like they would in front of a couple of cops? Annie, you're not thinking straight. All they've done is make themselves look more credible by asking to meet you and straighten it all out. Cops think they're on the up and up, and when you agreed and the place for the meeting was stated, who's going to be suspicious? Besides, I doubt asking for cash will be the first move. My guess is they'll come with something that looks legitimate to worry you even more. Then when they sense your panic, they'll offer to forget the whole thing for a settlement."

It sounded incredible, and McCoy, as annoying as he was, just didn't fit Annie's idea of a hustler. Then again, Betsy could be right. He wouldn't act in some shady way around the cops. "Okay, say he is a hustler. Then I'd be paying someone not to lie."

"And my guess is that you'd do it to protect Richard."

"Come on Betsy, I'm not that stupid."

"It's not stupid, it's desperation. And you wouldn't be the first one to get caught in that snare. Not a bad racket if it works. Especially because you'd have to reveal private and personally painful information to prove the kid wasn't yours, and as for Richard—they could bring some woman forward who claims she had his child. This wouldn't even fall into a she said/he said, because he's dead." She sat back and nodded. "Actually, it's a way to make some quick cash. Pay us or we'll make things so messy you'll wish you had."

"Shit."

"A good description, I would say."

Both women stared across the back lawn, watching some robins frolic in a stone birdbath. Annie stood and walked over to the railing. There was a small rose garden that Richard had planted for his sister. Annie remembered the precise instructions her husband had given on the care of roses. She wondered what he'd advise her to do about McCoy and Cullen. Recalling his strong attachment to Betsy's boys, it wasn't too big of a stretch to think he'd be more worried about Cullen than annoyed by some bogus accusation.

Annie wished he were there to tell her how to handle this. She knew he'd warn her against overreacting and making too quick a judgment. But still, she needed to do something. Annie took a deep breath and turned to face Betsy.

"I'm glad I came. You've been a big help. Maybe I'll report this McCoy to the state so they can check into how he's running Noah House."

Betsy's eyes widened. "Wait a minute. Did you say Noah House?"

"Yes."

"Then there is a connection to Richard."

Annie felt a sickening *whoosh* low in her tummy. "What are you talking about?"

"A few years ago, some of the local charities were asking for contributions from businesses in town. Noah House was one of them. I remember it because Jimmy and Ronnie had made friends with a boy who lived there. They thought it was cool being a kid who lived with a ton of other kids, so they told Richard all about it. I recall Richard emphasizing how lucky the boys were to have two parents, a nice house, and a family who cared about them. Apparently, though, their comments about the friend at Noah House stayed with Richard, because he later told me the business was looking for some more tax write-offs and he was going to look into Noah House."

"Richard told me about Noah House," Annie said dismissively, relieved that charity was his only connection.

"Seems a bit of a coincidence to me."

"So what are you saying, Betsy? That Richard has some particular connection to Cullen?"

"I don't know. That would be easy to find out. But if Richard went there and checked the place out, he could have met Cullen and taken an interest in him. Maybe the kid took that to mean more than Richard meant. Who knows? I'm simply saying that there might be more here than you first thought."

Suddenly Annie wanted to be alone, to erase the past few hours and pretend they had never happened. The day had been so strange and unsettling, and promised to get worse.

"What are you going to do?" Betsy asked when Annie opened the porch door to leave.

"I'm going to go home, take a shower, have some more wine, and finish reading that book on vintage fabrics."

"What about the meeting with the kid and McCoy?"

"I'm not going."

"Maybe you should."

Annie rolled her eyes. "You were the one who just told me not to let them intimidate me."

"I know, but—"

Annie held up her hand. "Stop. No more. I'm tired and I can't think about this anymore. I'll call you tomorrow."

"You gonna be okay?"

"I'll be fine." She hugged Betsy, cast one final longing look at the sleeping Lydia, and walked to her car.

Driving home, she tried unsuccessfully to put the past few hours from her mind. Mental hand-wringing. That's what she was doing. But as much as she wanted to airily dismiss all of this as so much garbage, she couldn't. The lovely, pristine, and safe world she'd created for herself had been altered, and she was at a loss as to how to put it back together.

After the ride back to Noah House, Linc took Cullen into his office and closed the door.

Books, a too-stuffed file cabinet, plus a desk that held a phone, a fax machine, a computer, a printer, and a giant jar of jelly beans. Cullen stood by the desk, head down, arms loose at his sides. He looked as scared as when he was first brought to Noah House.

Cullen asked, "You still believe me, don't you?"

Linc settled into the chair behind the desk. "About what?"

"About what I heard Sandy say?"

"It's not a matter of believing you, it's a matter of whether what you overheard was entirely accurate. And five years is plenty of time to apply a bit of revision."

"You think I'm blowin' smoke, or are you calling Sandy a liar?"

"All I'm saying is that she could have been mistaken or wrong or misinformed. You said she and Parker were arguing."

"But they was fightin' about me. Parker telling her it was a big mistake, that he never should have agreed, that I wasn't what he wanted. . . ."

The catch in his voice brought a gulp and an attempt to cover it. Linc had never asked Cullen directly about Parker Gallagher's side of this story; his own contacts at Social Services had told him more than enough—and that had been a sanitized version.

Gallagher, a staid Ivy League professor whose idea of adoption was to save the world from one more delinquent, had expected to form the child in his own image. His much younger wife understood that little boys needed more than Chaucer and quiet reflections on social cultures. Cullen was rambunctious and curious; he liked baseball and big dogs and rock music, while Gallagher preferred chess and caged birds and opera. The match turned out to be a disaster, with Cullen becoming the unwanted pariah when Sandra Gallagher was killed by a drunk driver.

Gallagher, distraught and incapable of caring for a devastated child, simply lost interest, ignoring Cullen until the boy ran away.

Watching Cullen now, Linc asked, "Before you went to the house, did you know Richard Hunter was dead?"

"How can you ask me that? You think I was pullin' some creepy jive? No, I didn't know," he snapped.

"Knock it off," Linc said. "If we're going to get anywhere with this, you can't be freaking out at every question." But how did he know Sandy had the right information? Or if it was even the same Richard Hunter? All he had was what a then-ten-year-old claimed to have overheard. And since the go-around with Annie Hunter, Linc was seriously beginning to wonder about his own involvement. Cullen's quest to hunt down his birth parents was his choice, and Linc had no problem with helping in any way he could. Still, his job at Noah House was cleaning up present-tense messes, not looking for future ones.

Already, in the space of a few hours, the police were involved, accusations had been made, and there was a very angry widow. And for sure, the Hunter woman wasn't going to be a bonanza of help, even with the meeting in some benign coffee shop.

A knock on the door, then it opened and Vesco stuck his head in. "The Hunter woman called, said she can't make it tonight."

"Damn."

"Yeah, doncha hate it when that happens?" Vesco smirked.

Linc raised his eyebrows. "Make yourself useful, smartass, and find a phone number or address for Evan Prew. Maybe we can mess up *his* evening plans."

Chapter
Four

Annie Hunter and Evan Prew, Richard's business
partner at Restorations, Inc, had a civil relationship.
Maybe not warm and touchy, but at least respectful. Annie
admitted to thinking that Evan mostly stood around while
Richard did all the work; Evan talked and bragged and
showed up at sites when he knew the owner would be
there. Richard had always defended his partner, saying
that Evan was brilliant in detail work, which was at the
heart of an authentic restoration.

For the most part, Annie had kept her opinions to herself; however, she knew for a fact that Restorations had
lost some clients since Richard's death. Her husband had
been trusted. Evan—even after ten years and Richard's
recent death—was still considered by some as the new
partner.

Given their cordial coolness, Annie wasn't surprised
when on Sunday afternoon after numerous attempts since
Saturday morning, she was still trying to track Evan
down. Seated in the den at Richard's rolltop desk, she
called him once more at home.

"He hasn't called you back, Annie?" Helen Prew
asked. "I gave him the message yesterday afternoon. He's

taking a shower. I'll tell him again, and this time I'll make sure he calls you."

"Thanks, Helen." She hung up, wishing she were dealing with Helen instead of Evan. While she waited, she returned to the box of Richard's papers that she'd taken from the den closet, where she'd stored it after his death. She'd looked briefly at the contents some months back during a closet-cleaning spree, but since they were mostly personal, she hadn't had the emotional energy or the desire to make specific decisions on each item's value.

Even this morning, when rain dampened her gardening plans, she'd hesitated about going through the box, partially because it would bring back a rush of memories, but she was also afraid that she might find something that couldn't easily be explained in this new light.

Silly, of course, for what could there be? Damning evidence about Richard's connection to Cullen? Pictures? A crumpled receipt from a baby store? Some sentimental object tucked among the mundane? How likely were any of those scenarios? Not likely at all, for if Richard had some dark secret, he certainly wouldn't have left evidence so easily discovered.

And so, relying on her trust of him and her annoyance at McCoy for planting suspicion, she'd hauled out the box. Sorting and reading, her faith in Richard didn't diminish when she found, as she'd expected . . . nothing.

She went to the kitchen and made a cup of tea, hoping to banish a plaguing internal chill due, no doubt, to a tangled nest of troubling and bogus thoughts. She absolutely refused to entertain the possibility of Richard being deceitful; it was so preposterous that she wouldn't allow her mind to play with a 'what if.'

Yet putting the entire issue of Cullen from her thoughts, as she'd hoped to do when she'd left Betsy's, had proven futile. Whether or not McCoy was a hustler, which she fervently wanted to believe he was, hadn't resolved the basic question—how Cullen knew Richard's name.

When she'd gotten home from Betsy's, she'd called Noah House and left the message that she couldn't meet McCoy. All evening and well into Saturday, she'd expected him to call and demand an explanation or simply show up unannounced and accuse her of cowardice for refusal to face his brand of truth. But he'd done neither, which instead of giving her relief had left her wondering why. Both he and Cullen had appeared determined at the police station. . . . What had changed?

After she'd canceled McCoy, she'd made the first call to Evan. If Restorations, Inc, had given regular donations to Noah House, rather than the one time Richard had mentioned, then there would be a record of it.

And who knows, perhaps the business never gave a dime. Perhaps Richard's interest had been as temporary as the polite but firm "not interested" coolness he'd reserved for vinyl-siding salesmen.

Back in the study, she picked up the phone on the second ring.

"Annie, what seems to be the problem?" Evan asked. She didn't miss the irritation in his clipped tone. No "how are you?" No "good to hear from you." No "is everything okay?"

Well, fine. She was irritated, too. It wasn't as if she were some stranger trying to track him down to harass him. "Did you get my messages?"

"It's been a hellish week and I've been swamped with messages." Implicit was that her calls carried no more weight than anyone else's. Perhaps she was being churlish, but the fact that her late husband had bankrolled Restorations and taken on Evan as a partner without asking for a dime of investment should have at least put her on the short list of calls to return.

"I'm looking into some local charities," she said, being

deliberately vague. "I wanted a list of the ones Restorations supported financially."

He was silent for a few seconds. "Why?"

Because it's raining and I had nothing else to do but call you and ask for irrelevant information. All her fury at McCoy and her worrisome weekend bubbled to the surface. Raging at Evan might be satisfying, but hardly productive.

She took a deep breath and spoke softly. "I'm doing some research."

"I would think the library would be a better source."

"Not when I want to know what charities Restorations supported," she said evenly.

"We didn't deal with whackos."

"I know that."

"The heart and cancer funds, the animal shelter, kids sports. That sort of thing."

"Restorations was indeed generous and diverse," she said, confirming the obvious. "I don't need amounts, just the names. And especially the names of the ones on your 'that sort of thing' list."

His sigh was heavy and long. "I guess I can find them."

"Thank you. I'll come by about noon tomorrow to get it."

"Tomorrow? What's the hurry? It could be a long list. If you could be more specific on which charities . . ."

She could, of course, but she didn't want any more questions. She already had too damn many. "I'm sorry, but a general list is what I'm looking for."

"Tomorrow is going be impossible. Friday would be better."

Annie hesitated. She didn't see how this could be all that complicated, but maybe it was a long list and she hadn't given Evan much notice. Maybe it had never been put into a database, but she couldn't imagine that. Still, if he'd returned her call sooner . . . "I'd really like to have it tomorrow."

She heard his mild profanity and ignored it. She guessed he wanted her to acquiesce, but she knew she couldn't wait all week.

"Evan, is there some kind of problem?"

"Richard always said you were impatient when you wanted something. All right. God knows how Richard filed them."

"Under charities, perhaps?"

"I wasn't in charge of files," he snapped as if she'd accused him of being a secretary. "I'll have to go to the office today and look for the file."

Probably she should feel like an ogre for sending him out on a rainy Sunday afternoon. But she didn't. If he'd called her back on Saturday morning when he'd been at the office . . .

"Is that all?" he asked in that iceberg tone that dared anyone to make another request.

"Yes, and thank—"

But he'd hung up before she could finish her sentence.

"Sanctimonious jerk," she muttered, and she punched the off button. She wondered how Helen could stand living with him.

She went back to the box. So far she'd found mostly papers relating to their house, an assortment of garden nursery bills for roses that he'd purchased, an array of matchbooks that Richard had collected, a framed picture of the two of them the first time she thought she might be pregnant—Annie even recalled the day the photo was taken. Betsy had stopped over to show off a new camera, always convinced that her usually bad photos were due to cheap equipment.

She and Richard had posed while Betsy aimed and shot. The photo had turned out to be remarkably crisp and clear, and Richard had had it enlarged and framed for his desk. That photo, filled with all the joy she'd felt at maybe having conceived, had made going to his office to pack up his personal things excruciatingly difficult. Others had offered to do it for her, but she'd balked against that intrusion. She'd brought the box and the photo home, then put them away to go through at a later time.

Now she set the framed photo aside, a raw shudder knotting inside her when she realized that Betsy had captured a moment when the two of them had been at their happiest.

She picked through the matchbooks; more memories. Their trip to the Rocky Mountains, a New Hampshire ski weekend, restaurants where they'd eaten when they'd vacationed, and Richard telling her he'd have to find another hobby, as finding matchbooks wasn't as easy anymore. Then she picked up one from Duke's Place. From the address it was north of Providence. Must be near one of the sites Restorations had been working. No doubt a business meeting. But she didn't recall Richard mentioning any projects north of Providence. This was silly, she decided. Although he'd always mentioned their work sites to her, perhaps he'd forgotten this one. Perhaps it was a small project. Perhaps *she'd* forgotten. She closed her eyes, blaming McCoy for turning the ordinary into the suspicious.

She added the matchbook to the others, then drew it back out again, then flung it down. It's a matchbook, for godsakes. Like she could walk into some public bar with a photo of Richard and the bartender would know him? Uh huh. Why not try and find some mysterious motive for a man going to a bar? Or maybe he never even went there, and the matchbook had been given to him by someone else. But that she rejected out of hand. Someone might have given it to him, but he never would have saved it. Richard never collected secondhand. His matchbooks always came exclusively from places he'd been. Surely there were others from places she didn't remember. She tossed the matchbook down and turned from the desk. Rain or no rain, she needed some fresh air and some clear thoughts.

She turned off the lights, pulled on her jacket, grabbed her umbrella, and when Rocky followed her to the back door, she took his leash off the hook.

"Okay, boy, let's you and I walk. It's just a light drizzle now."

Outside, she headed down the street, avoiding puddles but not quite able to step around the nagging pull of fear that Cullen Gallagher did indeed know something about Richard that wasn't going to go away.

"I'm sorry, but Mrs. Hunter has a busy day. Mondays are always very full. If you could make an appointment for next week—"

"This won't take long, Ms. . . . ?"

"Elaine. Length isn't the issue, an appointment is."

Elaine, the receptionist—or was it secretary? Linc wasn't sure—looked as if she'd been born in the job. Protective, serene in her position, and properly annoyed that a stranger could possibly expect to just "see" Annie Hunter.

Immaculate in her blue dress with white buttons and—what was that word Brooke always used? "Coifed," that was it. In fact, Elaine reminded him of Brooke; a woman he'd thought he'd loved once upon a time when he'd believed in that clichéd emotion and when he'd stupidly thought that lifestyle differences kept a relationship fresh and interesting.

What a crock that was, for he and Brooke both discovered that all their differences did was make a mess.

Now Elaine raised her eyebrows, then turned a few

pages in the appointment book. "Friday, she has an opening at two thirty."

"I had no idea interior decorators were that busy."

"She's very good and very much in demand."

"It would seem so. Exactly what does she do?"

"Pardon me?"

Linc repeated the question.

For a moment Elaine appeared flustered, as if she'd never been asked anything so dumb. But then, from when he'd walked in the door, she'd looked at him as if she'd never encountered a guy in jeans. Ah yes, he thought, in the rarified world of Annie Hunter, stupid questions and guys not wearing suits didn't exist.

"Yes, well, she consults and does interior design and decorating work for a number of Bedford's more expensive homes. She chairs two garden committees, plus she does four home decorating analysis classes at one of the furniture stores for their customers."

"I'm surprised she has an opening Friday."

"It is a little unusual. Shall I put you down for two thirty on Friday?"

Linc walked over to look at an array of photos on one wall. There were two rooms that looked expensive and empty, and there were three other photos of rooms that looked as if real people lived there. She was diverse, he had to give her that. Another photo showed Annie with two men holding some kind of award plaque. "Nice photo. These her partners?"

"No. The man on her left is her husband and the other is a local builder."

Linc stared at the image of Richard Hunter, noting that he stood somewhat behind Annie rather than directly beside her. A husband who wanted to make sure his wife dominated the photo? Was he intimidated by her success? Or proud and wanted her to have the limelight? Or was he in the photo only because he couldn't avoid it?

"So how is she to work for?" he asked.

"She's wonderful."

"And smart and efficient."

"Why, yes."

"And an understanding employer?"

"Absolutely."

"Then she won't fire you when I just walk past your desk and into her office."

"Wait a minute! You can't do that."

Linc deftly sidestepped Elaine, saying, "I promise this will only take a few minutes." Then he opened the door that he swore had been made of solid oak.

"Mr. McCoy, please. You can't—" Her words were a whispered hiss, but he already had the door open. The room was large and richly detailed, but it was also a working office. Wallpaper books, color charts, a basket overflowing with pieces of fabric, the desk scattered with papers and a computer. There were fresh yellow roses in a blue pitcher on a credenza—a carved monstrosity that, even considering the fact that he knew squat about furniture, he could tell hadn't come from an office-supply house.

Annie Hunter stood by the credenza, a folder in her hand, and then she glanced up, her expression was one of surprised apprehension. No question she hadn't anticipated that he would just show up. Which, of course, had been his intention. After she'd blown them off on Friday, Linc had decided that he wasn't going to let that happen again. If he simply showed, she couldn't duck.

Slim and startlingly attractive in a blue suit that mirrored the pitcher's color, her hair had been carefully combed into a roll that softly haloed her head. He was sure the do had some fancy name, but he immediately recalled how messy it had looked at the police station; he liked the frazzled Annie better.

Get it together, pal. Frazzled or proper were both irrelevant. *She* was irrelevant except in connection to Cullen. He didn't move further into the room. He was here to get some answers, not antagonize her.

"Nice office. Bet that view is incredible." The view from his office was an alley that served as a cut-through to another alley.

Annie Hunter, however, wasn't wasting time on polite chatter. "You were supposed to call me, not barge in here. I don't see anyone without an appointment."

"We had an appointment that you broke. I had serious doubts you'd take my call."

"Well, you were wrong."

"Noted. Why did you cancel Friday night?"

"Excuse me? I don't think I owe you an explanation."

"A bit testy, aren't we?"

"I am not testy! You are intrusive."

He was amazed at how quick her answers were. No stuttering or hemming and hawing. He grinned. "Hey, I've been stood up before. I can handle your reason."

"I didn't want to see you. Is that reason enough?" She glanced beyond him. "Elaine, if you could close the door please?"

"I'm sorry, Annie. He just barged past me. Is everything okay? I can call security."

"I'm fine. Mr. McCoy is a recent acquaintance I met through someone at my house. He'll be leaving in a few minutes."

Elaine backed out and pulled the door closed. Annie flung the folder down and walked over to him. Not close, but close enough that he felt the tension jump and spark off of her. Her eyes were wide and very brown, and the blush of color deepened on her cheeks.

Then came her voice, deep and brisk and steady. "You have a nerve acting like we really know one another. And I did not stand you up. We didn't have a date."

If Linc believed that old canard about angry women

being sexy and cute, he would have definitely applied it here. "You met me through someone at your house? Now, that, Mrs. Hunter, was creative. Oops, that's what you do, isn't it? Create, or is it recreate?"

"Elaine has a passion for drama. God knows what's she's thinking."

"And you care what people think."

"I care very much what people think. This is not a game, Mr. McCoy. I'm the widow of a man much beloved here in Bedford, and perception far too often carries more weight than facts. Reputations count and expectations of behavior count even more. And while my personal life should be just that, this is a small town, and having my receptionist think I'm involved in some personal relationship with you . . ." Her voice trailed off as though she'd wound herself into a corner with no exit.

"I didn't realize that seeing you without an appointment had such far-reaching consequences." Linc was amazed that a woman as sophisticated and put together as she appeared had been that rattled by him. Her defensiveness—that he expected—but this . . . When had this become about her and not about her husband?

Calmer now, she said, "I'm sure you startled Elaine. Men in jeans and a work shirt don't usually come in the front door."

"Next time, I'll obey the rules. But now I'm really curious. A guy in jeans coming in the front door and wanting to see you would send Elaine's mind rushing to what conclusion?"

"Look, I didn't say that very well."

"Ah, but you said it exactly right. Let me see if I can clarify it so there is no mistake."

"I have nothing more to say." She turned her back, folding her arms as though suddenly chilled.

A part of Linc warned him to back off. He had barged in, she owed him nothing, and for damn sure he wasn't looking for anything with her beyond finding out what information she could provide for Cullen. But this was too easy, too sweet, and he wanted to see her respond.

"Well, I have something to say." And before she could object, he said, "You're afraid she'll think we're having sex. Raunchy, secret, horny sex. And, you'd never do that with the likes of me."

She turned slowly, color bleached from her face, and Linc immediately regretted the smart-ass comment. He figured she'd get angry or act insulted that some blue-collar guy could even suggest such a ridiculous scenario. He hadn't expected plain old shock. There was more to Annie Hunter than he'd imagined.

"I apologize," he said, and meant it. "I shouldn't have said that."

She walked behind her desk, started to sit down, then must have thought better of it. Instead, she lifted a china cup from its saucer, raising it to her mouth and looking at him over the delicate rim. She took a sip and lowered the cup as if the gesture allowed her time to regather her emotions. Then, in a sturdy, even voice, she said, "Elaine is very protective of me and of my time. She knows I don't see anyone without an appointment. Especially anyone who Elaine would consider a threat."

Her explanation fascinated him. A threat to what? Her easy life? Her sophistication that was pretty and perfect, or was it a shell too easily cracked? It was hard to comprehend that a life lived in the wonderland of money, success, and influence could feel threatened by a guy in jeans with a smart mouth.

But he wasn't going to get sidetracked. This was business, and Cullen was his focus. "I won't take any more of your time, but Cullen wants to ask you some questions. Maybe he could make an appointment."

"Tell him to call me," she said, moving some papers around on the desk. She wants you gone, pal.

"I went to your house yesterday, but you weren't home."

She glanced up. "My dog and I went for a walk."

"Rocky the husky?" At her widened eyes, he quickly added, "Cullen told me. Like most kids, he likes dogs."

"I wish I'd been home. We could have settled all of this yesterday."

"Then you do have some information."

"Actually, I have no information that makes any connection between Cullen and my husband. It would appear the boy has indeed made a mistake."

Linc started to refute her denial, but let it stand. Instead, he added, "He shouldn't have jumped to the conclusion that you were his mother. I'm afraid his wishful thinking about his birth parents has made him too anxious to find them."

"Where did he get Richard's name?"

"That's more complicated."

"Yes, I'm sure. I would appreciate you just spelling it out instead of talking in vague generalities."

But then, before he could say anything, she did.

"I know what's at the bottom of this. Cullen is convinced Richard was his father."

Her directness astonished him, but also told him that at the heart of Annie Hunter was terror that the "beloved by Bedford" man she'd been married to was a liar and a cheat.

"Cullen believes that—yes."

"Then it would appear that he is once again engaging in wishful thinking."

"I'm afraid not. Your husband's name didn't just come out of nowhere. He overheard it during an argument between his adoptive parents. He heard Richard referred to as his father. Cullen's past is not a pretty story, Annie, and finding his birth father—"

"Look, I feel bad for Cullen. He seems like a nice boy,

but his father wasn't Richard. That's impossible."

"Why?"

"Because Richard never betrayed me."

"Annie, there's no way you can know that for sure."

"I knew Richard!" Her voice had risen, and Linc could see her desperate need to hold on to what she'd always believed. "You've damaged Richard's reputation with a ridiculous charge when he's unable to defend himself. What's even more alarming is that you've encouraged Cullen to believe it, too."

"Listen to me."

"No! I won't listen. I want you to get out of here and take all your lies with you."

Linc watched her, seeing pain and fear and a rampant loyalty to her husband. It was a familiar look—the face of a devastating possibility that was far easier to deny than deal with. He'd skidded and wallowed in it all when Michael had been killed. Pain, horror, denial, anger. And it was that shared terrifying bridge with Annie that made him nod and turn to leave.

At the door he glanced back at her. She had her back to him, her body stiff and unyielding. "Having sex with me would have been easier, wouldn't it, Annie?"

For an answer he got silence.

Chapter Five

*Annie sat for a long time after McCoy left. She be-*rated herself for verbalizing the issue that had plagued her all weekend. The issue that she'd avoided saying aloud even when she was alone. Richard and some other woman. Betrayal and lies and proof of such—Richard's son. She wasn't sure what was worse—that he might have betrayed her or that some other woman had had the child she'd so desperately yearned for.

It was a startling moment of clarity for Annie. She had valued Richard's instinct for the truth even when it had been messy and unvarnished. She and her mother had a strained relationship because she'd refused to provide Annie with answers about her father. Annie had to search on her own. And amazingly, that search-until-she-found approach was what she'd been prepared to do with this.

The pattern was so simple. Focus on searching and dismantling the facts, or revising them, then proclaiming that she'd discovered the entire truth. With her father, she'd discounted the few snippits she'd known growing up, and instead assumed her mother's refusal to talk was because she'd driven Annie's father away. Her mother trying to protect herself. Yet even when Annie had acknowledged that her mother might have been the victim, her mother still refused to be forthcoming. Why? Why hadn't she defended herself? Why hadn't she told the truth? Those were questions that to this day didn't have answers. But more important than not having answers was the flat refusal to even talk to Annie. It was the closed-mouthed "I won't discuss him" approach that had driven Annie crazy and in turn glorified Nathan Dawson.

And now Richard. And like her father, Richard wasn't here for her to go and ask for an explanation.

She rose and turned to look out the window. She realized that since Richard's death, she'd become a woman of observation without involvement. That was safe. No investment of emotion or heart or restless energy. She worked, went home, visited her mother, sought out friends on occasion, but she'd come to like her own company. She could watch what she wanted on TV, eat when she wanted, go to bed and get up without disturbing anyone. There was no stress, no effort, no surprises. And that was what was so disturbing about Cullen and McCoy. She'd been pulled into this, and now she was terrified of what would come next.

Annie didn't like surprises, whether in the form of parties or information. The view from her office always soothed her because it was so consistent. When change came, she saw it in the making. Brick and mortar buildings in a continuing state of refurbishment. The police officer directing traffic around some road resurfacing. Tourists with their cameras and totes. A skateboarder dodging traffic. This everyday ordinary view of the downtown area had sold her on this office space. It showed the bones of a growing community with all its struggles and wonder. A community hustling to keep up with the influx of tourists, swelling the small town in summer and then receding for the long winter, as businesses scrambled to stay open when their livelihood depended solely on the locals. If she looked toward the south she could almost imagine Noah House. She knew the area, an older part of town, but rarely had a reason to go there.

On Friday she'd looked out at this same scene, thinking about the first anniversary of Richard's death and realizing that yes, indeed, the shock and grief had softened with passing time. She'd left the office feeling melancholy about Richard but positive about her life and assuming the only knot in her life was her testy relationship with her mother.

But all that had changed with finding Cullen on her back porch, plunging her into a place she didn't know and didn't want to know.

As for McCoy . . . She pressed her hand to her chest, realizing her heart had just now returned to a normal beat. She'd handled him badly by getting defensive and snippy. She smiled a little. Her mother had called her snippy more than a few times when Annie had been annoyed that something hadn't gone her way. *Annie Jean, you take that snippy look off your face right now. Some things just aren't the way you want them to be.*

Ah yes, that huge gap between what she wanted and what was. In fact, she did understand Cullen's plight; she'd searched for her father, too, albeit under different circumstances. It was McCoy who unnerved her, McCoy who she didn't trust, and it was McCoy who'd set off a fuse inside of her that she'd thought long extinguished.

"Annie?"

She turned, startled.

"I knocked twice. Are you sure there's nothing wrong?"

"Just doing some thinking." She glanced down at her appointment sheet for the day.

"I wanted to remind you of Grace Tooley." Elaine stood in the doorway, trying very hard to not look curious.

"I was just about to leave." She checked the Tooley

folder, filled with swatches, designs, and some pictures from magazines that Grace had provided as guides of what kind of look she wanted in the master bedroom. Grace wanted Annie to help her choose from a number of wallpaper books.

"Annie, I know it's not my business—"

"It's going to be fine. Don't worry so hard about me."

"But I do. And he was so . . . so . . ."

"Yes, words fail me, too."

"I was going to say—" Annie detected a slight shiver in Elaine—"different."

"Definitely different."

"And dangerous-looking."

"I don't think we need to worry about him shooting up the office."

"I bet he's good in bed."

"I wouldn't know."

"He rides a motorcycle, you know."

That she did know.

"I saw it while he was in here with you. I even took down the plate number. He probably belongs to some gang."

"I think he's a bit old for a gang."

"A club, then."

He didn't strike Annie as the "clubby" type. "Maybe."

"I mean, he wore boots and he needed a haircut and, well, I don't think he's quite up to speed on the male sensitivity issue." Then she smiled knowingly. "Then again, I bet he doesn't have any trouble finding girl-friends."

"I'm sure he doesn't."

"But you can't get involved with someone like that. I mean, not in a serious way."

"Elaine, I'm not involved, either seriously or nonser-iously."

Elaine giggled, her eyes dancing as if they shared an

unspoken secret. "Oh, Annie, you can't fool me. Any ninny could have cut the tension." She drew closer. "I know it's been hard being alone. And maybe a secret fling is just what you need. Not serious, which it wouldn't be because he isn't your type at all. Crude and rough-looking . . . Intense and . . ." She sighed. "Very sexy. I predict—"

Annie rolled her eyes. "Sorry to blow away your romantic prediction, but we are barely even acquaintances."

"That's going to change."

"Oh?" Annie raised her eyebrows. "Let's see now." She tapped one finger against her cheek thoughtfully. "You predicted I'd meet a man in Aruba who would sweep me off my feet. All I got was a bad sunburn and a nest of green bugs in my room. Then, last March, you predicted I'd be invited to teach a design course at URI. I'm still waiting for that invitation. And now a secret fling with Mr. McCoy?"

"You left Aruba early, remember? And URI is still in play. And just wait and see about McCoy. I know I'm right."

Annie smiled. "And I know you're wrong." She took her shoulder bag from the small closet. "I have to get out of here or I'm going to be late. Oh, and I have a stop to make after I leave Grace's." She glanced at her watch. "Should be back around one."

She met with Grace Tooley, who had chosen ten wall-paper patterns from the four books Annie had left with her. The woman was clearly frustrated. Annie spent some time pointing out that a stripe would make the ceilings look higher, and since they were already twelve feet, Grace eliminated those two choices. One was very busy, nice for an accent wall but overall would close the room in too much. After eliminating others for various reasons from too contemporary to too dark, they settled on a traditional faux damask–style pattern in a soft blue with a dye-cut border.

"What would I do without you, Annie? So many choices . . . my goodness."

Annie grinned as she loaded the wallpaper books into her car. "I think the choice you settled on will be lovely. I'll get this ordered and call my paperhanger to set up a time."

She said goodbye and drove away. Her requested list from Evan was next. He wasn't in the office, but Julie, who worked the front desk in the building, gave Annie an envelope. "He said you'd be coming by."

"Thanks, Julie. And tell Evan I appreciate it."

"I will. How are you doing?"

"Good."

"Someone was here earlier to see Evan about Richard."

"Oh?"

"Evan was on his way out to the Browning site, but he did see him."

Annie's heart was pounding. McCoy? Perhaps. Whoever it was, Annie decided, she needed to brush up on her persuasion skills. Someone just drops in and is rewarded with an impromptu meeting when Evan is in a rush, and she couldn't get a returned phone call over a weekend? "Well, I imagine Evan gets a lot of people who knew Richard," she said as she unclasped the envelope and pulled out the sheet of paper with the charities list.

"Not really. I mean, he did for a few months after, but no one lately."

She scanned the row of names and noted that most were local. Restorations had always been community based; build your business at home with goodwill and honesty, and the rewards will reach the world. Annie had heard Richard say that so many times, but beyond sounding good, it had worked.

"Did the man say what he wanted?"

"Oh, it wasn't a man. It was a boy, a teenager about thirteen or fourteen."

Annie glanced up from the sheet. "Did you say a teenager?" She hoped she didn't look as stunned as she felt.

"Yeah, and he actually spoke words without mumbling. Nice-looking kid, but he needed a haircut and some better-fitting clothes. Some mothers these days, you just have to wonder."

And there it was on the charity list. Noah House. A thousand dollars three Christmases ago and the donation he'd mentioned months before his death. Annie stared at the name and the two figures as though their inclusion alone was damning.

Julie prattled on. "I mean, do these moms ever take a good look? Then again, I should talk. My daughter has a green streak in her hair."

Actually, the amounts weren't out of line with the other donations, and Betsy had said her sons had mentioned a friend at Noah House and Richard had told her Restorations was making a donation.

She slid the paper back into the envelope, making some benign comments about green streaks and sloppy clothes.

Finally, she and Julie said goodbye, and Annie, back in her car, again took out the sheet. She wondered if McCoy was at Noah House that Christmas that Restorations had made the donation. She wondered if a thousand dollars was high or low or average compared to other contributors. She wondered whether, if Richard were to suddenly appear to answer her questions, if the coincidence of Noah House and Cullen was really just that.

Before she returned to the office, she decided to stop at home and make sure she'd filled Rocky's water dish. In her driveway, she got out of her car, rounded a hedge of lilac bushes, and got a very slimy rubber ball right in the tummy about two seconds before a leaping Rocky knocked her to the ground.

The air whooshed out of her, and she found herself on her fanny with a slobbering Rocky trying to retrieve his ball from under a nearby bush where it had landed.

"Oh boy."

She looked into the frightened eyes of Cullen Gallagher.

"I didn't see you. Rocky and I—We were playin' and you sorta got in between." He leaned down, then hesitated, looking reluctant to get too close. "Oh, shit, I mean, I got you all dirty. Please don't call the cops. I'm sorry. I really am. I can get some money and pay to get your clothes cleaned."

"It's all right, Cullen. No harm done."

She got to her feet and brushed at her suit, but dog slime and grass stains weren't quite in the same league as lint and an occasional stray hair.

"Linc's gonna fry my ass," he muttered. "He told me I shouldn't come here without calling you first." Annie smiled at that, given that McCoy had no such standard for himself. "I was gonna wait in the driveway, you know, so you'd see me and if you didn't want me here, I could just leave. But Rocky here was jumpin' around and wanted to play. I didn't go on the porch or take any soda. Honest, we were just playing catch. You gonna call the cops?"

Rocky sat beside him, panting, body waiting and tail flopping. Annie hadn't seen him quite this happy since the last time her nephews had played with him.

"I don't think we need the police. Tell you what. We'll blame this on Rocky for missing the ball."

He grinned, and his eyes crinkled up and he cocked his head to the side in a motion so shockingly familiar, Annie actually got an ache in her chest. And in that moment, Annie knew. The boyish expression, the twink of a dimple low on his left cheek, the eyes were blue instead of hazel, but the shape was undeniably as clear and defined as a fingerprint. Cullen was Richard's son.

After all that had already happened today, this revelation seemed perfectly in tune with the others. And the significance of Cullen being Richard's son put all of this in a new light. No longer was this about Richard or betrayal or lies or her searching for facts to preserve his reputation. This wasn't even about her and her desperate efforts to keep things as they were in her perfect and serene and predictable life.

This was about Cullen.

Incredibly, she felt a kind of shocked relief, as if she'd been avoiding and denying and now that the pain of the truth was literally a foot away from her, it wasn't as horrible as she'd expected. What kind of sense did that make? None. But then little had made sense since she'd found him on her porch last Friday.

"How would you like to have lunch with me?"

"Together? Here?" He looked totally bewildered.

"I have some roast beef and potato chips, and I made some brownies for my nephews for when they came to mow the lawn on Saturday. But they didn't come because of the rain." She was babbling as if chatter would keep him here. Odd, a few hours ago she wanted nothing to do with him, now she was terrified he'd leave. She had a zillion questions, a jumble of feelings and, she hoped, a hungry boy. "I sure would appreciate it if you could eat some of those brownies."

"Brownies are my favorite. They got frosting?"

"Absolutely. Who wants brownies without frosting?"

"My old man." At Annie's start, he added, "Not your husband. The guy who adopted me. He didn't like anything I liked. He didn't even like me."

Annie started to tell him that that probably wasn't true,

but reminded herself that she had no idea anymore what was true and what was false.

He fell in beside her as they walked up onto the back porch. Rocky swaggered behind.

"Mrs. Hunter?"

"Call me Annie."

"Can I? Linc told me you wouldn't like that."

"Mr. McCoy doesn't know me well enough to know what I like."

"Yeah, he gets pissy about uptown women. Says they got money and time and don't know what to do with either."

"He should have asked me. I would have told him we shop, then we lunch and gossip."

"Yeah?"

"Perhaps Mr. McCoy has other suggestions."

Cullen eyed her. "You don't like him much, do you?"

"Now why would you think that?"

He grinned. "I think you're cool."

She smiled back. "Thank you, Cullen." She opened the back door and led the way into the kitchen. Cullen followed.

Then he looked once again at the stains on her suit. "I really can pay to get your clothes cleaned. I mean Linc would kill me if I didn't."

"First he's going to fry your ass and now he'll kill you."

"Nah, he wouldn't really do that stuff. It's just that he makes a big deal about taking responsibility and doing what's right."

That seemed to be where she was going, she mused. Taking responsibility for accepting a truth and then following through on it. "Mr. McCoy seems to have wide and diverse ways of looking at things."

"He's tough, and some of the kids get in trouble with him cuz he don't take no crap. How come you don't lock your door?" At Annie's look, he said, "I sorta saw that when I was here the first time. But I never came inside—Linc would've—"

"I know. Fried or killed you."

He grinned. "Yeah. Ain't you scared someone will just walk in and take stuff?"

"No."

"How come?"

"Because no one ever has."

"You mean you just trust strangers?"

"You didn't walk in and take anything last Friday, and you were a stranger."

"Oh yeah."

She laughed at his puzzled look that changed as he looked around the kitchen.

"Wow, this is awesome." Rocky flopped down out of the way like a sentry just relieved of duty.

"I like to cook, and once upon a time we used to have a lot of parties. A big kitchen is necessary for that."

"You don't have parties anymore?"

"Not very often." She took off her jacket, kicked off her pumps, then washed her hands before taking food from the refrigerator and setting it on the counter. Cullen slid into one of the chairs at the eating area, then looking at his hands, slid back down.

"Bathroom is through there and to your left," Annie said, pointing to a wide hall that arched off the kitchen.

She assembled sandwiches, piling beef and lettuce and tomatoes and cheese onto a bulky roll. She made a half-sized one for herself. She set out a cold Pepsi for Cullen and made a glass of iced tea for herself, then took out a bowl for the chips. Just as she was about to fill it, she stopped, put the bowl away, and put the bag on the counter. She didn't pour his Pepsi into a glass, either. She was learning not to be so proper.

"Hey, this looks great," Cullen said sliding back into

the chair and digging his hand into the chip bag.

Annie sat at the counter end and took a sip of tea. For a few moments she just watched him eat, taking a funny kind of contentment. To see him eat so enthusiastically made her feel like she'd gotten an A in nourishment. She thought he was too thin, but she decided it was more ill-fitting clothes than lack of flesh. Vaguely she recalled Betsy remarking that her two boys had hollow legs when it came to eating, but Annie had never really paid attention. Now she did.

"How about another sandwich?"

"Yeah?"

She grinned. "Yeah."

With the sandwiches eaten, Annie slid a plate of brownies onto the counter. "Another soda?"

"Got any milk?"

She nodded and poured him a glass.

He drank thirstily and dove into the brownies. Annie watched him eat the first one, and then he started on the second, washing it down with the milk. She tried to sound casual rather than curious. "Tell me about yourself."

He bit into the third brownie, stopped, put it down, and lowered his eyes. "If you mean about your husband, I don't know much."

"Right now I mean about you."

He was silent, thoughtful, and Annie saw a moment of suspicion as if he thought she was trying to trap him. Then it was gone. "My mom told me she and the old man adopted me when I was a baby. Her name was Sandy. Her friends called her that, but he called her Sandra." His expression pinched. "He always made a big deal out of using the real name. He made a big deal out of everything he didn't like. Mom always tried to make excuses for him, but he wasn't like a dad, you know, like the ones on TV who do things with their kids. He was a college professor and thought everyone should be proper and snobby like him."

Proper and snobby describes me, Annie thought, wincing. "Was your Mom? Proper and snobby, I mean?"

"Nah, she was neat. Real pretty and she liked kids. He didn't."

"He must have liked you," she said, realizing immediately she was contradicting what he'd said earlier.

"I don't remember if he did. All I remember is his scowl and him making me wear weird clothes and the other kids laughing. After she died he sent me away telling me I wasn't the kind of son he wanted. I was too rough and wild. He wanted me to wear suits, talk proper, and read with him in the library and I, well, I liked reading sometimes, but I also liked to hang with the kids outside and he . . ."

"Disapproved."

"Yeah." Cullen looked away and Annie's heart filled.

She couldn't imagine why a man would send away a child that he must have wanted enough to have gone through the adoption process. "Maybe he just didn't know how to handle a little boy."

"He never liked me. He never wanted to hear about anything I did—all he wanted was to make me do things the way he wanted. He wanted me to be like him and I couldn't. I tried, but I kept making mistakes. He called me stupid and hopeless."

Annie knew from her own experience with her father that one side of a story was never the whole story, and yet Cullen hadn't sounded vindictive or hostile—just sad and hurt. And even if this adoptive father had some justification, it was inconceivable that a man could turn away his own son.

And the instant that thought cleared her mind, in came the next one: Richard had. Richard had sent his son away. Not the same. Not the same. Not even close to the same.

Richard was nothing like the man Cullen described, yet obviously her husband's motives had been selfish, too. They'd been about self-preservation. He'd wanted to hide the boy and the woman and the affair.

"How did your mother die?"

"Some friggin' drunk hit her when she was coming home from the grocery store. He said it was my fault cuz she'd gone to the store to get stuff for cookies she was baking for a school bake sale."

"Oh, Cullen, words simply fail me."

His shoulders lifted and settled. "Yeah."

They sat a few feet from one another, the silence bouncing and restless between them. Rocky dozed, and from the dining room came the two-o'clock striking of the grandmother clock. Annie needed to get back to the office.

"I better go," Cullen finally said. He looked tired suddenly, convincing Annie that the retelling was nearly as painful as the actual experience had been.

"I'd like you to come back. Maybe we could talk some more."

He looked up at her and instead of nodding and sliding out of the chair, he said, "My mom told me Richard was my real father. Well, actually I overheard her arguing with the old man. She was telling him she was going to call Richard because *he* said he wanted me sent back. She believed he could do that, and she was afraid. She said even though Richard lived in Bedford he would help her."

"Help her do what?" Annie asked, intrigued by exactly what Richard would have done. She had so many questions—how he'd found Richard, how he'd gotten to Noah House. But there was time. "Do you know if she called him?"

He shrugged. "I dunno. She got killed the next day."

"What day, Cullen? Do you remember the date?"

"You gonna check to see if I'm lying?"

"No. I just thought that if I knew the date, I could check his appointment book and see if he'd planned to meet Sandy."

"November tenth. Five years ago. I was gonna be ten the next day."

The day before his birthday. This poor kid had lived with one disaster following another. "Cullen, I'm so sorry. I sincerely mean that."

He cocked his head, and again she saw the resemblance to Richard. "Yeah, I know. Everyone says that, but—"

"No one does anything."

He shrugged.

"Maybe I can," she murmured as her mind churned in two different directions. What had happened thirteen years earlier and what she could do about it today.

She'd have to dig out her old appointment books to refresh some of the details, but she remembered that in November thirteen years ago she had still been in denial about not having children. So Richard had been in contact with Cullen's mother for at least those months of her pregnancy and the giving up of the child. . . .

"I can try to help you get some answers." Annie realized that Cullen had seemed more intent on finding his father than his mother. From articles she'd read, it was usually the birth mother who was sought. Unless . . . "What about your birth mother? Was that Sandy?"

"I told you I was adopted." Then his eyes widened knowingly. "You think my mom and Richard? No way. She'd married *him* way before they got me. Besides, he watched her all the time."

Annie was relieved. She'd liked what Cullen had said about Sandy, and Annie wasn't prepared to like the woman Richard had betrayed her with. "Have you tried to find your birth mother?"

"I thought it was you. I mean since I knew about Richard, well, it seemed like a good place to start. But Linc said he was sure you weren't. You being upset and all was cuz of your husband, not me."

"Linc is very perceptive," she said, giving him the credit now that she couldn't have imagined giving just a few hours before.

"Do you know who she is?"

"No . . . no . . . Cullen, I'm not accusing you of making anything up, but I need something beyond you over-hearing a conversation. Richard's parents and his sister—they will be upset by this, and his parents especially won't just take your word."

"I don't have any other proof."

"You went to see Evan, Richard's business partner. Did he tell you anything?"

"No. Linc and I tried to see him Friday night but he wasn't home. Linc didn't go with me today—he had to deal with Eddie—a real jerk who just came to Noah House."

"Did you tell Evan you thought Richard was your fa-ther?"

He looked down, and Annie held her breath. If he'd told Evan, then any possibility that this would remain quiet was gone. Already too many people knew something was going on—the police, Betsy, Linc coming to her of-fice this morning . . . Although that had sent Elaine's imagination on one of her romantic scenarios, it would take very little for Elaine to change direction.

"I told him, but what's the big deal? It's the truth." Then he was off the stool and backing toward the door. "I figured he might be able to tell me something. You wouldn't."

Now she knew the result of canceling that meeting. Cullen wanted answers, and he'd do what was necessary to get them. Hardly an earth-shaking concept, and en-trenching even more within her was her earlier thought that none of this was going to go away.

"So Evan knew nothing?" she asked.

"Nah. Called me a troublemaker. Asked if I was lookin' for money and then told me to get out."

She didn't like the fact that her thoughts had been on the same track as Evan's. But she also noted that Evan hadn't really defended Richard; he hadn't said the very idea of Richard and betrayal and a child by another woman was outrageous. Evan hadn't said it was impossible because Richard would never do such a thing. Perhaps it was just the way Evan viewed honor and integrity—as concepts rather than ways of living. If Evan hadn't been faithful to Helen, it would follow that he figured Richard had been no better. Annie shuddered at the thought of asking Evan about Richard's faithfulness. But he'd been at Restorations only ten years; he'd come three years after Cullen had been born. She did not want to hear that there was yet another girlfriend. No. Asking Evan anything about Richard's private life made her skin crawl. Besides, why in the world should she believe him?

"Cullen, Evan was rude, no question. But an unknown teenage boy coming out of nowhere and accusing my husband would rattle him badly."

"I wasn't lyin'. It was the truth! My mother told me never to be afraid of the truth. She said that's why she told me I was adopted. She didn't want me to find out somewhere else."

Like I'm finding out about Richard. Sandy's lesson to Cullen about truth had no doubt given him the courage and grit to rise above a very painful rejection from his adoptive father. "I admit I didn't believe you."

"And what about now? You believe it now, or was all of this some trick to make me shut up? You just acting nice to get what you wanted? That's what he did. He was only nice when he wanted something."

Annie chafed at the comparison. "I believe you now."

He halted. "You do?"

"Yes."

"Why?"

Annie chuckled. "First you're angry because I didn't, and now you're suspicious that I do."

"Yeah, well, when someone who wasn't nice suddenly gets nice—"

"Like your father?"

"He wasn't my father! He didn't even try to play at being one." He paused, then said, "I saw a picture in the other room of your husband. You said you didn't have kids, but there were two kids in that picture."

"They're Richard's sister's boys."

"How come he didn't have any kids with you?"

Well, Annie thought. That's about as straightforward and to the point as she'd ever heard the question asked. Her admiration of Sandy climbed another notch. "We tried."

"So he knocked up some other woman and then gave me away because of you?"

"I don't know what he did. I didn't know about another woman." Her mind was reeling. If she thought she'd had questions before, now they were stacking up like dirty dishes in an all-night diner.

"He could've told you. You could've taken me."

"It wouldn't have been that simple."

"Why?"

"Because he—"

"Did it with someone else?"

God, she couldn't believe she was having this conversation. "Yes, because he betrayed me."

"So you would've hated me?"

"No . . . I don't know. I don't think so. It wouldn't have been your fault, but I would have been very angry with Richard."

"I don't see what's the big deal. You couldn't have kids so he has one with someone else and gives it to you.

Kinda like a gift. Like Noah House never has enough money so someone makes a donation and calls it a gift. No one gets worked up about where the cash comes from."

"It's not quite the same thing, Cullen."

"Yeah, well, lettin' your kid go with some guy who hates him isn't too cool."

"I'm sure Richard didn't know."

"Cuz he didn't want to know. Linc would've known. He can spot a jerk right away."

"Yes, I'm sure he can," she muttered, not willing to even think about comparing the two men. "Sandy loved you. That has to mean something."

"And she's dead! He's not. How fair is that?"

"It's not fair, Cullen. But it's the way it is. And most times we don't get choices, we just get results."

Annie cleared up the remaining dishes while Rocky sniffed under the chairs for crumbs and dropped morsels. She reached into the cupboard and took out two Oreos, giving them to the dog. He munched them down, looking for more. "You know the two-cookie limit."

Cullen grinned at all of this, and some detail dropped into place inside of her that she hadn't realized was missing. She didn't even precisely know what it was, but Annie felt a kind of resolve and peace—or maybe it was just a bit of that courage and grit that spilled from Cullen.

She glanced up at him where he leaned against the back doorjamb watching Rocky. "I'd like to help you, Cullen."

"How?"

Good question. If she totally accepted the premise that Cullen was Richard's son, there would be difficult decisions that, once made, would mean no turning back. She touched him briefly on the shoulder. "What's the best time to see Mr. McCoy?"

"You gonna come to Noah House?"

"Yes."

"Wow, he ain't gonna believe it."

She wasn't quite sure she did, either.

Chapter Six

Caroline Sheplin peered at the map in her lap while her husband, Gordon, looked for the street signs at the busy intersection.

"Typical of these small towns," he grumbled, easing through the green light. "No signs. What the hell good is a map if the town doesn't bother identifying the streets? Bartram's written analysis better match up with the site. Not too good for business if the customer can't find the place."

"I'm sure Maguires will make sure there's an abundance of signs."

He sighed. "Okay, Caroline. I know you detest billboards, but they do serve a purpose."

"What purpose beyond cluttering the view?"

"Never mind. If I can't even find the place, a billboard will be a moot point."

In the backseat sprawled eight-year-old Johnny, Red Sox cap turned backward, the plastic band creased into his forehead, tongue stuck between his teeth. He concentrated on the Game Boy he'd wheedled out of her just before this trip, much to his father's annoyance. "You buy them both too much stuff, Caroline. It's not child abuse to say no."

As far away from Johnny as she could manage and still be in the car was eleven-year-old Rose. Caroline bought "stuff" for her, too, but it was less noticeable because like her mother, Rose liked clothes and art supplies. Her daughter, wearing Gap shorts and a pink shirt over her first bra, had brought along art books, and because books never looked like toys, Gordon paid little attention.

"Turn right here," Caroline said, glancing at the art store on the corner and remembering. Mildred Perkins, the fluttery seventy-year-old owner who drove an industrial-sized Chrysler with a booster seat so she could see over the steering wheel, had always been solicitous of struggling artists. Caroline wondered if she was still living.

"Here? The directions said Ledyard Street. And at last we find a sign. This is County."

Caroline blinked. What had she been thinking? "Of course. Ledyard." She looked closely at the map. "My mistake. It's at the next light." She didn't tell him that County was a shortcut; she didn't tell him that she knew the unmarked streets of Bedford as well as the marked ones.

"Lots of construction going on," Gordon said, glancing around with a glow of approval. "That's good. A new housing boom means families, and families want yards and trees and bushes and flowers and mulch and garden gargoyles." His mood had obviously brightened.

Then from the backseat . . .

"Mom, tell him to move his feet."

"She's hogging the whole seat."

"Am not. You don't need room to play your idiot game."

"I've only got one game—you're the one with ten tons of stupid books."

"At least I have a brain. All you have is those dumb toys."

"Shut up."

"Stop it, right now, both of you," Caroline scolded. "As soon as we see the site we'll get some lunch."

"I want McDonald's," Johnny said.

Rose sighed heavily. "Please, Mom, can't we eat in a real restaurant?"

"What? You think Mickie's is the dump?"

"No, I think you're the dump."

"Will you two knock it off?" Gordon snapped. "I'm trying to concentrate."

Caroline turned and gave them both a stern look. "Put your feet on the floor, Johnny. And Rose, quit scowling. You'll get early wrinkles."

"She already looks like a prune," Johnny muttered.

"At least I don't have a snotty nose and grubby hands," Rose countered with a sniff, and moved even closer to the door.

"Piss on you."

Caroline caught Gordon's smile, and nudged him in the hip, giving him a "don't encourage him" look. To their son, she said, "Johnny Sheplin, is that any way to talk?"

"It is when's she's your sister."

"Please, just knowing we're related makes me sick."

"Shut up, fart-face."

"Johnny!"

Gordon slowed, eased to the right, out of traffic, and stopped. He put the car in park, and turning around, he said in that even, reasonable tone that Caroline had heard and admired for years, "Give it a break, guys, okay? I know you two can't stand the sight of one another and being stuck together for longer than forty-eight seconds is a trial worse than three life terms in prison, but do me a favor and deal with it. Next trip we'll leave you with your grandmother."

"No!" they chorused.

"Case closed." He moved back into traffic, giving a sideways look at Caroline.

"You always know how to settle them down," Caroline commented.

"Know what they *don't* want and make that the alternative. Works every time."

"I'm not sure I like my mother being the villain in this," she murmured. Her mother viewed children beyond two years old with a tenuous patience. Since being seen and not heard hadn't been taught by parents since the Truman administration—as she'd often reminded Caroline—her mother preferred visits that were short and reasonably silent.

"Come on, sweetheart," Gordon said. "You and I both know that your mother wouldn't want to endure them any more than they want to endure her."

"I suppose."

Silence returned to the backseat, and Gordon's attention turned back to the traffic as he made a right turn onto Ledyard Street.

Caroline's gaze wandered over the map, more amazed than she'd expected to be by the familiar names. Bedford had grown and expanded into a bustling town. When she'd lived here, it had been quaint and country and a bit doltish, struggling to find where it belonged in the rush for the tourist dollar. Newport, of course, commanded the biggest crowds, but many were finding the charm and uniqueness of interior Rhode Island.

At one time, she'd thought she'd live here permanently. She had everything she wanted—a cottage with a cutting garden, her art supplies, and her afternoon lover—how simple it all seemed back then. . . . An artist dedicated to her craft instead of the accumulation of money. Ah, the foolish idealism of being young and in love and believing she could be anything she wanted to be.

It wasn't sadness that made her throat raw, it was regret and the lies that she never spoke of. Looking back down at the map, she found the streets she'd traveled, the corner where she'd stood in the pouring rain . . . waiting and waiting. . . . The little dead-end street where she'd lived in that duplex, the roses she'd tried so hard to grow, the hours she'd sat in the yard with her sketchbook and watched the renovation of that house a few doors away. She wondered if it had ever been completed, if it had been placed and listed, as he'd said it would be, in the official register of historic Rhode Island places.

Gordon slowed down as Ledyard widened, and then to the left was a tired row of scattered stores trying to look like a shopping center. Once it had supported ten stores plus a JC Penny anchor store where Caroline had bought a winter coat, a toaster oven, and a blue-lace teddy because he loved her in blue. Now the center seemed barren and stark with a small office supply, a pet place, and a convenience store with a graffitti-splattered brick face.

If Gordon returned to Boston with a positive location report, Maguires would acquire, then level, and then build a huge home-garden complex.

He pulled into the lot and parked. "I'm going to do a walk around. Anybody want to come?"

"I do," Johnny said, scrambling out the door.

"Rose? Caroline?"

Rose opened the door. Caroline didn't.

"You three go ahead. I'll wait here."

Gordon waited until both kids were out of earshot. "Honey, are you okay? You seem a little wistful."

"Just tired from all the backseat wrangling."

"They're kids. Siblings fight and generally hate one another. I'd be more worried if they got along."

"Makes one see the benefit of being an only child."

"Only kids get spoiled."

"I was not spoiled."

"Okay, *most* only kids. Besides, big families are great. Then if one of the kids turns out to be a serial killer, you've still got some at home who will assure you that you're not a lousy parent."

"Now there's a consoling thought."

"Hey, I was one of six. Name-calling and fighting were put on the daily schedule."

"I don't think it's a lot to expect your children not to call each other disgusting names—at least where I can hear them."

He chuckled. "Ah, it's okay as long as you don't know about it."

"I just think that discretion and concern about the feelings of others are good traits."

Gordon cupped her chin and lifted until she looked at him. "You're a good mother and an even better wife. Our kids are lucky to have you, and I'm even luckier."

She slipped her arms around him and he kissed her. "We should have left the kids home," he murmured, touching the corners of her mouth with his.

She hugged him harder, reminding herself for the millionth time how very fortunate she was to have met and married Gordon. She'd closed the door on the past, and if it weren't for this trip to Bedford, old thoughts and memories would have stayed securely locked in history.

He cupped her breast lightly and squeezed, then kissed her again before releasing her. Winking, he growled in that deep, teasing way, "Later, we have a date."

She smiled, simply nodding.

Gordon opened the door and slipped out, glancing around. Johnny was looking at something on the ground—probably ants—and Rose had been checking out the animals in the pet-store window and now was walking back toward the car.

Gordon walked around to the passenger side scanning

the property. "Not a bad-looking site. Lot of potential here."

Caroline looked skeptical. "A little tight for a Maguires, don't you think?"

"Actually, it's perfect. We won't be dealing with a nursery, so a huge landmass isn't an issue. Getting into smaller towns and accommodating store size to the community landscape has been a popular trend. We've done it in two other places—mini-Maguires, we've been calling the more compact stores. They've proved successful in test markets. Corporate wants to stretch and diversify. Better to stay ahead of the trend than be stampeded by the competition. You know what they say about nothing ever staying the same. Sure you don't want to come and look with me?"

Some things do stay the same, she thought wistfully.

Gordon really was a dear man, always enthusiastic and positive about his job and his family. She loved him so much. He worked hard, had never given her even a moment of worry about faithfulness, adored his children, adored her. Caroline was very aware of just how blessed she was. She'd never been of the big-is-better mentality when it came to stores. In fact, she mostly avoided the superstores, preferring the small independents, but she had to credit Maguires for their realization that not every town wanted Godzilla-sized outlets. "On second thought, yes, I'd like to take a look."

He grinned as he pulled open the door. She got out and he took her hand.

"How does moving down here strike you?"

"Moving? Here to Bedford?" If he'd asked her to swim the Atlantic, she wouldn't have been more startled. "But we have a home in Wellesley."

"Maguires posed the offer. It would mean more money plus a chance to be on the inside at one of these smaller, town-friendly stores. If they work out as well as predicted, it could mean a promotion."

"But we have a home—" she repeated because she couldn't think of what else to say.

"Honey, it's called selling one house and buying another. Done every day. Besides, it's not as if I'm suggesting the Fiji Islands. Bedford isn't on the other side of the world."

"But the kids and school and . . ."

He squeezed her hand. "And don't forget leaving your mother."

"Very funny."

He turned serious again. "Just think about it as a possibility."

In other words, start getting used to the possibility. She knew Gordon. When he posed these scenarios, there was more at stake than just wanting her opinion and support. "I'll think about it," she murmured, because that was the easiest response.

"I love you," he said with so much meaning and warmth that Caroline felt as if she could handle any decision.

She slipped an arm around his waist. "I love you, too."

He lowered his head and kissed her lightly, then let her go. "Hey Johnny, how about we get sodas first? I know, Rose. Caffine-free Pepsi. Seven-Up for you, honey?"

"Yes, fine," she said absently.

And then he was trotting on ahead, grabbing his son in a playful neck hold as they headed inside for drinks.

"Mom, are we really going to move *here*?" Rose asked, obviously having overheard some of the conversation; she said it as if "here" were an artistic wasteland.

"It's a pretty town."

"Yuck. There's nothing here, just a lot of old houses and little stores. I didn't even see a mall."

A big plus for Bedford, Caroline thought. One less mall in the world was a benefit, in her opinion. To Rose, she nodded solemnly. "A definite minus."

"And did you see that place with all those disgusting boys playing basketball? I mean it looked like some gang center."

"I don't think there's such a place as a gang center."

"Looked gross."

She put an arm around her daughter. "When I was your age, I loved adventurous places."

"Here? How could anyone have an adventure here?"

"Guess it depends on where you look."

"I like Wellesley," she said stubbornly.

"I do, too."

"Then you won't make us move."

"It's not just my decision. Besides, I think you're getting ahead of yourself."

"Daddy had that look."

"What look?"

"The one he gets when he knows he can talk you into what he wants."

"Ahh."

"Usually men use it when they want sex."

Caroline's eyebrows lifted. "And, of course, you're an expert in that area."

"I go to movies and watch guys." She sighed dramatically. "They all think they're so cool and can get anything they want. They think girls are dumb."

Sometimes we are. "Are they?"

She shrugged. "I'm not."

"Good."

"I think sex is stupid. I'm going to be a virgin forever."

Caroline smiled. "Yes, I planned that, too, when I was your age. That is until—"

"I know. Until you met Daddy and fell madly in love.

But the guys I know aren't like daddy. He's handsome and cool and sophisticated."

"He's also forty-two. Hardly a fair comparison to a preteen boy."

"Just think, when you were eleven like me, daddy was nineteen. That's wild."

"Differences at those ages are immense. Not so when we're all adults. Better go help your dad. Looks as if he bought sandwiches and chips, too." Rose hurried toward them while Caroline regathered her thoughts and tucked them away with her memories.

One thing she was very sure of. She wasn't moving to Bedford.

"Okay, Eddie, we can do this the hard way or the easy way. Penny and Nick are willing to talk about taking you back, although God knows why."

Just an hour before, Linc had listened to a tearful, guilt-ridden Penny beg him to let Eddie return. Nick was less enthusiastic, but Penny was convinced she'd been too hard on the troubled teen. The empathetic instinct of exceptional mothers, Linc had concluded years ago, was unmatched by any social program or experiment he'd ever encountered.

One glance at the sullen Eddie should have been enough to make Penny never want to see him again, never mind take him back into her home. But Linc knew Penny wasn't seeing Eddie as a statistical success or failure. He'd become her son, not by birth but by grit and patience and love.

Looking at this surly, selfish, addicted kid slumped in the chair as if life being a bitch was someone else's fault, Linc guessed that in all probability, the creep would not grow up to be an exec with General Motors. More like a major-league addict, in prison or dead before he reached his twenty-first birthday.

Such raw cynicism had become his reaction too frequently lately, but he would have to be blind not to see the familiar pattern. Then again, Linc had wearied of excuses and blame going everywhere but on the one who created the chaos.

The vivid contrast between Cullen's actions and Eddie's were too obvious to miss. Cullen had survived a horrible experience—losing his mother and then a total rejection by his father followed by foster homes that hadn't worked out. Then the mess with Annie. The poor kid couldn't invent a break. Eddie, on the other hand, had been given one chance after another and systematically fucked up all of them.

Using his best affronted, who-needs-them tone, Eddie finally said, "Who says I wanna go back? They don't let me do nothin'. All they want is to make a buncha rules like I was in a friggin' jail."

"You mean they had a rule about you not getting drunk, shooting up, and leaving shit all over your room? Hard to imagine how they could be so nasty and mean."

"Yeah, I think so, too."

Linc sighed, taking a paper from a folder and sliding it across the desk.

"What's this?" he asked, picking it up and then scowling. "I don't know no Max and the Mops."

"It's a bill for the damages that you're going to pay for."

"Huh?"

"Damages, spelled D-A-M-A-G-E-S."

"I can spell."

"Excellent. Then we're making some progress. As I was saying, since you're paying for Max's crew to go in and clean up, and your cash flow isn't flowing, you can wash dishes here or wash them down at the homeless shelter."

"I don't wanna do neither."

"What you want ain't an option, pal. Social Services is leaving you here temporarily. So here's the deal—while you're taking up space, you'll do what I say."

"How come you don't make Gallagher do what you say? I ain't seen him washin' no dishes. I ain't seen him doin' nothing but comin' and goin' like he owned this dump."

"He didn't trash the people who loved him."

"He ain't no saint."

"No one here is." Linc walked to the door and opened it. "Dishes here or at the shelter. You got thirty seconds to make a choice or you're outta here."

"You said I'm stayin'. You can't toss me."

"Try me. Twenty seconds."

"I know my rights."

"Never heard of any. Ten seconds."

"I hate doin' dishes."

"Time's up." He opened the door. "Get out."

"No, wait. You can't. I ain't got nowhere to go."

"I'm crying big tears for you."

"Shit." He scowled and he muttered and he fisted his hands, but he got to his feet, slipped on his best cool expression, and swaggered out the door that Linc closed firmly as soon as he'd cleared it.

He went back to his desk, pushed his hands through his hair, and picked up the thick file on Eddie Montrosia. Somewhere in here was the buried hope Penny had for the kid.

Linc knew all about buried hope; it was the possibility of turning that hope for troubled kids into a bonfire of renewal and productivity that had brought him to Noah House. Yet, in the past few years, too many Eddies had beaten him down. No one knew how close Linc McCoy had come to walking away, giving it up for a job with money, decent hours, and a place to live that wasn't a littered teenage wasteland.

Close, until Cullen had come to Noah House.

There was something about the kid who wouldn't quit that inspired Linc when inspiration had become as sparse as happy endings.

Vesco popped his head in the door. "There's a real babe out here. Wants a 'tour.' Do we have 'tours,' whatever the hell they are?"

"Good word for you to look up. Who is it?"

He scrunched his face up. "Don't know. Never seen her before. Said she knew you; said she could make an appointment and come back. Made a big deal about making an appointment. Do we do appointments? Man, she talks funny."

Linc's eyes widened. Annie? Was she here to yank his chain after his unannounced visit? No way. Couldn't be. No entity on earth could have gotten her within twenty miles of Noah House.

"You want I should send her in or tell her you ain't got time."

"Send her in."

Vesco left, and Linc put Max's bill into Eddie's file and wondered if there'd be another one coming for broken dishes. When his door opened, he glanced up.

"Well, I'll be damned."

"Hi. I hope this isn't a bad time."

Chapter Seven

"This can't be Annie Hunter." His amazement was genuine. Both in the fact that she was standing in his office, and that the jeans and shirt were such a contrast to the business-woman suit she'd worn earlier.

"Guess I surprised you."

He detected the smile that lurked at the edges of her eyes. She was relishing catching him off guard, and he played along, feigning consternation. "No one told you that people in jeans have to come in the back door?"

She glanced around the messy too-small office. "Hmmm, you mean this isn't the back door? And here I thought I was doing it just right."

Linc chuckled. "You look, uh—" he wanted to say sexy and gorgeous. "Just right for a visit to Noah House."

He came around the desk, drawing closer to her and feeling as excited as a kid on his way to the circus. Such a juvenile reaction was a bit unsettling, but it felt too damn good to ignore. "Vesco said you wanted a tour, and since our regular tour guide is doing time—" Knock it off, he reminded himself. She just might take you seriously. "Guess you're stuck with me to show you around."

"What were you going to say?"

"Nothing. My cynicism of late has risen to a new level. Tell me, what made you decide to come over here?"

"Cullen, actually."

"Not another nap on your porch."

"Actually, he was playing with Rocky, who thinks Cullen is his ball-retrieving pal." She paused, the sounds of an outside basketball pick-up game drifting in the windows. "From what I've seen in the few minutes I've been here, this is a lively place. Tell me, Mr. McCoy, are all the kids here in as much awe of you as Cullen seems to be?"

"I hope so." He grinned. "Call me Linc. Mr. McCoy makes me feel like I'm in trouble."

"Not this time."

"Probably a first."

"So is the Linc for Lincoln?"

"Yes."

"A family name?"

"No, that would be too easy. The old man never did anything the simple way. He went in for the grand and complicated. He liked Abraham Lincoln. In fact, he collected books on Lincoln, read every one. He had some idea that if one of his sons was named for him, he might grow up to be some kind of hero-emancipator."

"Was he right?"

"No."

For a moment she looked taken aback by his bluntness, but she didn't press and he didn't explain. She might feel easier with him than she had that morning, but no way was she ready to hear that he'd gotten his kid brother killed. Or that the father who'd admired Lincoln had also been a drug dealer when he wasn't mowing his lawn, going to Little League games, and helping a neighbor shingle his roof. In fact he doubted she'd ever be ready for any of that.

Linc went to the door and said, "Hey Vesco, I'm going

to show the lady around. Check the kitchen and make sure Eddie is busy."

"Got it."

"Come on," he said to Annie, touching her back to ease her toward the central room in the house that housed a TV, a pool table, shelves sagging with magazines and books, and a lot of old, overstuffed chairs. A couple of boys were playing pool. They glanced up, and when they saw her, they looked at one another, then at him. Linc noted that both raised their eyebrows, and he could guess their question. *Not another Brooke.*

"This is the gathering room. Bobby and Figley—Fig for short—have been here the longest. Seven years." To the boys, he said, "This is Annie."

The two boys mumbled a hello, exchanged a "yep, another Brooke" look, and went back to their game.

Annie glanced around, again aware of an energy that she'd felt the moment she'd stepped into Noah House. Her decision to come had been for Cullen, but now that she was here, she realized not only that this was a whole new world, but also that it was one she couldn't have imagined even thinking about last week. She was fascinated.

"How many kids are here?" she asked.

"It varies. Right now we're full with twenty. Bobby and Fig came here when they were twelve. They've both turned their lives around—a remarkable story. I keep telling them that if they don't move on, they'll be permanently hired and stuck for life."

"So no one ever outgrows living here."

"Nineteen is the max. We allow that extra year to give them a fallback place as they ease into productive independence. It's not enough that they just have a job. They need to be able to support a place to live, pay their bills, and become useful citizens."

"And do they all do that?"

"Many do. A lot of the work is about changing their attitudes. Getting them to turn their focus legal instead of illegal. These kids have mostly had role models who break the laws. Part of what Noah House does is show them that being an honest citizen is cool, to convince them that they can do and be whatever they want, which at times sounds more like lofty words than reality. But these boys are smart and quick, and if they put just half of their intelligence into being productive citizens rather than criminals, they'll be successful."

"It must be very satisfying."

"Sometimes."

"And when it isn't?"

"We move on."

"They're lost, you mean."

"Human drives are powerful and instinctive. It's easier to follow the crowd than lead the crowd. All these kids have enemies, and they have friends who should be enemies. They know guys with big bucks, big cars, and sexy girlfriends. It's not easy to turn away from that and face a fifth-floor walk-up and boxed macaroni and cheese. They have to find within themselves something deeper. Part of what we do here is make them see that they have that deeper core just waiting for them to tap into it. Noah House is a respite, a place where they are safe and provided for while they learn skills. But most important they find that core of themselves that wants to reach beyond the easy."

Annie listened, struck by the enormous scope of such an undertaking. No buzz words that sounded good but often were more catchphrases than realistic. The landscape here was larger and grander, and most important, it had a goal and a conclusion.

She liked specific goals, and she prided herself on being goal-oriented. Decide specifically what you want, and then go about getting it done. And it was more than obvious that Cullen had that same approach. She had no doubt that Linc had been partially responsible for bringing that out.

"Where does Cullen fit?"

"He's a kid with a mission, and landing here gave him the opportunity to go after what he wants. It's easier to focus a kid once you've identified his problem. He'd been in a few foster homes, and none worked out. And in that time, he was angry and suspicious of anyone who tried to help him. That's not unusual, since a lot of these kids have trusted someone or something in the past and gotten dumped on in return, whether abandoned or rejected or used. Cullen was carrying all three. He's slept in alleys and lived for a few months with a hooker who had a maternal streak. He got into some drugs and got busted a couple of times. He ran away from the foster homes numerous times, and then when he was found and returned, he became even nastier. The last place he was, the guy was a pimp who sent the kids on weekend sex trips."

"My God."

"He'd been working that deal for years. Used another kid who ended up here, too. Cullen wasn't as cooperative as the guy liked, so he beat him into submission."

They were in a narrow hall that led to other areas of the house. Annie sagged back against the wall as she listened to a story that made her heart ache. How could an adoption become such a horror story?

"Cullen told me his adoptive father didn't want him after Sandy died. So all this awful stuff happened because of him."

"You could say that."

"Does he know? I mean didn't anyone ever try to make him see what he'd thrown his son into?"

"Probably, but for the bastard to do anything required him to care. Cullen was no choir boy, so Parker Gallagher had a lot of reasons to not care."

"Not care! The fact that he had some rebelliousness was exactly the reason his father should have cared. Cullen was his son!"

"Apparently Gallagher didn't start with that premise. He viewed Cullen as a mistake. A pariah was what he called him."

Annie turned away. He took her arm, and he could feel the hard beat of anger within her.

"The man should be shot," she said.

"My sentiments exactly." He'd seen these reactions before when an outsider heard a particularly devastating story. And while he knew the emotions were real, he also knew they were mostly fleeting. Momentary heat and outrage that would dissolve once they'd returned to their own lives. Linc understood that. A flash of anger, a need to do something, and then the inevitable something turned out to be a check. Generous and needed, a conscience salve, but also easier.

He turned to continue down the hall when she stopped him. "What happened to him?"

"Nothing. Unfortunately the family-court judge didn't set up a firing squad. He ordered Cullen sent here to get straightened out. The outrage was that it was Gallagher who needed a kick in the ass, but when you're a tenured professor at some big-time college and you count your friends in the judiciary, ass-kicking is frowned upon. Added to that is the attitude of family court. They bend their findings with pretzel logic trying to preserve family units, even though too often that's a bigger disaster."

"Something should be done."

"Yeah, and something should be done about drug dealers, serial killers, and abusers. But no one can fix everything. Here we focus on the things we can fix. Cullen is fixable. He's not thinking about getting even or dwelling on the things that are out of his control. His focus has been to find out who the people are who got him here."

The people who got him here. Richard and another woman. At her age, Annie thought she knew most of the important things in life. Like trust and faith and courtesy and being open-minded about those things she didn't understand. And yet her first instinct with Linc and Cullen had been suspicion because they threatened her life as she knew it.

Since talking with Cullen as a boy trying to find his father rather than a threat to her and Richard, she now saw the teenager in a different light—not as someone to fear or hide from, but someone a lot like her when she was trying to find answers about her own father. Stone walls of silence and mystery tended to strengthen tenacity rather than discourage it.

Still, Annie was too aware of the inevitable complications.

There were Richard's parents. There was her late husband's pristine reputation that would certainly be marred once it was learned he'd had a secret child. There was her own pride, and as prepared as she thought she was for the questions and pitiful looks, she knew she would bristle and hate all of it.

"Annie, he isn't your problem."

"But his story is a problem. Not because I don't believe him, but because I do. How much easier this visit here would be if I had proof that you and Cullen were con artists or worse."

"Sweetheart, if you had that kind of proof, a visit here would have included the cops and your lawyer."

She sighed. "I spent all weekend trying to convince myself you and Cullen were not only wrong, but were out to take advantage of a dead man. It was so much easier to believe you had bad motives, because the alternative was too horrifying to consider."

He stared down at her, finally saying softly, "Look, the toughest battle is realizing that what we've always believed might be wrong. It makes us angry and outraged and even a little desperate. We want to cover up news that can hurt or even destroy. In the end, we have to learn to live with the bad stuff. And once in awhile we become better people because of it."

"Very philosophical. And I don't disagree, but no child should have to experience what Cullen did."

He shrugged. "At the risk of a cliché, life's a bitch."

They walked through a laundry area, where three other boys were loading clothes into two washers. A door was open that led outside, where she could hear more boys talking and yelling. From overhead came the whine of a vacuum.

They walked into the sunshine and around the building to a yard and a vegetable garden. Another boy had a basket and was picking summer squash.

"Hey Linc. We got some early tomatoes. Puttin' them plants in early paid off."

"You got lucky."

"No way. I know how to grow 'em."

Linc said, "Jacko is our resident horticulturist. When he came here, the only thing he knew about gardening was harvesting his old man's pot plants and selling the stuff to support his own drug habit."

Annie walked closer to the garden. It was fairly large, with neat rows that were lush and green and without a weed in sight. He'd used newspapers to mulch. Not as pretty as the commercial landscaping products, but Annie recalled her own mother using newspapers on their small garden. And that garden had provided summer eating and a winter of canned tomatoes, green beans, and beets.

Annie knelt down. "Hi Jacko. I'm Annie."

"Cullen told me about you."

Annie felt a twitch of defensiveness. "Oh?"

"You here to raise stinkin' hell about him? Guys around here ain't gonna like it if you do. Guys around here know suck-up jive when they hear it. Linc knows it, too, so cash ain't gonna cut it."

Annie rocked back a bit. What was he talking about? Some kind of payoff?"

"Jacko, cool down the heat. You're gonna scare her away."

She appreciated his intervention, but she wanted to handle this. Her heart pumped, and her hands were suddenly clammy. It wasn't fear for herself physically, but a realization that how she responded would have to be different than a snippy retort if she expected to come back here and be taken seriously. It was important not to appear afraid, act nervous, or talk mealy-mouthed nonsense. "Payoffs for silence are a little out of my line," she said as if she'd been accused a hundred times before.

"Yeah? Well, cash don't work, but humpin' him don't, either. Brooke found that out."

Brooke? A woman slept with Linc because she wanted something?

"Knock it off, Jacko," Linc snapped, and although her back was to him, she could feel the tension and fury roll off of him.

Annie folded her hands and hoped she didn't look as rattled as she felt. While she should have been feeling insulted by Jacko's comments, she was more curious about this Brooke.

Instead of backing away as she guessed he expected, she gestured to the rows between the plants. "My mother swore by newspapers to keep the weeds down."

Jacko didn't miss a beat. No amazement that she was still there. No surprise that he hadn't forked up her outrage. "Yeah, Linc told me to try them cuz they're free. They rot right back into the ground and don't cause no sick dirt problems."

"An environmentalist."

"Huh?"

"Someone who worries about the land."

"Don't know nothin' about that. All I know is that if you work a garden right one year, then the next year it won't piss on you."

Annie smiled. One of life's truths that works with humans, too. Don't make a mess of your life and it won't come back and bite you. "I can't argue with that."

Jacko went back to picking squash.

She stood watching him, caught by his rhythm and exactness. For Annie, gardening always brought a basic sense of satisfaction, but to see a boy who lived in a halfway house connected to that same sense of productivity from the earth . . . she was indeed awed, but as much by the shattered stereotypes as by the fact that she'd have something in common with an ex–drug addict.

They resumed the tour with Linc saying nothing about Jacko's comments. Annie, however, was curious about Brooke; an interest that had nothing to do with Noah House and everything to do with Linc.

"Well? Can't you talk?"

Vesco, who indeed could, was too stunned by the sudden appearance of this woman who looked as out of place as a new Jag with his name on it. She was meaty, and he'd bet she'd never been hungry. She wore a pink suit, the jacket open, and a straw hat that flipped up at the sides reminding him of an empty bird's nest.

"Yes, ma'am," he muttered, figuring she must be a big shot so he better at least look official.

Her sigh was long and heavy. "Young man, I don't usually make personal visits to charities that I support, never mind those that I don't, and I don't write a donation check without my attorneys doing a thorough check on their credibility."

"You wanna give cash?"

She peered at him. "Certainly not."

Now he was really confused.

"I'm here because my niece insisted I see it myself." She pulled at her blouse in a cooling gesture. "Mercy, it's hot in here. Why don't you turn on the air conditioner?"

"Cuz we ain't got none."

"How did I ever let Penny talk me into this," she muttered to no one in particular.

"Hey, lady, I'm just here to answer the phone and keep out the jerks and bums."

The woman looked as if she'd had a sudden pain. She rolled her eyes. "Well, since I'm neither and I'd like to get out of this oven, will you please get someone who can answer my questions? I'd also like a tour, but not today."

"What's with all the tours," he mumbled, proud of the fact that he now knew what the word meant. "Uh, I'll have to get Linc, and he's busy right now."

"Well, interrupt him. I don't have all day."

Linc took two cold cans of Coke from the tiny refrigerator in his office and after Annie was seated with hers, he pushed aside a pile of papers and perched on the corner of the desk.

"So now you've seen the place, you've met some of the kids, what do you think?"

"The jelly beans are a nice touch," she said, indicating the tall jar on the desk.

"Some psyche guy told me that something familiar helps kids to relax, so I decided to try it."

"Does it make them relax?"

He shrugged. "It gives them something to do with their mouthes besides swear."

She took a sip of the Coke. "Jacko was particularly informative."

"He's the garden expert."

"I was talking about Brooke."

He tipped the can to his mouth and took a long swallow. "Ah yes, Brooke."

"You don't strike me as the kind of man to be taken in by a woman."

He raised his eyebrows.

"Bad choice of words. What I mean is you seem too savvy to—"

"To get hosed for stupidity?" He rolled the cold can between his hands. "Don't bet on it. Look around, Annie Hunter. No one here wants to be studied and analyzed so you can decide they're heroes with altruism running in their veins."

"I'm not looking for any hero."

"Then a heroic cause. You're experiencing a rush of interest, enthusiasm, pity, or some other inner enlightenment, and now you want us all wrapped up in a neat little package that you can tuck away as your good deed of the month."

Annie stayed calm. He was not going to ruffle her. "You don't know my motives, and to assume they're that shallow is insulting. I came here hoping to learn something about Noah House, and yes something about you. I made a lot of assumptions over the weekend and today, after talking with Cullen, I realized that I wasn't being fair."

"Fair? And that would be? You deciding a boy has a right to know who his birth parents are?"

Annie got to her feet and set her Coke can down a few inches from his thigh. She wanted to dump it in his lap. "You know what? You're not going to get rid of me by insulting me. And since we were getting along fairly well until Jacko mentioned Brooke . . . Obviously, I don't know what this Brooke did—"

"She donated money, a lot of money."

"And that's bad?"

He rose, turning away from her. "And between her writing checks, we had an affair." He swung back to face her. "Want the salacious details?"

To Annie's horror she did. "Of course not."

"You're a lousy liar."

She lifted her chin and looked straight at him. "All right. You said affair. Was she married?"

"It doesn't matter. It's over."

Annie stared at him for a long time before finally saying, "You loved her, didn't you? You loved her and she hurt you and—"

"She dumped me. End of love, end of story. Let's drop it, okay? I want to know what's going on with Annie Hunter." He set the can down and folded his arms. "You coming down here, acting as if we were old high school classmates who just rediscovered one another at a reunion. If this is about nixing Cullen's attempt to find out about his father—"

"And how would my coming here accomplish that?"

"You tell me."

"You're the one with the suspicions."

"You being here doesn't fit."

"Doesn't fit your stereotype of women like me? You know, those with too much money who just shop, gossip, and do lunch?"

"I've known more than a few," he muttered, but offered no apology.

She walked to the window and then back, suddenly restless with the tension that flared. It was too hot for arguments, but his false assumptions annoyed her. And she was still curious about his involvement with Brooke. There was more between them than an affair. Had he fallen in love with her? He hadn't denied it. Then she curbed her speculation. It didn't concern her and she didn't care anyway. "I came here to talk about Cullen, not who *you* think I am."

He had powerful eyes and they cut deep; she guessed he could be very dangerous if he wanted to be. This was not a man raised with polite manners and good breeding, as Richard had been.

Then he sighed and urged her to sit down again. When she had, he said, "Talk to me about Cullen."

"I believe him."

He didn't pretend ignorance. "Okay."

"I want to help him."

"I'm listening."

"If Richard was his father, there has to be someone somewhere who knows about it."

"The birth mother for one."

"Yes, but from talking to Cullen, he isn't that interested in finding her. Might that be because he loved Sandy? To Cullen, she *was* his mother. I got the impression he thinks he'll betray her memory if he focuses on the other woman."

"Good observation. Plus Richard is dead, therefore he can't hurt Cullen. He can't reject him the way a surprised birth mother could."

"So Richard is a safer search."

"Yes. Plus Cullen genuinely likes you, and therefore he's presumed that since you're pretty cool and rich and not howling to anyone who'll listen that he's trashing your husband, that his birth father would be the same if he was alive."

"I'm afraid my reaction hasn't been that straightforward. If Richard were alive . . ." She let her voice trail off.

"Look, your marriage is none of my business, nor Cullen's, but a husband cheating is not big news."

"That doesn't change the fact that it's wrong and selfish and destroys trust and honor. Just because a marriage survives doesn't mean it's happy."

"So I've heard," he muttered.

Annie continued. "I have a couple of friends with cheating husbands. One pretends it isn't happening and the other has taken the view that all men cheat so she might as well make the best of it. With both, the idea of divorce horrifies them, so they continue living the lie that they are happily married."

"Maybe they are. It would depend on what you want out of the marriage."

"I couldn't live like that."

"No, I don't imagine that you could."

"Besides, this thing between Richard and the other woman was a lot more than an affair. They had a child. A child I never had with Richard. If he were still alive, I can't imagine that I would be so understanding."

"Yet you're managing to be understanding now."

Annie realized he was right. Her tolerant attitude made no sense. She should be hurt and horrified and furious with Richard. Perhaps resent Cullen. Or she should be determined to maintain a cloak of denial that any of it was true. Then again, she'd felt those things and more—all weekend and to what end? She certainly hadn't awakened that morning feeling smug and justified. And was this turning genuine or just another buffer against what she knew would be difficult days ahead?

She just didn't know.

Chapter Eight

Annie rose, adjusting the strap of her shoulder bag. "I think I'd better be going."

Linc nodded. "So what's next?"

"I have to tell Richard's parents. They've been in Italy on vacation. Richard's mother collects Italian art and the trip is a yearly event. They're due back on Wednesday."

"Were they close to their son? Are they close to you?"

"They adored Richard. James and I get along fine, but Vera is another story. We were never close. She blames me because Richard and I didn't have children. Then when he died so unexpectedly . . ." She stopped herself.

"She blamed you for his death?"

Annie heard the incredulity in his tone. "No, no, she wanted grandchildren and because that didn't happen she blamed me. At first she was patient and seemingly understanding, but I don't think she ever believed that no matter how hard we tried, I couldn't get pregnant. And for sure she never thought I was even more disappointed than Richard. Then with his sudden death, they both grew distant, although in recent months it's been better. James especially has been kind. I think Vera still believes I wasted his life." She looked away, recalling the stretch of years where getting pregnant had dominated all their energy to the point where she, more than Richard, couldn't think about anything else. Desperation and disappointment had plagued her days, and she shuddered now with the memories of those endless cycles of frustration.

"Annie, I know this isn't my business, but did your husband feel the way you think his mother did?"

"That I'd wasted his life? I don't know."

And even as she said it, her thoughts came to an abrupt stop. Why didn't she know? Of course he'd never said anything overt, but perhaps there had been some regret. He certainly seemed to love kids, and they'd built the house with kids in mind. Of course, he'd been disappointed, but had he regretted marrying her? It was a question she'd never considered.

Then, as though waiting to pop into her thoughts, she recalled Iris Moffitt. "Richard had been dating another woman when we met, the daughter of friends of the Hunters. Iris married about a year after Richard and I, and she and her husband at last count had four kids. We would run into them occasionally at a dinner party and they would show pictures and brag about what their kids had accomplished. Richard was always gracious and interested, where most of the other men would be looking for ways to escape."

"So you think Richard might have been thinking that if he'd married this Iris those kids could have been his."

"Maybe. For sure the Hunters felt that way. His mother, especially, said so to Richard."

"And he told you?"

She nodded.

"What a guy," he said with no shortage of sarcasm.

"I can understand their disappointment. Richard was their only son and, well, they feel cheated."

"They? So even though your father-in-law was less critical, you think he felt cheated, too."

"I'm sure he did."

"You're an amazing woman. You're concerned about them when it should have been the other way around."

He was watching her, not, she sensed, out of idle curiosity, but with genuine interest. It seemed a bit late, but she wanted someone to be outraged that she had been cheated—not blaming her but angry right along with her. Annie's hostility, however, hadn't been directed at Richard or even at the Hunters, but at whatever enmity had decided she would be barren.

"It just seemed so unfair that some women get pregnant so easily and others like me can't even once." She sighed. "We had such plans. Financially, we could easily have afforded kids, plus I wanted to stay home, so I planned to scale back my business and work at home until they were in school all day. . . . It all seemed like an easy plan and I assumed the baby would come just like falling in love and getting married. . . . How incredibly naïve I was." Her words softened into silence, and she realized she was on the verge of telling him things that were too personal and too painful.

"Earlier, you said Vera blamed you . . ."

"Obviously she was right, since Richard has a son." She heard her own bitterness. The appearance of Cullen proved beyond any doubt that their childless marriage had been her fault.

She was a bit surprised that he hadn't asked why she hadn't conceived—it certainly would have been the obvious next question. But he hadn't, and she felt little incentive to detail the compounded conception failures of irregular ovulation and sperm allergies.

"Want me to go with you?"

For a moment she was confused, so caught up in her past sadness and regrets. "You mean to see the Hunters?"

"Yes."

"Why?"

He shrugged. "It's tough breaking unexpected news."

"Yes, but you coming with me . . . I don't know whether that would be a good idea." She shuddered. Actually, because her relationship with the Hunters, while cordial, couldn't be called fuzzy warm; she had no idea what they would do. Would they even believe her? For sure they'd be skeptical of a stranger she presented.

"Annie, I'm not talking about for them. I mean for you."

When she looked blank, he added, "They're not going to believe you. I can back you up."

And suddenly she wanted to embrace the offer. Someone on her side, someone unfazed by what she knew would be the Hunters' outrage and denial. "They won't understand."

"Come on. They're adults. And you're not telling them to hurt them, but in fact to prepare them. How can they not understand that?"

"I'm just trying to imagine how I would feel in their place."

"You already know how you felt. Shocked denial and anger. The thing with shooting the messenger is that afterward all you have is the message. In other words, the truth is the truth. They'll have to decide if they want to deal with it and in the end have a grandson, or deny it and deny Cullen."

"You make it sound so simple."

"Guaranteed, it won't be simple."

The more they talked, the more she realized that she'd slipped from distrust and suspicion into a reliance on him that seemed too smooth a transition of emotions. She knew better than to allow her feelings to overwhelm facts, and facts about him were what she didn't have. "Why are you doing this? For Cullen, I know, but what do you get out of it?"

He stood and walked to the window where outside the late-afternoon sun had slipped behind some clouds. "I haven't decided yet."

"That's hardly reassuring."

He turned. "You want a lie so you can put me into some safe box that won't mess up whatever your perception is?"

"My original perception was that you were a hustler and a con artist."

"And now?"

"I don't know."

"Then we've made some progress." He came around the desk and touched her back to ease her toward the door. "So are we on for Thursday? I'll even wear a suit."

She turned and he was so close that with the slightest turn of her body, she would have been in his arms. The idea excited her and alarmed her. Without moving, she said, "You in a suit? How could I turn down such an offer? Thursday around two?"

"Done. You want to pick me up? Or if you're feeling reckless, we can go on the bike."

Annie's eyes widened. Ride on his motorcycle? The idea intrigued her. And once again, she was a bit over-whelmed by her fast-changing thoughts about him. "I'll pick you up."

"Chicken."

"Absolutely."

He cupped her chin, pressing his thumb lightly below her lower lip. She stood staring at him, unable to move. For some crazy and totally unexplained reason her head was buzzing and the room seemed to close around her. If he kissed her or she reached up and kissed him . . .

"Thanks for believing Cullen," he whispered, then withdrew his hand.

She stepped back, feeling sheepish and embarrassed.

Fumbling a bit, she reached for the door knob, turning it and pulling.

Linc stepped aside, saying nothing. Suddenly she was hot and weary and wanted only to escape. But once she'd stepped into the main public area, she came to an abrupt and surprised halt.

Standing just a few feet away was Grace Tooley, the client Annie had seen earlier. The woman looked as much out of her element as sterling silver at a biker picnic.

"Grace! What are you doing here?"

The expensively dressed woman seemed equally startled. "Why Annie Hunter, you aren't what I expected either. Are you here making a donation?"

"No, actually, I wanted to see how Noah House worked."

"Really. I had no idea you were interested in local charities. I would have filled you in on what I knew when we met earlier. Although truth to tell, I don't know much." She tossed Vesco a perturbed look. "I still don't." She patted her forehead and her throat with a lace-trimmed handkerchief. "The dreadful heat here is enough to make me never want to return."

Annie glanced back at Linc, who stood as though he were nothing more than a bored passerby. Odd. Shouldn't he be the one making nice and asking questions? Well, if he wasn't curious, she was. To Grace, she asked, "How did you come to know about Noah House?"

"Well, not from any attempt by anyone here to tell me, that's for sure." She sent a darkish look in Vesco's direction; he looked even more engrossed in his comic book. She barely looked at Linc. "I've been trying to get some information. My niece has been raving and pushing me to consider it for my charities list."

"Your niece." Annie's mind sorted through what she knew about Grace's family. She didn't recall any mention of a niece.

"From the poorer side of the family, but a dear child just the same. God knows she could use some charity herself, but she insisted Noah House is more worthy. She wanted me to come down in person and talk to Lincoln McCoy." She peered over her glasses at Linc, and whispered to Annie, "Is that him?"

"Yes, it is."

Grace watched him, and when he said nothing, she said to Annie, "Is he usually so unresponsive? It seems to me that if this place were legitimate, they'd have some people working here who could talk. First him," she gestured toward Vesco, who continued to ignore the conversation, "and now this Lincoln person."

How Annie had suddenly been thrust into the role of handling a potential contributor mystified her, but she knew Grace and understood she needed special handling. And the woman was known for charitable generosity, and Lord knew, Noah house could use some. It was really quite amusing—from getting her first tour to securing a contributor. And McCoy had better be suitably grateful.

Annie took the woman's arm and guided her to a chair, where a bit of a breeze was struggling through the front door. "I assure you Noah House is legitimate. Richard had made several donations, and he was always careful about charities."

"Humph." But there was no doubt that the mention of Richard had reassured her. "From what I've seen, they certainly need something more than a few dollars. Paint and air conditioning would be a good place to start. I'll have to have my lawyer do some more checking." Once more she looked at Linc, who seemed to be taking it all in with a kind of scowling expression that clearly said he'd rather be listening to nails down a chalkboard. Vesco was still deep in the adventures of some superhero.

"How are you funded, Mr. McCoy?"

"State and private donations."

"And do you have a list of the private donors?"

"Somewhere."

"Sounds very slipshod to me."

"We try."

Grace's eyes widened, and Annie gave Linc a withering look.

"Linc prefers to spend his time with the kids rather than shuffling papers," Annie said, trying to cover his rudeness and then wondering why. If Grace decided against contributing, the loss could probably be blamed on Linc's less-than-friendly attitude. "I've met some of the boys, and Noah House has done a fine job."

"You certainly sound like their head spokeswoman."

"Just my impressions, Grace."

"So you're a volunteer?" Her gaze slid over the jeans and tee shirt. Annie wasn't sure if the look was approval or distaste.

"No, an observer."

She scowled as though trying to figure out what an observer was. "Oh my, but it's hot," she said fanning herself and blotting more with her hankie.

Annie walked over to Linc. "Are you usually this annoyingly taciturn about a potential donor?"

"Is that what she is? So far all I've heard is complaints."

"She's accustomed to attention."

"No, really? I would have never guessed."

"It wouldn't hurt you to be a bit solicitous."

"She wants to donate, let her write a check and put it in the mail."

"Maybe she'd like to see where her money is going and for what?"

"Well, she's seen it, and so far all I've heard is a cranky whine. My job is with the kids, not wet-nursing some uptown broad who wants to be stroked for a few bucks." He gave her a dark look. "I thought you had to go."

"What's the matter with you?"

Instead of answering, he glanced beyond her. "Hey, Vesco!"

"Yeah?"

"Get Mrs. Tooley a glass of ice water." Then to Annie, "My contribution to the care and feeding of Queen Grace."

He started around Annie, when she took his arm. "How can you be so mean and judgmental? You don't even know her."

"Oh, I know her, Annie. I know her like I know the over-dressed, pinched-nose snobs that venture into the wrong side of town with some self-enlightened babble about helping poor kids with cash rather than sweat. It's old and predictable and I'm goddamned tired of doing the suck-up. I'll see you on Thursday."

And then he walked over to Grace just as Vesco returned with the ice water. Then, to Annie's amazement, he rattled off the names of donors to Noah House followed by a summary of the house's goals and that any donation she wanted to make would be appreciated. It was all concise, bereft of cheerleading details, and refreshingly lacking in promises that were too optimistic.

Grace, appearing a bit overwhelmed by the man who'd gone from near total silence to dishing out a plethora of information nonetheless, was obviously impressed.

Annie slipped out the door, pondering what she knew about Linc McCoy and wondering whether he'd considered the time he'd spent with her as sucking up for the benefit of Cullen.

By late Thursday morning, thanks to her sister-in-law, Annie was having second thoughts about telling Richard's parents about Cullen. She'd taken a few hours off from work to see the Hunters, so when Betsy dropped the boys off to mow the lawn, Annie invited her in for a glass of iced coffee.

"What are you doing home in the middle of the day?" Betsy asked once they were seated on the porch with the hum of the lawn tractor in the front yard. "Anything wrong?"

"It's a long story."

"Uh oh."

"Don't look like that."

"Like what?"

"As if you think I've gotten myself in trouble."

"Have you?"

"I hope not."

Betsy leaned forward, a playful spark dancing in her eyes. "You finally broke that stupid self-imposed rule about keeping men at a distance." Then she nodded knowingly. "I've got it. You're having sex. Well, it's about damn time."

Annie rolled her eyes. "If it were only that."

"It's more? An orgy?"

"Will you be serious. It's about Cullen." When Betsy scowled, she added, "The boy I found on this porch last Friday? Remember?"

"I know who you mean. I thought that went away. You weren't going to meet with them, and since I heard no more from you, I assumed—"

"There've been some new developments." Annie filled Betsy in on the events of the past few days. The real sticking point for Betsy was what she called Annie's sudden reversal about believing Cullen.

Betsy, framed by the vigorous wisteria that climbed up the side of the porch, said, "This is crazy. You don't have any proof beyond what two strangers have told you."

"You had to be here to listen to Cullen, and then Linc. Plus Cullen looks like Richard."

"Yeah, well, I like to write. That doesn't make me the daughter of Faulkner."

"Very amusing, but hardly an apt comparison. I dug around in some pictures Vera gave me and I found one of Richard when he started high school. The resemblance to Cullen is uncanny."

Betsy shrugged. "All kids, especially at the scruffy age, look alike. What other proof?"

"At this point? None."

"Annie, I know there was tension with Richard because the two of you weren't able to have kids, and my parents didn't help with their chorus of disappointments—"

"And blame."

"Okay, blame. But you going to them with this . . . is a horrible idea. It's just as likely that it's a huge scam on the kid's part."

"I don't think so."

Besty huffed. "What about this McCoy? You left my house on Friday convinced the guy was a dirty liar with nefarious motives. Now you're telling me you want to go take him to talk to Mom and Dad. What the hell happened?"

"I did a lot of thinking this past weekend, plus listening to Cullen and talking quite a bit with Linc . . . and well, I just keep coming back to a gut instinct and how much—"

Betsy cut her off. "Yeah, yeah, he looks like Richard." She leaned forward. "Annie, think about what you're doing. Some scruffy kid with a sob story and you're ready to present him to my parents as Richard's son."

Annie stood, sliding her hands into her shorts pockets. The day was a beauty—sunshine and a light breeze with a cloudless sky. She'd awakened this morning with a sense of anticipation that had sent her scurrying about with a burst of energy. Even a phone call to her mother had gone well, with Annie promising to drop by the next day. She would have to be told about Cullen too, and Annie was more than curious as to how she would react, given her mother's tendency to close down when uncomfortable information was presented. But that was later. First the Hunters.

"This isn't about running to them with a flimsy story. I simply think they need to be prepared. Cullen told Evan. He'll probably tell Helen. Word will get around, and I don't want James and Vera to learn it from gossip."

"So you're going to head off gossip by dropping this bombshell? The cure is worse than the disease."

"Do you think I want to upset them? Come on, Betsy."

"Of course I don't. But if this Linc is anything like I've heard, Mom and Dad will be beside themselves that he's even in their house."

Annie's eyes widened. "What do you mean, what you've heard? What?"

"I made some phone calls over the weekend." She gave Annie a stern look. "Calls you should have been making."

She was right. Annie had spent the time wondering about Richard and whether he'd betrayed her when she should have been checking up on the two strangers. But if Betsy had been told something pertinent . . . "I sure appreciate you calling me and telling me what you learned." She knew she sounded sarcastic.

Going on the defensive, Betsy sniffed. "I thought you'd dismissed the whole thing on Friday. I only did the checking for ammunition if they tried something. Looks like they have, and you're falling for it."

Ammunition? Already, Annie didn't like where this was going. Annie sighed. "What did you hear?"

"That this Linc makes most bad boys look like saints. Let's see. His old man was a drug dealer who is now in prison for killing the guy who killed his son. Seems your boy Lincoln saw all this and did nothing, then instead of getting some guts, he partied and rebelled and generally raised hell. His mother threw him out and he bummed around, got arrested a few times for drugs, then did rehab, and got himself connected to the guy who built Noah House. That got him a job working there and he just kept moving up."

"Sounds to me as if he rehabilitated himself," Annie muttered. "The Linc I know doesn't come close to being that self-absorbed. So who told you all of this?"

"Different people," she said vaguely.

"Obviously not his friends."

"Who goes to friends when you want the truth?"

"So you ask the enemies?"

"Why are you defending him?"

"I'm simply trying to understand why you're so inflexible. So he had a tough life—"

"A tough life! He had a life that he pretty much screwed up all by himself. Please don't tell me we should feel sorry for him."

"He's not the same man as you've described."

"And how would you know? Because he's charmed and cajoled you into thinking that his interest is only in the boy's future? I'll bet my next paycheck he didn't tell you any of his past."

"He told me some. There was a woman that he loved—"

"Uh, let me guess. She hurt him and he's never gotten over it."

Annie looked down at the melting ice cubes in her glass. Sure she thought Betsy was being a bit over-aggressive in her opinions, but Linc's unease about a past lover hadn't disturbed her as much as his reaction to Grace. It seemed counterproductive to the man who wanted so much success for Noah House. Then again, not for a moment had she ever thought that Linc McCoy came out of a privileged prep school with all the social accouterments. But so what? None of this was about Linc and her anyway. This was about Cullen.

"Annie, the guy isn't stupid and he probably knows that the nice widow with a soft spot for kids would likely turn tail and run if he'd provided the details about his real past."

Annie bristled at Betsy's summary. "You make me sound like some hothouse flower."

"Around a guy like McCoy? Absolutely." She stood and went and put her arm around Annie. "I don't want to see you and my parents have an even less cordial relationship than now. I'm telling you, Annie, they would be appalled by McCoy."

Annie thought of how delighted she'd been at his offer to go with her. The gesture had seemed unselfish and certainly unexpected. And he'd been clear, he was going for her, not the Hunters. That had pleased her immensely. And yet Betsy was their daughter, and Annie understood her need to protect them.

"I'll have to think about this, Betsy."

"Don't take this to my parents," she warned.

And then Annie glanced up at her sister-in-law and for just an instant saw terror in her eyes. Then in a blink the expression was gone.

"They don't need to hear a lot of junk that can't be proven."

Reluctantly Annie nodded.

"Tell the boys I'll meet them at the bike shop to pick up their bikes. I have to run an errand."

And with that, Betsy marched down the steps across the lawn and the next sound Annie heard was her car starting.

She let out a long breath, then gathered up their glasses and took them into the house. Postponing this concerned her, but at the same time . . . Saying something too soon and especially if it weren't true ... And Betsy sure seemed convinced it wasn't.

Annie glanced at the clock. She had to meet Linc in an hour. But what she couldn't get out of her mind was that unguarded expression she'd seen on Betsy's face. Then in a dawning bit of insight, Annie realized that she'd seen a similar terror years ago in her mother's eyes when she told her she was going to find her father.

Self-protection, an unwillingness to step into the unknown, fear that the present can never be helped by the past. Annie felt as if she teetered on some precipice between what she believed was true and those who would resent her for pursuing it. Plus she bristled at Betsy's insinuation that she was too delicate and dumb for the machinations of Linc McCoy.

Her nephews had finished the lawn, she paid them, and gave them the bike shop message from their mother. Then she tried to call Linc; she learned from Vesco that he was busy with one of the kids. "Tell him I have to cancel this afternoon."

She hung up and picked up her car keys and her purse. She needed to get some answers of her own.

Chapter Nine

The last time Cullen had been in a cemetery was when he was being chased by the cops for the money he'd stolen out of that unlocked Mercedes. Back then he'd been running in zigzags to avoid the stones and hoping like hell he could get over the wall and under the overpass and across the tracks before the train came. He could hear the whistle and the rumble of the old freight lumbering down the rusted tracks. Timing would either kill him or save him.

He'd made it, and when the train had roared by, separating those dumbass cops from him, he knew he was home free.

Now, he looked around at the rows of stones—some small and square and flat to the ground, some old and broken with the words barely visible, some huge monuments as though to say, "Hey, I'm dead but I'm still important." Cullen read names and walked the rows. He concentrated on the bigger headstones, skipping the small ones. He just knew that Richard Hunter would have an important-looking gravestone.

The day was hot, but the trees and the abundance of shade not only cooled but added a sense of serenity and refreshment. This wasn't a scary place, or one of shadows and ghosts, and as Cullen walked and read, he realized that while his wish had been to find his father and have him be pleased and excited, at this point he just wanted to find him. Even in the cemetery.

In the distance, he saw a man in a green worker's uniform running a Weedwacker. Cullen hurried over.

The man was old and small, sun-weathered and with the name "Gus" on an oval over his left front pocket. A wad of tobacco pumped out his right cheek. He looked at Cullen with a craggy curiosity as if a kid looking at gravestones was an unheard-of adventure. Cullen talked fast.

"You ain't been lookin' too hard, kid. The Hunters have a family plot. Over there." He pointed to his left. "There's a rose bush blooming near the stone."

"Thanks." Cullen started off.

"Sure was a nice guy that Richard Hunter." The man sat down on a flat-topped headstone.

Cullen stopped and turned. "You knew him?"

"I've lived in Bedford all my life. Know most everyone, or I know about them. 'Course I knew him. Used to have coffee with him at the Victory every morning."

Cullen tried to imagine the Richard Hunter who lived in that big fancy house on Morning Glory Drive eating at the Victory Diner. He knew the place. It was cool. Loud and crowded and greasy. "I think I'm looking for a different Richard Hunter."

"Nope. He owned a business fixing up old houses. He figured that the best way to get good workers was to go where they went."

"I don't know," he said skeptically.

"Shows what you know. Lots of guys with bucks stopped at the Victory every morning. Good coffee and good talk. He was a regular guy. We chewed the fat about the Yankees. Tough being a Yankee fan in this here state."

"He was a Yankee fan? Really?"

"Yep."

"Me, too."

The man grinned, reeling off names and batting averages, and while Cullen, under other circumstances, would have done the same, not today.

"Yep, real friendly sorta guy, Hunter was. Good to people he didn't have to be good to."

Cullen's sense of pride swelled. "Like how?" he asked, eager now to hear everything.

Gus, who'd always had a soft spot for redemption stories, was just as eager to talk. "Hired my kid when no one else would touch him. Boy done some bad stuff. He was right about your age back then. Mr. Hunter gave him a job with one of his carpenters. Kid really took to the work and helped on a big downtown project. That was years ago. Today, he's a master carpenter."

The story gave Cullen such a rush. This was his father, the father he'd always wanted, a father who did good things, a father who cared what happened to other people, a father who, in the time since he'd learned who he was, Cullen had painstakingly tried to recreate. He wanted to ask Annie, but he'd been too scared he wouldn't like what she said. Now, deep inside, a kind of burning to know had just gotten hotter. "He was a cool guy."

"Yep. Say, you talk like you know him. He help you out, too?"

"Well, not exactly. I never met him." At the man's puzzled look, he quickly added, "I've heard about him and kinda wanted to know more." It was a dopey thing to say, but Linc had ragged him out about tellin' that Evan jerk who he was. The guy didn't look convinced, so Cullen didn't know why it was such a big deal, but Linc said he needed more proof before he started flapping his mouth. Cullen gestured toward the distance. "He's buried over there?"

"Yep." The old man reached for the pull cord on the weed trimmer.

"Wait."

"Kid, I gotta get back to work."

"You said your son was about my age when my—uh, when Mr. Hunter helped him. I'm thirteen."

"Boy was fifteen. So?"

"Would it be okay if I talked to him?" Cullen soon realized how weird he must have sounded. "I mean, I'm doing a paper for, uh . . . uh a summer school project on—" He fished desperately for something that sounded credible. "On people who make a difference."

"You lookin' in the cemetery for them?"

"No, I mean yes . . ." he laughed nervously. "Look, I'm just looking for some stuff on Mr. Hunter. Like I said, I didn't know him, but well, it's a big deal to me to find out about him."

The man swiped a kerchief across his forehead. "A big deal huh? What are you? His long lost kid or something?"

Cullen blinked, but the man laughed, obviously making a joke. "Don't know if my kid'll talk to you, but guess you can ask. Lives over on Decker. Forty-six Decker. Probably at work now. Simmons Construction. They're building a house a few blocks from here. Go down the road and take your third right. You'll see the trucks."

"Thanks."

"Hey!"

Cullen turned around.

"You need his name if you're gonna talk to him."

"Oh yeah." Jeez, Cullen thought, Gus probably thought he was an idiot.

"Danny Costello." Gus started the Weedwacker and continued trimming around the graves.

Cullen made his way to the Hunter family plot. As he'd guessed, the gravestone was big and fancy.

RICHARD JAMES HUNTER
Husband of Annie. Son of James and Vera Hunter
February 18, 1959–July 10, 2001
Wisdom and Integrity were his friends

Cullen studied, not really sure what it meant, but one thing he'd learned so far: Richard Hunter had been nothing like that bastard who had adopted him.

He looked at the other gravestones. A set of grandparents and great-grandparents. Cullen made note of the dates for the grandparents, and of course for Richard.

He stood for a moment staring hard at the stone and wondering if his father was watching. He wanted to believe he was. He wanted to believe his dad was sorry he gave him away. He wanted his father to be happy that Cullen wanted to know him.

Cullen swallowed the lump that crowded his throat. He wanted to know the father that had helped out that kid, he wanted to know the father in the smiling picture in Annie's house. And as he took one last look at the gravestone, he realized that he wanted to know his grandparents. Not fake ones who pretended, but real ones. His father's parents.

There was much to do, he decided as he unlocked his bike from the post at the cemetery entrance. Riding down the street, he turned right three blocks up and just as Gus had said, there were Simmons Construction trucks. Now all he had to do was find Danny Costello.

"Come on in, Annie Jean. I thought you weren't coming." Her mother ushered her into the kitchen that, despite efforts by Annie, her mother had refused to update. *No need,* she'd said. *Everything works just fine.* A few months ago her mother had taken great delight in showing Annie a magazine picture that displayed a retro kitchen with appliances almost exactly like the ones in Marge's kitchen.

"Mom, it just *looks* like your kitchen, but it's more efficient and the appliances are state of the art."

"Don't care nothing about art for my stove. Had this one for twenty years and it works just fine."

It was a discussion that Annie wasn't going to win, so she had long since stopped saying anything.

Despite its age, the kitchen was immaculate. Her mother had always been a fierce housekeeper, adhering to the philosophy that a clean house leads to a clean life. Annie had never been quite sure how those two interconnected, but her mother had little use for modern views about women working at outside jobs because they liked them. Mostly, Annie imagined, that was because Marge Dawson had worked for years, and loving her job had nothing to do with it. She'd been an in-house seamstress at a dry-cleaning establishment, not because she liked it but because, as she'd pointed out in a rare burst of honesty years ago, *I worked because he drew pictures that nobody bought.*

"Come and sit down," Marge said. "I made a lemon pie for the church bazaar and a smaller one for myself."

Annie slid into the familiar slat-backed kitchen chair. On the table was a bright cotton tablecloth she'd seen a thousand times. In the center was a small vase of pansies, a sugar bowl, and a set of salt-and-pepper shakers from her mother's collection. This particular set, of a hen and a rooster, had been from Richard; he'd gotten them when he'd been on a trip. The thoughtful gesture had endeared him to her, and Marge soon forged a closeness with him she and Annie had never quite achieved.

She got out plates and forks while Annie wondered if coming here was more about pointing out that Richard wasn't all that perfect. Or perhaps her intent was emphasizing that she, unlike her mother, wasn't going to hide in some hovel of silence.

"So are you volunteering again this year?" Annie asked, disturbed by her own potential motives.

"I was requested," Marge said with the dignity and pride of an invitation to see the cardinal.

"Requested. Well, that's quite an honor." Annie knew her mother was one of the hardest workers at St. Luke's yearly bazaar, where the preparations began in late January. Even though Annie's own attendance at Mass was sporadic, anyone with any acquaintance with the St. Luke's Bazaar knew that they had so many volunteers that many were turned away. To be invited to work carried some status.

Her mother cut into the small lemon pie and slid a slice onto Annie's plate. "They even gave me one of the biggest moneymakers. I'm in charge of the white-elephant room."

Annie was impressed. The white elephant was a huge draw with people coming from all over the state and long lines waiting for the doors to open. "What happened to Edie?" Or was it Ernestine? Annie could never keep them all straight.

Her mother, knife poised above the second piece, gave her a blank look. "Edie? She just hands out plastic bags at checkout. How could you forget what happened to Ernestine?"

Uh oh. Had she died? Been banned for theft? Gone to a nursing home? Just her mother's tone boded nothing good. No doubt she'd been told in one of her mother's rambling chats that Annie heard but usually didn't register. It always amazed her that her mother was a fount of information on every topic but the one Annie had wanted to know about—her own father.

"I'm sorry."

"I don't know why I tell you anything," she said, obviously hurt. "You probably won't even remember by September that I had the white elephant this year."

"I won't forget."

"Are you going to come?"

"Of course."

"Richard always came for the auctions."

"Yes, he did."

"Sometimes you didn't." Only her mother could make missing a summer bazaar akin to a mortal sin. Annie was again reminded of her mother's phone call about meeting her at the cemetery. In her mother's world there were conventions and must-dos and to avoid, forget, or, God forbid, simply blow off any one of them was not easily forgiven and never forgotten. Annie imagined that her own father had been permanently placed in his own category of never forgiven.

"Well, I'll be there this year. I promise."

Her mother smiled, the whereabouts of Ernestine forgotten. Annie didn't ask again.

With the pie cut and iced tea poured, her mother clasped her hands together and whispered, "I have something for you. Something I found yesterday."

"Sounds intriguing. What?"

She went to a pine hutch and opened one of the doors. She brought a tissue-wrapped object to Annie and set it down. "I found it when I was unpacking stuff. It was in a box marked fifty-cents items so I paid for it. Wouldn't want you to think I'd just take something."

"Mom, that I would never believe." Annie unwrapped the tissue, revealing a brown wishing well with lots of details in the glazed pottery. It had a small bucket on a chain that still worked—it raised and lowered the bucket if the handle on the side was turned. Around the piece were the words "Oh wishing well, grant a wish to me." Annie immediately turned it over and her eyes widened. "You got this for fifty cents?"

"It's a McCoy," she said, proud of her knowledge about collectibles. "I heard on one of the shows that the markings on the bottom of pieces are very important."

"Yes. But how did it get into a fifty-cent box? I thought there were some ladies who were experts on the valuable stuff. How did this get by them?"

"I unpacked the boxes."

"I know that. But aren't you supposed to let them look before the items are priced?"

"These items were already priced," she said stiffly, and Annie knew immediately she shouldn't have asked. "I told you the box was marked fifty cents. Don't you ever listen to me? Look, you don't want it I'll give it to Evelyn. She collects McCoy stuff. Was gonna give it to her first, but I know you like wishing wells." She put the pie back in the refrigerator and then sat down, but she pushed her own plate aside. "Don't know why I bother. Richard would have just been grateful. You gotta turn it into the theft of the century. Can't you ever just say thank you?"

Annie apologized. "You're right. It's a lovely piece. Thank you." And she was right about Richard. He wouldn't have questioned, but then he rarely did if it was a matter that didn't interest him. He lacked curiosity in details that weren't directly related to his work. To be sure if her mother had found a set of 1880 house plans, Richard would have been all over her with questions and quizzing her as if she'd discovered the lost secrets of restoration.

"I just don't want you to get in trouble," Annie said, and meant it. It was certainly possible it had slipped by the pricing experts. "I would say you scored a major find with this." Her mother's scowl began to fade. "It's a lovely piece."

"Lovely? It's ugly."

Annie grinned. "Maybe a little."

"Do you think it's worth a lot?"

"Definitely far more than fifty cents."

"Maybe I should ask Evelyn."

Annie wasn't going to ask. No doubt her mother had told her about Evelyn a dozen times, too. One thing was clear—she needed to pay closer attention. She set the wishing well aside. "I'll add this to my collection with pleasure."

Then she got the full benefit of her mother's approval. Annie realized once again that one of the reasons her mother adored Richard was that he always praised and complimented. Annie tried, she really did, but on the other hand, that constant effusive approach could be cloying. Richard detested conflicts and went out of his way to avoid them. It wasn't that Annie liked dissension, but sometimes it was necessary, for there was a core of honesty in being candid.

And on that thought, she cut into her pie. Savoring the tart lemon, she said in total truthfulness, "You make the best lemon pie."

"I do, don't I."

And for a few moments, they ate and sipped tea. Finally Annie said, "Something about Richard has come up and I don't know what to do."

Her mother gave her a puzzled look. "I can't imagine."

Annie began with finding Cullen on the porch and brought the story details up to her talk with Betsy that morning. "I should be at the Hunters right now, but Betsy was adamant about not telling them."

Her mother had sat back in her chair, her eyes getting wider with each detail. Finally, she said, "Richard cheated on you?"

"If Cullen's story is true."

"And you believe a stranger and not your husband?"

"Mom, I never asked Richard if he ever cheated. I had no reason to."

"A wife knows," she said, causing a rush of questions

to stack up in Annie's mind about her father.

"Perhaps if there were signs or reasons or problems in our marriage. I don't know of any."

"Well, I know of one. He wanted children."

"So did I."

"Maybe not as much as he did."

"The end justifies the means? That's preposterous. He wouldn't get a woman pregnant and then give the baby up for adoption if his intent was to have the child."

"Maybe he was ashamed. Maybe he knew no one would understand. Maybe he knew you wouldn't understand."

Annie was taken aback by her mother's reaction. She'd expected a defense of Richard, but not one like this. "Wait a minute. Now it's my fault?"

"I'm telling you that he was very upset that you didn't get pregnant."

"He was upset?" Annie rose to her feet, amazed and irritated that the conversation had turned into a criticism of her. "That sounds like I refused. It wasn't like that. I saw doctors, I was tested—I did it all—*we* did it all—and nothing worked. We tried and tried, but I couldn't . . ." Annie turned away, the smarting tears blurring her eyes.

And for a few beats of tension, all Annie heard was her own heart hammering.

Then, "I heard it kind of different," her mother said softly, and there was no mistaking her obvious confusion.

"What did he tell you?" Annie asked, hard-pressed to believe that her husband would have deliberately lied about her.

"Richard told me—poor man, he nearly broke down and cried—he said that you and he weren't going to have any children."

Annie relaxed. They had made that decision a time or two. Both felt that if they convinced themselves pregnancy was impossible, that it then might happen. "Mom, I told you how we were tested. I told you how upset I was and how much . . ." She cleared her throat. "If there was any decision, it was to quit being so obsessed about it. The doctors said we were too uptight, that we should relax. We decided to look into adoption."

"Maybe that's what he meant."

"Do you remember when he told you there would be no children?"

Her mother thought for a moment. "I know it was in the spring, because he'd brought me a new rose bush." She thought some more. "I don't know. I can't remember which spring."

Annie did. It had been March, three years before. She remembered because she and Richard and another couple had driven down to Newport for the St. Patrick's Day parade. Richard had brought up adoption that morning as they were getting ready to leave.

Where did this come from?

Come on, Annie. We've discussed it on and off for years.

I know, but it takes so long, and getting an infant—

Then we should try private adoption.

That has its own risks.

Do you want me to look into it or not? I can call Drew and have him do some investigating.

He does corporate law.

Do you want me to look into it or not?

He'd been annoyed by her questions, by her seeming caution or, as Richard called it, indecisiveness. Regular-channeled adoption took a long time, especially when an infant was wanted. Private adoptions sounded ideal if you had the money. They had that, but Annie knew from her own reading and research that it was far from ideal or a guaranteed happy ending. Birth mothers changed their minds or birth fathers showed up claiming they never knew about the baby. Laws were more favorable to the natural parents, which often meant a fight in court. Annie had seen too many of those TV pictures of babies wrenched from the adoptive parents and returned to birth parents. Just thinking about that kind of scenario made her shudder.

But she had agreed and he'd called Drew. To Annie's amazement, the lawyer had answers and even two college girls who were pregnant. The young women were interviewing other prospective parents along with Annie and Richard, and they chose other couples for their babies. Despite disappointment, she'd been encouraged for the first time in years. Annie was beginning to believe that her dream of a baby might really come true . . . and then Richard had died.

"Why, here comes Evelyn. I wonder what happened to her car. We were going to walk over to church together and finish up some last-minute things. Evelyn does the face painting."

Annie pushed aside the old thoughts and carried the dishes to the sink while her mother opened the back door. Annie turned to say hello. The woman was petite and lovely, with black hair cut in a bouncy bob. She wore khaki jeans and a blousy top and standing behind her was Linc McCoy.

Chapter Ten

Amidst the flurry of introductions, Annie felt just a bit stupified to be standing in her mother's kitchen looking at Linc and being introduced to his mother. Only in Bedford, where the person you thought was a stranger is really someone your mother knows. Why bother with surnames when everyone knows everyone else?

Obviously the two women were well acquainted, but what really jarred Annie was that for the past few days while she'd been obsessing on Linc and who he was, here was her mother and his mother . . .

"Now, Annie Jean, you're not going to forget to come tomorrow."

"I wouldn't miss it." She turned to Linc, who hadn't looked anywhere near as surprised as she had. Had he known all along? That seemed pretty far-fetched. "Perhaps Mr. McCoy will be going, too."

She expected an "I don't think so" and instead got an "Is that an invitation? I humbly accept, Mrs. Hunter. Given all the stand-ups I've gotten lately, I wouldn't want to blow a new opportunity."

Her mother managed one of those forced smiles indicating she had no idea what he was talking about but wanted to appear as though she did.

Evelyn reached up and kissed his cheek. "Thanks for the ride." It was then that Annie realized the "ride" had been on his motorcycle. Apparently catching Annie's realization, Evelyn added, "Linc took your mom for the first time a few weeks ago. She loved it."

For sure, this was all a dream; it couldn't get any more surreal. "My mother on a motorcycle?"

"An adventurous lady. We had a great time, didn't we Margie?"

Margie? No one but her mother's brother had ever called her Margie.

"It was fun," *Margie* said, her eyes bright, her smile wide. "A little scary at first, but Linc was wonderful."

Annie folded her arms. "Yes, I'm sure he was the model of safety and decorum."

Evelyn patted her arm. "We need to go, Marge." She offered her hand, and when Annie responded, she enclosed their hands with her other one. "It was so good to meet you." She said it with so much warmth and sincerity that Annie knew this wasn't mere politeness but genuine. "Your mother speaks of you often, and of course, she spoke glowingly of your late husband. I'm so sorry. You are much too young for such a loss."

"How kind of you."

Evelyn gave her hand one more gentle squeeze before the two ladies set off. Marge stopped and turned. "Annie Jean, don't forget your wishing well and please lock the door."

Annie nodded and then the two ladies, with their heads down and close like two teenagers in a serious chat, walked down the sidewalk.

As they turned the corner, an echo of laughter drifted back and Annie was reminded that just a few days ago she'd wished her mother would find something to do beyond canonizing Richard and criticizing her. How short-sighted and utterly self-absorbed had been that thinking, Annie now realized with some awe. Marge Dawson had had a whole other life and it was Annie who needed to get up to speed.

Her never having mentioned the motorcycle ride with Linc McCoy baffled Annie. Then again, Annie had hardly been more than an infrequently visiting daughter. But that wouldn't have been true if their relationship had been closer.

And who's fault was that? Annie wasn't yet willing to divide the blame. If years ago her mother had offered, provided, even reluctantly revealed the answers Annie had needed about her father . . . but she hadn't, and to this day, all the information Annie had about Nathan Dawson had been learned or accidentally stumbled upon by her own persistence.

She glanced at her wristwatch and realized she'd been standing here in silence for more than three minutes. She turned to find that Linc was fiddling with something on his motorcycle. She went into the house, retrieved the wishing well and recalled her mother's words: *I was going to give it to Evelyn. She collects McCoy stuff. . . .* Well, of course she did. Why wouldn't she? It was a more interesting hobby when you could claim your last name was on a piece of pottery.

It had definitely been an eye-opener of an afternoon, Annie thought, as she locked the door. An afternoon she wouldn't soon forget.

She set the wishing well on the floor of the front seat of her car, and then walked to where Linc had hunched down by the front tire of his bike. The Harley was a sleek animal of steel and chrome and black leather. A single helmet hung near the rear seat. Picturing her mother straddling this all swathed in protective headgear was an astonishing image. Linc finished fiddling with a piece of chrome and then rose, tugging off a pair of black gloves.

"Problems?" she asked sliding her hands into the side pockets of her sun dress.

"Fender was kinked and rubbing on the wheel. All fixed." He brushed off his hands and then slid his sunglasses back on. He wore jeans and a white, albeit a bit dirty, tee shirt and a silver chain around his neck that disappeared inside the shirt.

"So how long have you been riding a motorcycle?"

"Since I was sixteen."

"What do you do when it rains?"

"Get wet."

"And in the winter, you just get cold?"

"Nope. In the winter I use my truck." He swung a leg over the bike and reached to start it.

Take a step back and he'll drive away and that will be that. Then you can go to the office and spend the rest of the afternoon returning phone calls. Which needed to be done, which she'd planned to do, which would certainly be wiser.

Instead, she said, "I'm sorry I had to cancel earlier today."

He shrugged. "I'm getting used to it."

"It's just that Richard's sister felt that Cullen and you saying so and me agreeing wasn't enough proof that Richard was Cullen's father—she was worried that her parents would be upset needlessly."

"She prefers to wait and upset them at a better time?"

"Of course not. She's protective of them, and if this story of Cullen's turns out to be wrong—"

"So she's convinced you, too."

Annie heard his disappointment in her and for no reason that made a scintilla of sense, she felt as if she'd let him down. "It's not a matter of convincing me, but simply considering that there could be a mistake. Mind you, I do believe Cullen, but he could have gotten some bad information."

"You mean his mother pulling Richard's name out of the air? That would be a pretty incredible mistake."

"Betsy just thought it was better—Why are you shaking your head?"

"Because you've allowed her to seize control of this, and that's stupid."

"Don't call me stupid," she snapped.

"Christ, knock off the defensiveness. You know that's not what I said. You need to get off the dime, Annie. Your husband had a kid by another woman thirteen years ago. The kid was Cullen. That's a fact."

"Yours and Cullen's fact."

"You believed it a few days ago."

"I know, but Betsy's concern is valid."

"So what's her stake in this?"

"Her stake? You make it sound as if her motives are suspicious. I would say she has a valid interest in preserving her brother's good name, for one. Her parents learning about a grandson that may or may not be theirs could be troublesome."

"Whatever," he said, dismissing her explanation. "Here's what I see: You allowing someone with only a marginal stake in the outcome to set the parameters tells me you'd rather wait and hope it will go away." He paused as if waiting for her to deny what he'd said. When she remained silent, he continued. "Cullen's intent is to find information about his father. And if a few honorary monuments to Richard Hunter's sterling character get a bit tarnished, then so be it."

"And if Cullen is wrong?"

"If it's another Richard Hunter? Is that your question?" he asked, with so much incredulity Annie winced. "We checked out the other Richard Hunters in the area. All but your husband were false choices."

"All right. But why make this all about Richard? What about the birth mother? Neither of you seem at all interested in finding out who she is."

"Only a matter of time." Then he reached behind him and unstrapped the helmet. "Put this on. We'll go for a ride."

"Wait a minute. What do you mean 'a matter of time.' Do you know something?"

"Nope."

"You think she's going to just reveal herself?"

"I think eventually she'll be flushed out."

"Flushed out? God, that kind of comment makes me want to defend her." She took the helmet and settled it on her head, her curiosity about Richard's girlfriend taking a new turn. The questions of who she was and where she was had floated around her thoughts, but more in connection to Richard.

In considering her just as Cullen's mother, Annie wondered what her reaction would be. Pleased to meet her son? She'd read stories about reunions, and that while they might initially go okay, in time they often became resentful or simply faded away from too many differences and too much past pain. Would she be horrified that she'd been found and how that discovery would affect her life now? Perhaps even a staunch denial that Cullen was her son. Annie realized that these last two were similar to her own reactions.

And what about Cullen in all this? He'd impressed Annie by his levelheadedness, but so far his discoveries about his father had been more factual than emotional. How he would fare, should his mother be found, would be revealing.

"Let's go," he said cutting into her wandering thoughts. He reached out to help her onto the cycle. "Tuck your dress up and away from the metal."

"Wait, I have other questions."

"Annie, you always have questions. And when you get the answers they only last until someone throws a tantrum or disagrees. Sweetheart, you need to trust your instincts and not get so jittery about what others think."

"You make me sound indecisive and wishy-washy."

"You are."

Annie opened her mouth to object and then closed it. Maybe he wasn't exactly right, but he was close. Linc started the cycle, the roar filling the air. She shouldn't do this, she really shouldn't. He was a pain with his blunt comments and surprise appearances, but he intrigued and fascinated her, and though the last thing she wanted was any involvement with him, he excited her. And excitement was a sadly missing component in her life.

"Where are we going?" she asked.

"No rules. No boundaries. No turning back."

"Some biker code?"

"Nah, I adopted it when I met you."

"Oh," was all she could think of to say.

"Hold on to me."

She did as she was told, getting as comfortable as possible on a hot leather seat that had none of the cushy comfort of her car. She slid her arms around his waist and instinctively tightened them.

He turned his head and winked. "Good girl."

And then they were off and Annie held on, hands clasped tightly around his waist. The air tore at them, and houses and trees and cars and joggers whizzed past as though getting out of their way. Annie watched it all, paying little attention to where they were going, only feeling a sense of anticipation that she'd embarked with growing enthusiasm on an adventure that a week ago would have been as unlikely as a date with one of the local plumbers.

No rules.

No boundaries.

No turning back.
She grinned and held on even tighter.

In Wellesley, Massachusetts, Caroline Sheplin poured her second vodka, drank, then braced herself for the shudder when it raced down her throat. This time the shudder was muted, and the liquor securely blunted her fear, which had been the whole point. Apprehension along with dread had been steadily working through her for the past twenty-four hours. A few steps away, outside on the covered section of the deck, where Caroline's hand-painted flowers showcased its floor and grape vines twined on a nearby arbor, her husband waited.

She put the glass in the sink, tightened the cap on the vodka bottle, and wished she could just take the bottle upstairs and lock herself in the bedroom with it. Instead, she willed herself to be firm and not be pushed into getting either angry or hysterical. She picked up a tray with two tall glasses of iced tea, and Gordon looked up as she came through the doors.

He was seated at the small glass-topped table, some papers spread out in front of him, talking on his cell. Caroline set the tray down, removed the glasses, and placed one on a napkin near him. She lifted her own as a comforting buzz settled in. The vodka had done its work; she felt relaxed and sure of herself. She could handle this.

"Yeah, just have to iron out the final details." Pause. "In the next couple of weeks." Pause. "Thanks for that info I asked you to check on." Pause. "Yeah. Sure. Bye."

He stacked the papers and slipped them into his briefcase, then lifted his glass and settled back in the chair. He was a handsome man, looking, as usual, a little frazzled in his loosened tie and rolled-up shirtsleeves. She hated adding to that frazzle. Oh, for the early days of their marriage, luring him into some fanciful afternoon sex extinguished most any problem. The fact that fanciful afternoon sex in her unmarried days could be a huge threat today accounted for her need for this vodka buzz.

"You're awfully quiet," he said.

"I'm not happy about this."

"I know that. But please, try to at least act supportive when the kids come home. They're going to freak and whine, and I need you to help convince them."

"Yes, you will," she said, with a bit too much flipness. Never mind. He needed to be very aware of just how annoyed she was. She sipped, wishing the tea were vodka.

"Your anger is clear, Caroline."

"As well it should be." She sat in a cushioned wicker chair that she'd bought the summer she'd lived in Bedford. "When we were in Bedford, you gave no indication that the move was already decided, nor that it would happen in two weeks."

"Look, I agree this was more sudden than usual. And God knows, I'm aware of how you hate moving, but we've made location changes in the past and you've never been this negative about it."

"I don't like being lied to."

"Do you think I wanted it this way? It's my job. I sure don't see you complaining when I bring home my paycheck."

She chose to ignore that, and softened her tone. "We'll hardly ever see you until the building is up and open for business. You'll be gone and the kids and I are stuck in a strange place with no friends."

"Caroline, we're moving about a hundred miles south of here. As I said to you when I first mentioned this—it's not the Fiji Islands."

"It might as well be."

His eyes narrowed and his mouth thinned.

He was annoyed and beginning to look not only more

frazzled, but very impatient. She didn't want that; she wanted things as they'd been before his company had decided to build in Bedford. She didn't want to go back there; she didn't want to be anywhere near ... Then a moment of clarity. Why, of course. Why hadn't she thought of it earlier. Why, they'd even done it before.

"Gordon, I think I have a solution."

"I can only imagine."

"It's very simple. The kids and I should just stay here like we did a few years ago when you had to be on site in Springfield."

When he didn't immediately say no, she seized the silence, softening her voice. "Please, Gordon, understand this the way the kids and I see it. No school changes, no tiresome move, and you know what a mess moving is. It's not like you'd be so far away we'd never see you."

"You want me to commute."

"Lots of people commute. From Providence to Boston every day." She knew it sounded as if she were heartless and selfish, forcing him into this when she knew he would hate it. But this wasn't just any move. This was simply impossible for her to do.

He rose and walked to where the backyard rolled out with garden rooms and her wonderful borders of rose bushes.

"Let me think about it."

Caroline could hardly believe that he hadn't roared about families being together and that he didn't want to live by himself in some sterile town house. And the fact that he was open to her suggestion meant she would get her way. An indecisive Gordon always meant he would do as she asked. She quickly moved to slip her arms around him and press herself against him. "Oh darling, I love you."

"I haven't agreed."

"I know, but at least you're open to the idea. I don't

think we should say anything to the kids until we've definitely decided what will be done."

He turned and gathered her to him, making her sure she'd convinced him. But then he scowled, and it was too late to get away. She tried to pull back, lowering her head, but he gripped her chin, forcing her head up. "Okay, Caroline, what the hell is going on?"

"Going on?" *Damn, damn, damn.* "I don't know what you mean."

"The vodka. You drink when you're scared."

"Well, I am scared. I don't want to move. And the kids don't, either," she added quickly.

He gripped her arms and moved her out of the way.

"Gordon, wait. It was one drink." She hurried after him but didn't reach him before he pulled the bottle from the liquor cabinet.

He held it up and then looked at her. "This was full two days ago."

"What are you, the alcohol police?" but she couldn't look at him. She'd meant to buy a new bottle so he wouldn't know.

He walked to the sink, dumped what was left, and then dropped the bottle in the trash. Then he leveled her with a hard, direct look. "It's Richard Hunter you're scared about, isn't it?"

Suddenly all the air in the room evaporated, and Caroline felt the floor roll beneath her, her mind going totally blank. She backed up a step, her hands gripping one of the breakfast-counter chairs. *Oh God, Oh my God.* She wanted to look puzzled and confused and innocent, but it was too late for that. Just staying on her feet took all her concentration. How had he found out? How could she make him understand? How could she defend herself? Questions tumbled in succinct order despite the vodka.

"Your silence is as loud as a megaphone."

"How did you know?"

"Secrets keep better when they aren't written down."

"What?" Her voice was barely a whisper as she tried to focus. Then she knew. "Goddammit Gordon, you read my journals!" Which meant he'd been in her studio, which meant he'd been doing more than closing windows during a rain storm.

"With great interest."

"How could you!"

He folded his arms, seeming to evaluate whether he should feel guilty. "It was a few years ago and I didn't give it a lot of thought, actually."

"Years ago and you've never said anything? Why?"

"I have to admit I was startled that you would have had an affair with a married man, but since you weren't my wife at the time, I decided it wasn't worth mentioning—"

"But apparently worth it now?"

"Your actions have made it an issue. He lived in Bedford and you don't want to go there—close enough of a connection to make me reconsider it, yes. The drinking just added credibility to my instincts."

"Well, aren't we the all-knowing judge," she said sourly.

"Would you have rathered I confronted you and demanded an explanation?"

"Like you're doing now? I would rather you'd respected my privacy which obviously you didn't." But nothing she said rattled or shamed him. "What were you waiting for—the best possible moment?"

"You know better than that. Actually, I hadn't thought about it until we were touring Bedford and you acted as if every corner had a hidden billboard announcing the relationship. And of course now, the contorted refusal to move. If you'd acted as you have with every other location change, I never would have said anything."

He had her there. Despite wanting to be neutral and disinterested, her actions proved otherwise.

"So did you know Hunter was married when you met him?"

"If you read the journal, you'd know I didn't."

"And he didn't feel any need to tell you."

"No. Not at first."

"Sounds like a real up-front guy," he said, and Caroline didn't miss the sarcasm or the disgust.

"It wasn't an issue," she said defensively. "We were just friends. We talked about my art and his knack for growing roses." At his disbelieving smirk, she snapped, "It wasn't some bar pickup."

"Uh huh. Not like us."

"I met you at a club, not a bar."

"Come on, Caroline. The only difference is whether they give away generic or designer rubbers."

"Do you want to know or do you want to draw your own conclusions?"

"I'm listening."

"He was working near where I lived and passed my house every day. It all sort of evolved when he offered some gardening advice on some roses I was trying to coax into blooming. I don't know how the affair started. It just did."

"Honey, affairs don't just begin like mushrooms in the dark. But no matter, did you find out he was married before or after you slept with him?"

"I loved him!"

"Before then, and it didn't matter?"

"No, it didn't matter," she said, just because she was so pissed at his oh-so-superior attitude. "We were in love."

"And you thought he'd leave his wife for you?" His expression was incredulous.

"Yes, no . . . I mean at the time I didn't care." She was

going to add that the sex was the best she'd ever had, but
prudently didn't. "Stop looking at me like I was a dolt
who committed the crime of the century. I was barely into
my twenties."

But he did look a bit shaken. Good. If this conversation
were about his sexual past, she knew damn well he'd blow
it off as old news.

"What ended it? His wife catch you?"

"Her? No way. She was too busy taking her tempera-
ture." At his frown, she added, "She wanted kids, and the
sex became functional for him. He said she made it so
clinical and forced, he lost interest." Then, because Caroline couldn't just let this go, because she was so angry
that he'd invaded what had been private and perfect and
hers alone, she added, "It was never clinical or forced with
me."

Suddenly he didn't look as interested anymore.

Caroline, however, realized that if the gods of kept
secrets existed, they'd just blessed her. "Despite his wife
being such a jerk, I knew he'd never leave her. And I
came to realize I had no future with him—"

"You broke it off?"

"Yes." Of course that wasn't entirely true. The break-
up had been much more complicated. "Now you know
why I don't want to move to Bedford. It would be awkward if I were to run into him."

"You won't have to worry about that."

She was still reeling from his snoop into her journals,
but now he was acting *so* blasé and *so* sure that Richard
was in her past that she said, "You seem awfully secure.
I might find running into him . . ." she deliberately paused,
"interesting."

But that didn't even raise his eyebrows. "I doubt it."
He went out to the deck, retrieved his briefcase, and re-
turned. "Subject is closed. I found a house in Bedford that
I know you'll love, and I want you to see it. We move in

two weeks. Kids need to get settled before they start school."

She folded her arms. "No. I'm not moving."

They stared at one another, her eyes narrowed and just begging him to order her, his expression one she'd seen often—the savvy businessman waiting for the right payoff moment.

And then it came.

"He's dead."

She blinked through a rush of stunned silence. "Richard? He can't be. That's impossible."

"Maybe his female friendships finally did him in."

She was too unhinged to respond to the dig. "How did you know?"

"Called a buddy in Bedford when you acted so weird about moving and I'd put together a few pieces. I asked him if he could check into Hunter. Figured he might be divorced or maybe had six kids to occupy his spare time. I was on the phone with him when you brought out the iced tea. It seems Hunter had a heart attack about a year ago. Left a grieving widow a lot of money and no kids to spend it on."

The words all flowed together like some mass of echoing noise. Richard dead. She couldn't grasp it.

He actually looked surprised at her reaction. "You really didn't know."

"No . . . No . . . I didn't know."

"What about the wife? You afraid you'll run into her?"

"She doesn't know about me."

"Unless Hunter left a few writings like you did."

"You're a bastard, you know that?"

He drew close to her. "Don't go all weepy and outraged with the victim routine, Caroline. I have a problem with married men who cheat. Since most twenty-year-olds have little experience beyond their hormones and dewy-eyed feelings about love and romance, I can understand you. But Hunter? He has no excuse. He was married and he knew exactly what he was doing. As far as him being in love with you and trapped with a wife who made sex clinical? Please. Even you don't really believe that old chestnut."

But she had believed it. Then and now. They had been in love. And truth be known, some deep longing had stirred, causing her to fear seeing Richard, not because of Gordon but because of herself. For she knew that if Richard wanted her, if he'd wanted to renew their relationship, if he'd wanted to sleep with her . . . she would have done it.

"Caroline?"

"Looks as if you'll get your way. I'll move to Bedford."

"I'll make an appointment with the movers when I get back to the office." He touched her cheek. "We don't need to mention this again. But I suggest you get those journals put somewhere else so the kids don't find them."

By the time Gordon had left, Caroline felt as wrung-out and weary as an old mop. She wanted a drink. She took a bottle of scotch from the bar and poured some. She took the glass and went into her studio, where she got out the journals of her past. Sitting in the leather chair, she held the closed books on her lap—she didn't need to read them, she knew them by heart. All the angst and longing and all the hurt and the tears. Finally, she lowered her head and wept. Not about the exposed secrets, not about the move that was now going forward, but for the passing of the man she'd once loved so fiercely.

Chapter Eleven

"*I lied.*"

He felt her tight against his back, arms wrapped securely around his chest, legs spread so that her thighs nestled his hips. Her body was warm and relaxed despite a few harrowing corners, a car without brake lights that he had to swerve to miss, and a bumpy side road he'd taken to avoid a traffic snarl in the downtown area.

"About what?" he asked, easing the bike to a stop in front of a high, flat wall of vinyl-sided housing punched with discount windows. Some kids danced in front of an open hydrant and an old man with enough hair on his face to pass for a grizzly checked through a fist of lottery tickets.

Behind him, Annie stirred. "Lied about never riding on a motorcycle."

He chuckled. "Okay."

She slid off the cycle and removed the helmet, shaking out her hair. Dampness made the ends curl. "You don't want to know why?" she asked.

"Honey, in the world of lies, that doesn't even reach the status of a yawn." He pocketed the cycle's key. "Confess something to me worth knowing."

"Like what?"

"That you've wanted to go to bed with me since we met at the police station."

"Before that," she said so smoothly, so assuredly, he was sure he misunderstood.

He took his sunglasses off and hooked them on the neck of his tee shirt. "Before you knew me? I think I missed something."

"Just the threads of an old fantasy."

"You have fantasies about sex with strangers?" Linc was both amused and amazed. First that they were even having this conversation, and second that this was an entirely different Annie Hunter than the one he'd had to talk into going for a ride.

"Well, you're hardly a stranger."

"Close."

"You remind me of a guy I once had this terrible crush on. A real bad boy that I was sure I could reform if he'd only go out with me."

He grimaced. Not another woman bent on redemption. Was that where this was going? She wanted to reform him? Now he was certain he'd misunderstood her. "Let me guess. He rode a motorcycle."

"He did, and I rode with him a few times. I loved it. My mother didn't. She was sure I'd be splattered all over the road, and if that didn't do me in, surely a reputation as a biker babe would. Mom always assumed the worse when it came to me."

"Maternal preparedness. My mother had the same disease. Prepare for the worst. Then when it happens you'll handle it. So who was this guy?"

"His name was Cal, and he wore leather and had dark smoldering eyes that looked at me like I had no clothes on."

"Not a good beginning in reformation one-oh-one. So what happened? You have sex with him?" Linc surprised himself with his own question. Careful here, pal, or you're gonna be in a soup of potential trouble.

Yet here she was shaking her head as if he'd asked her whether she'd ever had a burger with the guy. "We did go out a couple of times, we kissed some, but he never really touched me. I think he was scared."

"A chicken biker? Never met one of those." At her puzzled look, he added, "Biker rule number four—if a girl scares you, you're out of the club. And to a biker, the club is it. Girls recycle, biker buddies are there forever."

"Sounds like you know the rules from experience."

"One or two."

"How intriguing."

"Trust me, you don't want to know."

"I bet I know more than you think."

"Uh oh."

"Seriously, Linc. I did hear about when your brother was killed. I can't even imagine how awful that must have been for you and your family."

"Yeah, it was pretty bad. Had no idea Mickie was behind the old man until I knocked him down. My brother died instantly."

Annie blinked. "You saved your father's life," she whispered, recalling how Betsy had missed or neglected to tell her that important fact.

"It was more reaction than heroics. My dad had a lot of enemies and I grew up suspicious. When I saw the guy with the rifle . . ."

Her admiration for him soared. For the act, yes, but also because he clearly wanted nothing to do with credit for saving his father's life. "Please tell me you're not blaming yourself."

"Not as much now. The other choice would have been the old man dead. If that had happened, I'd probably be dead or in prison."

"You'd have gone after the shooter and killed him."

"Yes, and the bastard who'd ordered it. Instead, my dad did the honors."

"And he went to prison." At Linc's nod, she asked, "Do you see him often?"

"I was there last month. I take Mom a couple of times a month. And I go sometimes by myself."

"I liked your mother. You seem to have a good relationship with her."

"She's a saint, and believe me, if you piss off a saint you're in pot full of trouble. So," he said, folding his arms and leaning against the bike, "the reason you lied about never riding on a cycle is . . . ?"

"Richard's widow would never admit to having bad-boy fantasies. Annie Hunter would. At least I would have years ago before I became all sanitized and proper and fearful of what everyone thinks."

She stood next to him, her sundress billowing when a car drove past. She'd clipped her hair back and the messy style made her even prettier. Her hands were expressive, gesturing as she talked, and he noted she still wore her wedding ring. Not unusual, but then she twisted it off her hand and slipped it into her dress pocket.

He always figured the removal of a wedding ring would be bittersweet or sad or because another guy was on the scene. Doing it on Godfrey Street in the midst of bad-boy fantasies startled him, but then again, given the weird direction of their conversation, this gesture seemed normal.

"Guess one cycle ride has more power than I thought."

"I found it very freeing. It cleared my head and made me see things as they are and not how I've believed they were."

"God bless insight. So what do you know now that you didn't before?"

"That being stupid and naïve isn't limited to kids. All through my marriage, I believed Richard and I had something perfect and special. And while I was believing that, he was having an affair, a baby, and giving it away while I'm trying desperately to get pregnant. Is that a sick irony or what? And the fact that he's dead and I can't confront him is horribly frustrating. If not for you and Cullen, I would have lived out my life believing I'd had the ideal, loving marriage, when in fact it was all a lie."

Linc didn't say anything. He sure wasn't going to defend Hunter, but the guy was dead and who knows, he might have had his own reasons for bonking some other woman. Long ago, he'd learned from his old man that what appears to be unexplainable is perfectly logical in different hands. Most things in life aren't what they appear, and offbeat stuff begs the questions: "What's this really about?" and "What's really going on?" Of course, getting a straight answer could be as frustrating as putting socks on a centipede.

He tried to imagine Hunter's reaction when the woman announced she was pregnant. He had to be pissed and angry and more than a little freaked. A knocked-up girlfriend had to be handled very gently. One messy argument could equal one dropped dime and good-bye marriage. Getting those socks on that centipede would have been a game of jacks by comparison.

What Linc didn't understand was why the woman hadn't gotten an abortion. It would have been a helluva lot easier to arrange than an adoption. Had Hunter thought that maybe he and Annie could adopt the boy? Perhaps given their own no-baby situation, Hunter figured a half-natural kid was better than none. But it hadn't happened that way. Cullen was placed in a private adoption, Hunter went home to Annie, and the girlfriend went where? Or did she go anywhere? Maybe she was still around, and maybe Hunter had stayed in touch. He wondered if Annie had considered that.

Linc shook out the plethora of thoughts when Annie

tipped her head to the side and said, "What are you thinking?"

"About you. About us. About where we're going."

"You look uneasy."

"And you're not?"

She thought for a moment. "No. Actually, I can't wait."

He had to admit, she looked and acted like a woman set free. What that might mean—God, please not some redemption plan—left him a bit jittery. Sure he'd like to take her to bed, but then what? He wasn't so sop-eyed that he'd lost his focus. Ever since Brooke—and before—he and serious relationships didn't cement for the long haul. It wasn't because some other woman had hurt him; he never waited that long. It wasn't even because he liked being alone, although he did. It wasn't even monogamy, although he'd always been pretty particular about who and where and when. No, his reluctance sprang from a bone-deep restlessness, a boredom of imagination, an uncertainty that he could sustain anyone but himself. Women came and went in his life, but his interest never reached beyond the surface. Bailing out always called louder to him than settling in.

As for Annie, it was better, safer, and not so sticky for him when she clutched at those widow memories. This new "freed" version presented real complications.

"You're too much of a turn-on, Annie Hunter. I think I was safer when you were breaking dates."

She laughed, pressed her fingers into his arm and then danced away. "We're going to have a good time."

Something inside of him stirred, and he wished liked hell it were in his crotch instead of his soul.

A few minutes later, they'd crossed the street, stepping onto a badly cracked sidewalk and walking toward a craggy-faced apartment house with grafitti splatters on the worn shingles and a first-floor broken window. When Linc turned to climb the steps, Annie balked.

"What are we doing here?"

"Sorry, forgot to mention it in all the my-past-life and fantasy and cycle talk. Remember I told you about kids that leave Noah House and how they have to be able to make it on their own? One of the kids, Tim Jofer, lives here with his girlfriend. I want to check on him, see how he's doing."

But instead of a nod and a smile, she backed away. "I don't think I should go with you."

"Why not?"

"I don't know them, and well, I'd feel funny."

"I'd feel funny leaving you out here."

She tried to back even farther away, and he stopped her. "Whoa. This isn't a choice. Annie?" And he saw a real terror in her eyes.

"I can't, Linc. I can't."

She'd begun to shake, and because he didn't know what else to do, he gathered her into his arms. She shuddered against him like a frightened animal. He didn't ask questions, nor did he release her. She burrowed in as though he were a bulwark and she had no intention of letting it go. So there they stood with a few neighbors gawking and a couple of kids stopping, dripping from the hydrant, giggling and then running off to get wet again. Still Linc held her, waiting for her shivers to stop.

Finally, she eased her way back. "You must think I'm some nutcase."

"The range and span of change in the past hour does make me a tad curious. Come on," he said taking her hand and moving away from the building.

"You changed your mind?"

Ignoring her question, he said, "Let's get a frozen lemonade."

They walked to a small area three doors down where a vendor's lemonade stand tried desperately to stay cool in the shade of an old oak tree. Linc bought two paper cones, grabbed some napkins, and led her to the other side of the tree. A bench would have been nice, but this was Godfrey Street, where if it wasn't chained to a pole, it disappeared faster than a druggie's last high.

They both ate the frozen ice, and then Linc said, "Okay, why the panic?" It wasn't a question as much as an observation.

"I don't like old apartment buildings."

"That's not the reason."

She glanced around as if hoping a new rationalization might fly by and she could grab onto it. "And how do you know?"

"Because no one gets the panic in their eyes that I just saw in yours over walking into a building. What's the connection? You know someone who lives here?"

"Here?" She looked appalled. "I've never even been on Godfrey Street."

"Now that I believe," he muttered.

"I'm supposed to apologize because I don't hang out in crummy neighborhoods?"

"Did I say that?"

"You implied it."

He sighed. "Yeah, I guess I did. Guess I'm a bit sensitive about streets that used to be families and good neighbors who looked out for one another. Now Godfrey is struggling against the creeps that have invaded. Look, I've got to see Tim. If you don't want to come, then I'll take you back to get your car. I can't leave you out here."

"I'll be fine. Outside doesn't bother me. I'll stay right here under the tree."

"No."

"No?" She looked genuinely puzzled. "How can you tell me no?"

"I'm the guy who brought you here—it's called responsibility, and while it might sound like a goofy line from a B movie, it's the way things are."

She leaned back against the tree, and he hoped her silence meant she wasn't going to give him any more grief.

Finally, she said, "You think I'm a clueless pain, don't you?"

"No, I just think you need to open your eyes and see things the way they are. This is a long way from Morning Glory Drive."

"I'm not as much of a hothouse flower as you think," she said simply.

He shrugged.

After a sigh, she said, "I should have just told you, but it's hard and—it's just that—" Then she simply spoke, "My father lived in a lousy apartment building just like that one—in Boston." Her words sounded forced, like getting them out was a struggle. "I'd been looking for him for years and I was overjoyed when I learned where he was. I went to his apartment all nervous and excited, and when I found him . . ." She took a breath as though she'd run out of oxygen.

"He wasn't what you expected?"

"He was dead. He died all alone in a cheap dirty two-room walk-up that smelled like burned peas." She shuddered. "I'll never forget that smell."

He already knew the answer, but he asked the question anyway. "You found his body didn't you?"

"Yes."

"I'm sorry, Annie." Linc had no other words, for there were none worth saying. He knew about shock and despair and grief, but he also knew that sad stories weren't made less painful by someone's vapid attempt to understand.

"I hadn't seen him since I was seven. He left us to follow his dream. He was an artist."

Her father walked out and then she marries a guy who had some secret life. Christ. To Annie he said, "Parents separate, they get divorced and start new lives—sometimes, it's the best way."

"They never divorced." She tipped her head, watching him closely. "Your mother never told you?"

"Evelyn 'my lips are eternally sealed' McCoy? No way. Hell, she wouldn't gossip or pass on any information if someone jammed a gun into the back of her head. Too many years of living with my old man. Loyalty and silence were her best buddies."

"She could give my mother a run for her money on being silent. She probably never did say anything. To this day, she refuses to talk about him with me."

"And you're still pissed."

"Gee, does it show?" she said, sarcasm obvious.

"Maybe she had her reasons. Maybe it was to protect you."

"I'm thirty-eight, Linc. At seven, yes. Maybe marginally at seventeen. But now? It's too silly and ridiculous."

"Obviously not to her if she's refused to talk about him."

"You're defending her?"

"She has an opinion. You don't like it, but that's not her problem."

"All I want to know is why the silence."

"If not to shield you, then to protect herself."

"From admitting that she drove him away."

"Or that she wouldn't give him what he wanted or needed, so he went out to find it for himself."

She looked at him for a long time, then whispered, "His freedom?"

"Probably."

"He could have been free right at home if she hadn't

nagged him. She wanted him to give up his art and go work for a local plumber."

Linc lowered his head to hide a grin he couldn't help. Poor bastard. A plumber-in-waiting by day and an artist by night. No wonder he took a hike. "What a deal. He refused, right?"

"Damn right. They were always fighting about money—she wanted him to work all the time, and he didn't want to. He'd say they had enough money. She said they'd have had more if he worked instead of expecting her to do it all."

"She worked while he drew pictures? Nice."

"She knew what she was getting when she married him."

Linc shook his head. It was a huge question as to who was the bigger fool. Annie's mother for believing marriage would change him, or her father for thinking she would forever financially support him while he pursued some artistic dream.

". . . I came from school and he was gone," she was saying. "For months afterward I was told he'd come back, and then one winter day, she said he'd died and was buried somewhere in the midwest. Because I was so upset, she arranged for a memorial service and we got sympathy cards and she even had it put in the newspaper." She paused, staring down at the melted ice. "It was all a made-up story, a lie. And to this day she refuses to acknowledge even that."

Lies. Lies about her father. Lies about her husband. That explains the basis for her shedding her marriage memories of Hunter so quickly. She'd been gullible once, but not a second time.

"You obviously found out something about your dad despite your mother. What convinced you he wasn't dead?"

"I saw his name in an article on tramp art that I was

researching at the library. I then went digging and learned a lot about Nathan Dawson."

"Doesn't sound as if he was too hard to find."

"Meaning?"

He shrugged. "Just that if someone seriously wants to disappear, he doesn't leave a trail as obvious as newspaper interviews."

"Maybe he just wanted to get away from my mother," she said, so quickly he knew she didn't really believe that.

"Perhaps." Or, Linc thought, he didn't give a damn. Found or not, he wouldn't have come home.

"Do you want to hear this or not?" At his nod, she continued. "He'd lived in a lot of different states, and he had trouble paying his rent because what money he had went for food and supplies. He stayed with some other artists, really struggled to get his work noticed, and then he moved to Boston. I found some papers in his apartment about an outdoor art show where some of his work would be sold. Finally he'd found some success, but he didn't live to see it."

"So how did you find all of this out?"

"I talked to two of his friends."

"How did he die?"

"I was told he was diabetic and didn't take care of himself."

Linc nodded. "When he was in Boston, did he call or ever come home?"

"Home to my mother? After the way she treated him?"

"I was thinking more along the lines of wanting to see his daughter."

"She would have never let him see me."

He squashed the lemonade cone, remaining silent and deciding to let this conversation just die. Clearly Annie wanted to hear nothing good in her mother's actions, but Linc was surprised at her vigorous defense of a father who'd abandoned his family for his own self-interest. He guessed that the artistic Nathan probably relished in the fact that his wife had declared him dead and held a service. The guy couldn't have invented a better reason to stay away. If he'd felt any love or regret about Annie, he sure hadn't let that interfere. And yet she clung to her ideal of him. Not so with her husband; she'd cast off her rosy view and no wonder—the truth of Cullen couldn't be denied like the mystery motives of an absent father and silent mother.

"Finished?" At her nod he took her paper cone and threw them both in a nearby trash can. He glanced around. By daylight the neighborhood still looked seedy and tired with an element of danger permanently lurking like a masked mugger hiding in a dim doorway. Linc had warned Tim about moving here, but the kid couldn't make the rent on a better street. "So you coming up with me or am I taking you back to your car?"

She hesitated, glancing at the building, then back at him. Her expression was troubled, a mixture of regret and sadness. "Linc, I'm sorry. I must have sounded like some wild-eyed shrew with a vendetta against my mother. It's just that I never talk about it, and then when you pushed me about going into the apartment—"

He held up his hand. "Hey, it's okay. Venting without apologizing for honest feelings is better than pretense."

"I know I sounded bitchy. I don't hate her, really I don't. In fact, except for her tendency to tell me what to do, we get along pretty well. It's only about my father that we lock horns." She was thoughtful for a moment. "She's not going to change, is she?"

It wasn't a question but more of a quiet acknowledgment.

"Doesn't sound like it," he said.

"And you think I should just let it go?"

"Annie, keeping anger and resentment stirred up requires a lot of energy, and to what end? The relationship doesn't improve, it's either tight and strained or bobs around in neutral. Apparently your mother's feelings and what she knows about your father are hers alone." He paused, not sure how far he wanted to push, but he figured she was about as open as she'd ever be right now. Nevertheless, he spoke carefully. "Maybe the reason you hold so tight to the anger is that you're afraid if you let it go, you'll learn that your mother was justified in resenting your father."

"That she's been right all these years?" She drew in a sharp breath. "That's ridiculous."

"Okay. Just tossing it out as a possibility."

She frowned, as if she expected him to push his point. "You really don't understand."

"Fine."

"I mean, if she offered me some explanation, anything—"

"You'd see her side," he said, glancing at the building. "I agree."

"No you don't," she said. "You just want to change the subject."

"Women," he grumbled. "Disagree and they get pissed. Agree and they're sure it's a trick."

"You always have an answer, don't you?"

"Nah, I just know when to fold and leave the table." He dropped his arm around her shoulders. "Come on, let's go see Tim. I'd like you to meet Tiffany. Tim and Tiffany—it sounds like twin cats."

She smiled, and the tension eased as they walked back down the sidewalk to the apartment building.

Chapter Twelve

A few moments later, Linc said, "By the way, Tif-
fany likes that decorating stuff. She told me once she
wanted to be as rich as a New York decorator."

"Don't we all."

As they made their way up the stairs to the second
floor, she whispered, "How old are they?"

"He's nineteen, she's eighteen going on thirty-five."

"She doesn't have parents?"

"Oh she's got them, but they give the word a bad
name. Most times they can't remember who they are
never mind that they have a daughter. Tiffany has pretty
much been on her own since she was twelve. She can be
tough and direct, but she's not a bad kid."

At the apartment door, music swarmed through the
walls, competing with a sportscaster screaming about a
home run over the green monster at Fenway. The hall was
shadowed, the only light coming from a window high on
the stairwell.

Annie stood close and he swore he could hear her heart
pounding. Then, on impulse, he tipped her chin up, lowered his head, and kissed her. She didn't stiffen or resist,

but sagged into him as though this had been the relief she'd been waiting for.

Linc had thought about when and where and what manner of kiss it would be—he'd thought about it since he'd watched her at the police station. Despite her being too rich and too sophisticated and way out of his league, he'd known this would happen. His instincts, more than usual, had faithfully and persistently warned him. Yet reminders and vibes about complications hadn't stopped his mind from roaming, considering, and mapping a method.

A run-down apartment building on Godfrey Street hadn't been in the mix of choices, yet here the moment presented itself. Here in the midst of loud noise, sticky summer humidity, the stench of pee and decayed sweat, here the touch and taste of her mouth was sweet indeed. And when her arms slid around him, her mouth was pliant and just eager enough to fire up new thoughts about Annie Hunter.

He allowed them a second more, then slowly drew back. Her eyes were bright and open, searching his for something—an explanation? Reassurance?

"I didn't plan to do that here," he murmured, his hand gliding down her back, finding the hollows and the curves and the softness.

"Me neither."

"You should have resisted." He drew her close, savoring the feel and scent of her. It had been too damn long since he'd felt anything this good. "But I'm glad you didn't."

"So am I."

And there in this very unromantic place, they remained quiet as though trying to absorb what had just happened. Then, as if standing close were some kind of commitment in and of itself, they stepped away from one another, each trying to get their bearings from the implications of one simple kiss.

You need to get a grip, Annie chided herself. Just a kiss—one kiss, hardly worth more than a momentary buzz—and yet her insides were reeling and churning with raw feelings that made her feel deprived and bereft and hungry. Instead of her practical, more cautious nature putting on the brakes, she wanted more from him, more with him. Even knowing that any connection with Linc McCoy would probably go nowhere, the freedom she'd found on the cycle ride made him all the more compelling.

No, she thought with a wave of new clarity. This wasn't about tension or kisses or even an attraction to a compelling man. This was about a change in her, a change she hadn't known she'd wanted and yet now seemed natural and right. She liked him, really liked him. He excited her. She felt safe and wanted and even a little special. And hadn't she told him more about her father than she'd ever told anyone? That had to mean something.

The tumble of new perceptions made her smile, and she squeezed his arm.

Then the door opened a crack. Peeking out was a very young woman who had the eyes of age in a face that looked more like fifteen than eighteen. She had wet cheeks, streaky mascara, a trembling mouth, and a balled-up sock in her hand.

Her eyes darted to Annie then back to Linc. "He ain't here."

"I told him I was coming by this afternoon."

"Well, he didn't tell me nothin'."

"You two have a fight?"

"When don't we."

She started to turn away, and Linc said, "Come on, sweetheart. Tell me what's goin' down. Maybe I can fix it."

Annie noted he didn't push his way inside, and she liked that he showed respect for her and genuinely wanted to help.

"You can't do nothin'. No one can." New tears formed, and she pushed the sock against her eyes, then looked away as if showing that sadness made her too vulnerable.

"You know better, Tiffany."

"You always say that."

"Because it's true."

"Well, this can't be fixed." She folded her arms, the move hiking up her tee shirt to reveal the edge of gray-looking cotton panties. Then a door across the hall opened and a young woman with an explosion of blood-red hair and wearing skimpy shorts and a halter that showed more breasts than it covered lounged in the doorway.

Tiffany stiffened as if a board had suddenly been rammed against her back. Glaring, she lifted her chin. "What are you lookin' at?"

The redhead gave a bland look of indifference. Then her gaze ran down Linc; her grin blatantly sexual. "Timmy ain't come back, huh? What'd you do, dump him for the new guy?"

Tiffany propelled herself forward, and if not for Linc grabbing her around the waist, she would have been across the hall and clawing.

"Let me go. I'll kill the goddamn bitch."

"Too messy and then I'll have to call the cops," Linc said smoothly. With his arm around the struggling Tiffany, he pushed her apartment door wider.

Annie stared at the redhead, mesmerized by the unchecked nastiness. It was so vivid it didn't seem real.

"Better hurry on in, honey. They be doin' it without you."

"Shut up," Tiffany yelled, gesturing over Linc's shoulder.

"Come on, Annie," Linc said as though just remembering she was there.

He carried the still-struggling and screeching Tiffany inside and Annie, feeling like a clueless intruder, followed. She should have let Linc take her back to her car. She had no business here. Mentally, she calculated how far the walk and—

"Forget it," he said, tossing the words back to her, and then he turned to calm Tiffany, who seemed now to be as furious with the redhead as she'd been with Tim.

Annie sighed and stepped into the room that would have made a matchbox look spacious. Overcrowded, cheap, and messy, it was also stuffy, stale, and hot.

A squeaky ceiling fan tried to work through the stifling air. Fast-food cartons lay on the floor, and decorating magazines were stacked and spilling off of a low table. A basketball lolled in one corner next to the wheel of a bicycle. Food-crusted dishes were piled on the counters. Clothes were flung about over and on the sagging furniture. A door to the left stood open, hanging precariously from loose hinges. A mattress was in the middle on the floor with a sheet and two pillows. There wasn't even a bed frame. Linc had to be mistaken about Tiffany's interest in decorating; she might look at the pictures, but that's all she did.

"Tim giving you trouble?" Linc asked as if nothing around him were amiss, as if that redhead had been only white noise, as if none of this either surprised or shocked or even annoyed him. Annie expected something, although she wasn't sure what, but he remained calm and focused as if this were simply a summer afternoon visit.

"I hate him." Her eyes darted to Annie as if seeing her for the first time. "She don't talk?"

"You haven't given her much of a chance."

"Bet she's some freakin' social worker. I had all of them I need. All they do is make it worse. I don't need no more goody girls messin' up my life."

"She's a friend. Her name is Annie."

"You sleepin' with her?"

The question hung in the air.

Tiffany waited as if the answer might mean world peace.

Linc raised an eyebrow as if his answer might start a war right here in the room.

Annie answered it. "I haven't decided yet," she said and to her amazement Tiffany smiled.

"Good for you. Don't let him hustle you into any quick hook-ups. A girl needs to consider what's in it for her. "Just 'tween you and me, you could do worse. Linc's okay."

"Ah, a seal of approval. I knew there was something holding me back," Annie said, sure she had completely lost her mind.

"Ladies, enough, okay?" But Annie didn't miss his smile. He was enjoying this.

Tiffany shrugged, seemingly already bored by the conversation. She went into the bedroom and Annie stepped back toward the still-open door, but Linc took hold of her arm as if she might flee the apartment and escape down the stairs. What earthly reason would she have for leaving this garden of delights?

"Don't run away," he whispered.

"Me? Run? From this lovely scenario? May God strike me dead at the very thought," she snapped, her sarcasm as biting as she could make it.

"Okay, I know this wasn't what you were expecting—"

"I was expecting a simple visit to a kid who had his act together. If this is an example of a Noah House success story, you have a lot of work to do."

"Take it easy. This was unexpected. I'll make it up to you, I promise."

"How? With a quick hook-up?"

"With an explanation." He gestured to Tiffany who was coming out of the bedroom. She'd pulled on a pair of red shorts and clipped her dark hair up off her neck.

To Annie, Linc whispered, "Something's wrong here. Something beyond a lover's spat."

Annie was wide-eyed at his insight. His slow, easy-going questioning now took on meaning beyond the gentle handling of Tiffany.

To Tiffany he said, "So when's Tim coming back?"

"I don't know and I don't care. He don't want nothin' to do with me. He wants to hook with that skinny blonde downstairs." She stomped over to a pack of cigarettes, started to light it then changed her mind.

"What did you fight about? Besides the skinny blonde."

She looked at him, eyes narrowed. "The fat redhead next door."

"Ah, he's doin' her, too."

"He's doin' um all, the bastard." Tiffany perched on the edge of the sagging couch and folded her arms in against her. She looked up and Annie saw in that moment how terrified she was—a little girl lost—and she was reminded of herself when she was a teenager and wanted the father she never had.

The teenager spat the next words out. "Wanna know what else we was fightin' about? He knocked me up."

Annie heard Linc swear.

So did Tiffany. "Yeah, that's right. And you know what he tells me? Get rid of it. Just like that. No askin' me what I want. Just what he wants. Like I give a skunk's ass what he wants and I told him so. So he gets pissed and walks out."

"I'll talk to him."

"I don't want nothin' from him. I hate him."

Linc knelt down in front of her and slipped his hands around her wrists. "Tiffany, we both know Tim loves you and if he walked out it wasn't to get sex. Tell me where he is."

She twisted her hands trying to pull away from Linc's

grip, but he held tight. New tears flowed down her cheeks. "He needed money on account of he got laid off—I know, he was supposed to call you—"

"Never mind that. Where did he go for money?"

Her bleached out expression said something. Annie had no idea what, but Linc's tightened jaw indicated Tim wasn't around the corner applying for work at the local convenience store.

Linc let her go, rose, and then leaned down and kissed her forehead. "I'll take care of it. I want you to get things cleaned up here."

"You won't call the cops will you? He ain't doin' it cuz he likes it—it's just that the money—the money is too good."

Linc squeezed her shoulder. "No cops. I'm going to leave Annie here with you."

Annie blinked. Was he insane? "Linc, I can't—"

"I don't need her. What's she gonna do besides look at me like I climbed out of some sewer."

Instantly Annie knew that was exactly what she'd already done. Oh, not in so many words, but clearly she'd telegraphed her feelings and Tiffany had picked up on them immediately. It was a horrid and dead-on true assessment that Annie realized showed her up to be a total snob.

Suddenly Tiffany grinned. "You're scared of me. Linc's girlfriend in her big-bucks sundress is scared I might get her dirty."

"Back it off, Tiffany. And lose the whipped-up bitch attitude. It's not Annie's fault that you and Tim are fighting."

"Not my fault either. He walked out, I didn't."

Annie took a deep breath. "I'll stay."

Tiffany shrugged. "Who cares." And the teenager went into the small kitchen area and turned on the water in the sink.

Linc was at the door when Annie stopped him. "When are you coming back?"

"I won't be long."

"You know where Tim is?"

"Let's put it this way. I know who knows where he is."

"Where?"

"Getting paid to have sex with rich old women."

"My God."

"Nice world out there for kids looking to make fast cash."

"He did this before?"

"Yeah to support his mother. I don't want to see him back in that life to support a kid. By the way, Cullen was recruited, too, remember I told you about that? Well, it was Tim who hauled him out before he got suckered in. I gotta go." He tipped her chin up and dropped a kiss on her mouth that she barely had time to taste before he was out the door and moving down the hall.

Annie stood for a long time after he'd gone. His words about Tim and Cullen numbed her. Not the fact of it, although that was disgusting enough, but that Linc seemed not only calm but so confident that he could fix it. This was the world he lived in, the world he was constantly trying to right. He wasn't doing it with money or speeches or adding problems to a list of worthy causes. No fanfare, no look-at-me, no conditions. Simply seeing the pain and the frustration and wanting to fix it.

Her respect for him and for Noah House were one thing, but this—the moments with Tiffany and now the hunt for Tim—this was walking into the lives of these kids when most wouldn't have bothered. Easier to call the cops, simpler to call State Services, less trouble to just dispense cliched advice along with a pat of assurance.

Basic involvement was the key. Just as he'd done with Cullen. But it was more than words; it was action with a passion for answers. And for Annie, this was a turning point. She knew that a week ago she would have fled here . . . No, a week ago, she would have never come here.

"Hey, you can leave. I ain't gonna stop you." Tiffany stood at the sink with steam rising into her face and bubbles swelling up to her wrists as she pulled plates out from the soapy water.

"No, I'd like to stay."

"Lookin' for Linc to give you a gold star?"

"I was hoping maybe you would."

"Hah. I ain't never even seen a gold star." She gestured with a dripping hand toward a rickety cupboard. "You wanna stay, make yourself useful and dry these dishes. Towel's in the drawer."

Annie had to smile. Tiffany was young enough to be her daughter, and yet there was no question who was giving orders. From the drawer, she took a sage green cotton towel with a Martha Stewart label on the edge. It was exactly like one she had in her kitchen.

Back at the sink, she took one of the plates and dried it.

"Bet you didn't think you'd be doin' this," Tiffany said.

"No, I sure didn't."

"Bet you got a dishwasher and other stuff. Tim, you know, he's always telling me that someday we'll have things. Looks like that's all shot to hell."

"Tim will be fine and so will you."

"Yeah, you know somethin' I don't?"

"I know Linc."

She thought for a moment. "Yeah, he does get stuff done. Watch out you don't break that bowl. I ain't got another one."

"I have some extras that I don't use."

She put a handful of silverware in the drainer. "Oh, I bet you got lots of extras of everything. I like bowls. When they're filled with stuff it feels like I'm rich."

"I'll bring a couple over for you."

"They aren't gray, are they?"

"Why no. One is yellow and the other is the green sage color of this towel."

She nodded. "I hate gray."

"Me, too."

And Tiffany smiled.

They fell silent, the only noise being the dishes in and out of the drainer—the rhythms of an era past, and Annie realized how fortunate she was: not to have all the modern conveniences that Tiffany didn't have, including no gray bowls, but that she'd stayed and not run. She wasn't sure that meant anything, but for the first time in a long time, Annie felt accomplished and satisfied.

Linc made the rounds of the bars where Fiper usually hung out. At the fifth stop he found him. As skinny as a longshoreman's rope, Fiper's taste for leather clothes wasn't diminished by hot summer days. Linc wasted no time.

"Where's Tim?"

"Well, well, if it ain't my old buddy McCoy. Got tired of turnin' all those devils into angels—?"

Linc had him slammed face first up against a wall, his arm twisted up behind him. That was the thing about guys like Fiper—all mouth and no muscle. Linc ignored the howls. "Where's Tim?"

"I ain't seen him—Christ, let up will ya, you're breakin' my arm."

"Talk." And Linc yanked harder.

"Okay, okay, I saw the kid, was gonna set him with this forty-year-old who thinks she's a princess, but he assed out. He was headin' down toward County 'bout twenty minutes ago. Said somethin' about construction."

Linc shoved him away. "If you're lying to me, Fiper, I'm gonna hunt you down and take your eyeballs out with a dull knife."

"I ain't lyin'. I ain't."

Linc got back on the cycle and roared down the street, circled back to the boulevard and headed toward County. About midway, he spotted a Simmons Construction site sign and slowed down. He drew to a stop near the porta-heads, swung off the bike, and headed toward the work area where trucks, a cement mixer pouring into forms, and a main trailer dotted the landscape.

"Hey Linc!" a man in jeans and a Red Sox shirt and cap called out before trotting over to shake hands. "You ain't lookin for a job, are you?"

"Not today. I am looking for a kid though. He's lookin' for work."

"Gotta be Tim. The other kid was just looking for information."

"Other kid?"

"Name's Cullen."

"Cullen?" He sighed. "What's he doing here?"

"Asking some questions about Richard Hunter. No trouble. Danny answered them, and as he was leaving Tim came in. The two of them are over by the drink cooler."

"Thanks."

Linc walked across the site, stepping over lumber and a spilled bag of nails. It was Tim and Cullen all right, slugging down sodas as if this were just any old summer day. When they saw Linc both came to immediate attention.

"Oh God, Linc, I forgot. Honest. Tiff and I had this big showdown with her screechin' at me to get out. I was gonna call you but then I ran into Cullen, and we well, we were just sorta shooting the shit . . . and . . . and . . . well, you know how it goes."

Without saying anything, Linc turned to Cullen. "It was like he said, Linc. We just sorta met. I was here to find out some stuff about my father from a guy who he helped. It's a really cool story . . . Tim met the guy, his name is Danny and he told me what a great guy my dad was. Tim and me, we was just talkin' about, well, lots of stuff . . ."

And both boys shuffled, heads down, hands crunching their soda cans.

"I should be royally pissed at both of you. You, Cullen, for giving Eddie that black eye, and you, Tim, for getting Tiffany pregnant."

The boys glanced at one another, looking more puzzled than relieved.

"How did you know?" Cullen ventured.

"He ratted you out."

"Figures."

"He deserved it," Linc said. "And you don't need to tell anyone I said that."

"Yes, sir." And Cullen let out a long breath.

Finally, to Tim, he asked, "You get a job?"

"Yes sir."

"Here?"

He nodded. "I start tomorrow morning."

"Good. Cullen you get on back to the House. Vesco needs some help. As for you, Tim . . ." he paused, then said, "Next time you get jammed, call me. That doesn't make you a baby, it makes you smart." He glanced around the site. "Then again, I'd say you're already on your way to being smart."

Cullen went to his bike and Tim followed Linc.

"Want a ride home?" Linc asked.

"Nah. Think I'll get some flowers for Tiff. She's pregnant and I figure that's kinda special."

Linc squeezed his shoulder and watched as he went on down the street.

Some days just plain turned out good.

Chapter
Thirteen

After a night of thunder and lightning, Monday dawned rainy and gray, which nicely matched Annie's mood.

She spent the morning with a new client and her cute but too pampered ten-year-old daughter, who wanted her bedroom instantly redecorated. Annie generally took impossible requests in stride, but while this would be a profitable project, she found herself impatient and testy. It all seemed so pointless; another wealthy woman spending gobs of money to indulge the whim of a child that in two years would be whining that the room was horrible and she hated it. Annie had been down this road more than a few times in the past. By next year the mother would want a new decor and in a few years it would be redone once more, then a fourth time for a guest room when the daughter went off to some six-figure Ivy League college. It was all so predictable, but in the past Annie had simply smiled and happily watched her profit margin rise because of the whims of the wealthy.

This time was different. She smiled, slid all her notes and the mother's ideas along with the preliminary sketches into her briefcase, but she wasn't happy. Back in her office an hour later, she left her wet umbrella in the reception area in a gold-edged Italian stand from Richard's mother. She greeted Elaine, handing her the sketches, notes, and ideas.

"Want to work on this project?" Annie asked the surprised receptionist.

"Really?"

"Time you got both feet in."

Elaine had been taking design courses, but Annie knew hands-on experience combined with an instinctive eye for pattern and color worked better than classes. Elaine had those instincts and she'd worked enthusiastically with Annie in the past. And if Annie needed anything right now, it was enthusiasm.

Eagerly, Elaine opened the sketchbook. "Oh, it's a little girl's room. Ruffles and lace."

"Uh, no. She wants jungle animals and a garden theme."

"The Lion King meets Mary, Mary, Quite Contrary."

"Excellent," Annie said. "I knew you'd be right for this project. Write up some of your ideas and we'll throw them around."

"But Annie, don't you want to give me a starting point? You never just hand something over."

No, she never had. "The King meets Mary is pretty basic. Build on that. Then let me see what you come up with."

"Wow, I can't wait to dive in."

"Coffee fresh?" Annie asked glancing at the beverage table.

"Just made it. I'll bring you a cup."

In her office, she eased the door closed, slipped out of her pumps, hung up her suit jacket, and thanked Elaine when she came in with the steaming cup. She sipped carefully while she paged through her notes from another project with as much ardor as she reserved for junk mail.

But the scarier moment had been the morning she'd just spent. Instead of looking forward to the process of this new project, all she'd envisioned were endless days of changes and redesign. Her swamp of disinterest was an odd sensation, because Annie never looked that far into the future of any decorating job. She'd learned to be creatively flexible, for there were always panic phone calls on the way to completion. Oftentimes these changes were for the better, and from a financial perspective the new ideas and alterations yielded found money for her business when a project deviated from the original estimate.

And given the mother and daughter's diverse ideas of what that bedroom needed, Annie knew "additions and changes" would be the order of the day.

Yet despite her own apathy, she'd nodded, given advice, and helped select the preliminary colors and patterns. Both the client and her daughter seemed thrilled with her general suggestions so that by the time Annie drove back to the office she was pretty sure she had the job; the real truth was that she didn't care. In fact, she'd almost hoped the woman would call to say she'd had a better price from another decorator or that they were going to wait another year or that they'd decided to donate the money to charity.

Annie couldn't help but imagine how many air conditioners could be purchased for Noah House with the money that would be spent on that bedroom.

All this inner churning about what she wanted and didn't want certainly indicated a restlessness, a need for something different. In her career, in her life, in her heart? A kind of life-choices overhaul? Was that what had been dragging at her this past weekend?

Or did it all boil down to this *thing* she had for Linc McCoy? Not just a passing interest, but a think-about-all-the-time interest. If she were sixteen, this would be a very ordinary I-can't-live-without-him crush. But she wasn't sixteen and more importantly, they had no relationship, so what was the source for this deep wanting that ached? Her heart seemed to be illogically out of kilter, but did that mean the other areas of her life were, too? Apparently so.

What was really weird was the issue of Cullen and a kind of inner calm that she settled into whenever she thought about him. Maybe if he'd been a messed-up nasty-mouthed kid or a teenager harvesting illegal trouble, she'd be more conflicted. But he was a nice kid who wanted to learn all he could about his birth father; a boy who was so infatuated with being Richard's son that he told whoever would listen. Like Richard's business partner, like Danny at the construction site, like Tim and God knows who else since Friday. Vera and James Hunter would not be in the dark for long at this rate.

Word from Linc, delivered after he found Tim, that Cullen was telling others that Richard was his father had propelled Annie's decision to talk to the Hunters. She shouldn't have caved last week when Betsy raised a fuss. Linc had been right. Richard's parents must be informed, and just because it was awkward for Annie and Betsy was vehemently opposed changed nothing. Further delay would only be embarrassingly painful.

She hadn't spoken with Betsy, and debated now whether to call her first. But why bother? She'd only get annoyed and try to bully Annie out of it.

Annie picked up the phone, punching numbers. When Vera Hunter answered the phone, and after the polite pleasantries, Annie asked, "Would it be okay if I dropped by this afternoon?"

"We'd love to see you, Annie," Vera said with her polished enthusiasm. "I thought you would have visited before now. We did just return from Italy."

"Yes, I know. I intended to, but—"

"Your decorating business, I know," Vera said, cutting her off. "Betsy told us."

Vera could be direct, and had no doubt questioned Betsy as to Annie's absence, and her sister-in-law had to say something. Annie should have stopped by sooner, even if she'd never mentioned Cullen. She had no excuse for simply ignoring them. Yet if she'd visited, in all good conscience, she could not have stayed silent, not with the truth of Cullen lurking like some ticking fuse on an emotional stick of dynamite.

"It will be good to see you," Annie said, wondering if she sounded as lame to Vera as she did to herself.

"It was a fascinating trip, and you'll want to see the painting I purchased. A small oil by a young artist. A boy, actually—so young and so obviously talented." Her sigh was audible, and Annie knew that she was thinking of Richard's childhood drawings that she'd had framed and now hung in the den. Talent only a mother could love. Vera continued. "What time can we expect you?"

"I have another stop to make, so about two o'clock?"

"That's fine for me. I don't know about James. He has his Monday afternoon chess game at his club. You know he doesn't like his routine disturbed."

"If two is too late, then I can make it earlier. I'd really like to see both of you."

"Is there something wrong?"

How did she answer that? "I do have something to tell you."

"Are you okay? You're not sick or in trouble, are you?"

"No, no, nothing like that."

"Then do make it one." She paused. "Annie, is this about another man?"

The question threw her. "No. Why would you ask that?"

"A friend in Providence called last night and was very upset that her son was remarrying so soon after his wife's death. She kept saying you would be snatched up soon, too. It was very disturbing."

Snatched up? Annie shuddered at the distasteful image. "I think widowers tend to remarry sooner than widows. I'll see you both at one."

Annie punched the off button, trying to imagine their mood after she told them about Cullen. And what would they think of Linc if she were to introduce him? It was a question she didn't need to think too hard about.

She punched out another number and when he answered, she said, "I'm surprised you're there."

"Annie?"

"Hmmm, remember me?" It was a snippish question, but she didn't care. Not once since she'd last seen him on Friday had he called or tried to see her.

"Uh oh. Sounds like I'm in trouble."

"You *are* trouble."

He chuckled and she felt a little better, but not much.

"I wanted to let you know I'm seeing the Hunters at one today."

"Good."

"No offer to come with me? Like you offered last week?" she asked, unable to keep silent.

"Can't. Not today." No "I wish I could." No "you'll do fine" encouragement. No apology. Instead, he said, "I've got a staff meeting plus two social workers coming in. Why don't you stop by when you're done? No, forget that. We'll get interrupted. I'll swing by your house about four."

Actually she liked that idea better. "That'll be fine."

"Annie, you okay? Is there something wrong?"

She'd had no intention of saying anything. Nevertheless, she said, "I don't know what's wrong. Nothing is what I expected it to be."

"Like what?"

"I thought I'd be uneasy or scared or reluctant about

the Hunters, but I don't feel any of those things. It's like it has to be done and I'm going to do it."

"This is a bad thing?" he asked.

"It just doesn't feel right to me."

"Just because you're not wringing your hands and looking for an exit sign doesn't mean that you don't care."

"But I feel so disconnected from all of it, Linc. It's like I don't care anymore about what Richard did to me, and I should." *But I care very much what you're doing to me and I shouldn't.* "I should be furious, or on some hunt for the other woman, or digging through Richard's past for clues on why he betrayed me. Cullen told me that first time we talked that *Sandy* had said she was going to call Richard. I intended to check his appointment books to see if she had, and if he'd planned to see her. I checked the books, and found no record, by the way, but it was as if it didn't matter. Like his having a secret meeting with the woman who adopted his son was irrelevant to me. It's as if Cullen simply slid into my life, and after some denial and some anger at Richard, there's no conflict there anymore." *All my feelings are toward you and that scares me.* "It as if it's all okay, and making Cullen's appearance some big deal is too much effort, when actually, I wish Richard were here so he could have known his son." She paused, and when the silence stretched between them, she said, "I know I'm rambling and it probably sounds all disconnected." Another beat of silence. "Say something."

But if she'd expected some soothing pet of fuzzy warm understanding, she should have known better. He said, "I'm trying to figure out what."

"I never should have said anything."

"Sweetheart, you're asking me to look into your soul— a little tough over the phone."

"Are you making fun of me?" She hated the whiny tone of that question.

"You know I wouldn't do that."

"I don't know. I don't know anything anymore." Oh God, she was going to cry and she absolutely didn't want to do that. She literally swallowed down the rawness in her throat. "I'm sorry. I know you have to go."

He paused as if hunting for something more to say, then finally, "I'll see you at four."

And then he was gone, leaving Annie staring at the phone, feeling ruffled and edgy and confused. How could she be so mixed-up about so many things? She sighed, then slid her chair back from the desk and rose to her feet.

It was a puzzle all right, this inner disconnect. And tears. Annie never thought of herself as so sensitive that one remark could bring her to tears. Maybe she was having too many premenopausal moments.

Something had happened to her between her first learning of Cullen and this past weekend. For one, Cullen's paternity was no longer a question for her. It was patently obvious, and while she knew that legally more would be needed than simple belief and acceptance, she wasn't pursuing a legal course. The Hunters might, and that was their right given that Cullen would be a potential grandson.

Admittedly, Annie was mildly curious about the birth mother, but again, there was no burning need to know who she was. Her burning need, apparently, was to know herself. Or Linc McCoy.

My God, she was almost forty and still discovering things about herself. What had changed had been her outlook, her perspective, and her heart. From that visit to Noah House, her discovery that her mother had been friends with Linc's mother, that freewheeling motorcycle ride capped off with Tiffany—Annie had been part of it all in a way she'd never been part of her marriage to Richard. It was as if she'd willingly exchanged the staid, routine world she'd known for fifteen years with Richard for a new world of energy and surprises and a fantasy or two.

Linc. He was the linchpin in this. And where was she going with him? Obviously he wasn't sexually attracted to her in that making love didn't ride high on his list. When they'd left a grateful Tiffany and a solicitous Tim, Linc had taken her to get her car at her mother's, given her a sort-of-maybe-perhaps-I'm-interested-in-you kiss goodbye, saying he had some things to do. Then he'd ridden off as if the suggestive comments during the day had been thrown confetti, promptly forgotten. Perhaps sexy talk to him was as vacuous as a handful of bubbles. Her dwelling on the possibility of intimacy had been the imagination of a too-fertile mind.

On Saturday, she'd gone to the church bazaar, pleasing her mother, but not pleasing herself, for Linc never showed up. All his mother said was that he was busy with the boys. And then after she'd left the bazaar, Annie had done something really stupid. She'd driven over to Noah House to see if his motorcycle was there. It wasn't, and that had upset and hurt her, for she was sure he was off having a good time with someone else. Someone female. Maybe that Brooke who he'd been involved with.

Sick. That's what she was. My God, riding by a guy's place to see if he was there? She hadn't done anything that juvenile since she was a teenager and hung out for hours at the music store because Doug Demers worked there and she wanted desperately for him to notice her enough to ask her out. Back then it was harmless teenage infatuation. Now it was pathetic and sad. She'd driven home vowing to not think about Linc, to not like him, and definitely to not call him.

By Sunday, she was miserable. Too much solace wine from the night before gave her a raging headache. She read through the Sunday newspaper, took Rocky for a long walk, and came back hoping to find a message from Linc. But there was none.

Then she got angry, at herself for wanting him and at him for not wanting her.

By Monday morning, she wasn't any happier, but she was determined to act cool, undisturbed, and distant. Of course she hadn't talked to him, because he hadn't called her, so once she'd talked to Vera, she had an excuse, a Cullen excuse rather than just calling him.

Then she'd almost blubbered into the phone.

As to his coming to her house at four, she could already guess the outcome—he'd listen to how the visit went, make a few comments about when Cullen would meet the Hunters, and probably toss her a light kiss and leave.

She sighed in resignation. It was probably better to be prepared for just such a scenario—then she wouldn't be disappointed when it happened.

Annie put on her jacket, shouldered her purse, and looked around the spacious office that she'd always loved. Even her business had slid in importance. Maybe she needed a vacation or some counseling about getting her head on straight. She had the perfect life—a business she loved, money enough to try new things, a gorgeous home—and yet she felt empty and cold and disconnected.

Instead of looking forward to designing a client's daughter's bedroom, she was leaving those details to Elaine so she could dash home and get the two bowls to take to Tiffany. Excitement bubbled in her over that visit. Two bowls to a pregnant teenager with bad English on Godfrey Street?

My God, who had Annie Hunter become?

At home, Annie filled one bowl with a bundle of *Martha Stewart's Living* magazines and took the other one from the refrigerator. It held a pasta salad she'd made earlier. She felt a little foolish taking food, but at the same time the bowl looked naked just left empty.

Her concern was for naught when Tiffany opened the door and whooped at the sight of the magazines, fell in love with the bowls, and told Annie she didn't eat pasta, but Tim would gobble it down.

"Working construction makes him eat." She looked much better, and the apartment was straightened up and actually felt cooler. She invited Annie in.

"For a few minutes," she said. Tiffany had a pretty smile and she certainly looked more content than she had on Friday.

"So you goin' to see Linc? I mean you're kinda dressed dressy to just come here."

Annie smiled, realizing this was one of the things she liked about Tiffany. She simply said what she meant with no attempt to couch it in phony diplomacy. "I came from work and then I'm going to see my in-laws. They just got back from Italy."

"Wow, you mean you're married?"

"I'm a widow."

"Oh. So how did he die?"

"A heart attack about a year ago."

"You miss him?"

Two weeks ago she would have given an unqualified yes.

"Yes, but not in the same way I did right after he died. I'm more circumspect now."

Tiffany nodded in that way people do when they don't quite understand. "You got kids?"

Annie shook her head.

"Yeah? That's weird. I don't know nobody who don't have kids."

"Now you know me."

"You don't like 'em?"

"I love children and babies, but I couldn't have them."

That seemed to fascinate her. "You one of them I read about got too many aborts?"

"No, I never was pregnant. My husband and I had tests done, saw a lot of infertility experts, followed all the advice, but nothing worked."

Tiffany nodded. "Maybe you needed to like relax and think about other stuff. I read that, too."

"That's what my husband always said." This time Annie looked away, feeling the sting of what might have been. Talking about not being able to get pregnant wasn't new, and here, in a conversation with an eighteen-year-old, she should be all together, not on the verge of looking back in endless regret.

Tiffany tipped her head to the side. "Hey, it really bugs you, huh?"

"It's been disappointing, yes."

She nodded, solemnly. "Yeah, gotta be tough to have all those nice things but can't get what you really want."

"An astute observation."

"Huh?"

Annie smiled. "In other words, you're smart."

"Yeah? Jeez, nobody ever called me smart. So far the ones who know Tim knocked me up all said I was stupid."

"Linc didn't say that."

"Oh, he didn't say the words, but he's thinkin' it."

"And how 'bout Tim? Is anyone saying he's stupid?"

"Me. I told him we couldn't be doin' it all the time like he likes—he hates them rubbers—when we don't have no money for my pills. But he didn't want to hear that, so here I am. Relaxin' weren't never a problem for us. That's what we fighted about. I called him stupid for gettin' me this way. He don't like to be called stupid. He tells me to get rid of it—like he's got a right to say shit. But, you know what? He's been real good since Linc talked to him . . . not like happy, happy, but not tellin' me I gotta get rid of it."

Annie was too aware of the sweep of envy that gripped her. Tiffany prattling on about a pregnancy that neither wanted, made halfhearted attempts to prevent, and yet here they were. Whereas she and Richard had not only tried, but spent money, seen doctors, had tests, and she'd wept endless tears.

Stop it. It's all in the past and too late and not to be. In her mind she'd resigned herself, but in her heart, well that was a different place. Listening to Tiffany brought back all her own hurt and disappointment, and yet she was happy for Tiffany. How could she not be?

"Guess I yammered too much, huh?" Tiffany asked, looking unsure, as if Annie's contemplation meant she was angry.

"No, actually, it's given me some perspective. I'm glad things are working out for you and Tim."

"For now we're cool."

And they both stood in the living room where a cool summer breeze came through the windows. Then Annie said, "I better go."

"Hey thanks for the bowls, and uh, the other stuff."

"You're welcome."

Again crevices of silence looped between them.

"Well, goodbye . . ."

"Yeah." But as Annie started down the hall to the stairs, Tiffany called out, "If you ever want to come back, I'll be here. I mean like I ain't got nowhere to go, and uh, well maybe sometime, when you ain't busy, maybe we could . . ."

Annie walked back. "Get together? I'd like that."

"For real? You ain't just saying' that?"

Annie laughed. "I'm not just saying it."

Tiffany grinned. "You wanna like come back or somethin' I could look in those Martha mags and get some ideas. I could fix somethin'."

Annie started to say that wasn't necessary for she knew the couple didn't have a lot of extra money, but Tiffany looked so eager Annie simply accepted. "What day?"

"Uh, Wednesday."

"I have to check my appointments. I'll call you."

"Yeah sure."

"Tiffany, I promise."

"Sure."

Annie didn't know what to say, but she didn't want to leave with Tiffany thinking she was putting her off.

"Okay, Wednesday, it is."

"You mean it? What about them appoints?"

"They're not as important."

The teenager beamed. "Okay."

"I'll see you then."

Back in her car, she wondered what she was getting into. It was hard to understand how the unexpected find of a boy on her back porch had propelled her life into such a diverse direction. But it had happened.

Chapter Fourteen

The Hunters lived in a sprawling Tudor-style house on a street as far away from Godfrey as July heat was from a January frost.

Annie parked in the drive, left her umbrella in the car since the rain had tapered off, and walked up the brick path that wound through a fence of widely spaced hydrangea bushes. The front door was oak and brass with long etched windows framing each side. Two pots of red geraniums in cement urns stood sentry.

She rang the bell, and in a few moments the door was opened by James Hunter, dressed in pressed pants and a pristine white shirt. Tall and boxy, his body looked as steady physically as Annie knew him to be when it came to life in general. James never blustered or reacted wildly to any news that Annie could recall. When she'd called them about Richard, James had been calm and almost stoic; only later did she find him weeping in the den. He was a private man who had little use for public outbursts no matter the reason. Remembering that now reassured her about what she had to say.

"Come in, come in," he said, smiling and slipping his hand around her arm to draw her close. He kissed her cheek, and if Annie had closed her eyes she could almost have believed this was Richard.

"It's good to see you, James." And she meant it. He was a fine man and she was reminded today of just how fond of him she was.

"You are looking lovelier than ever, Annie."

"And you look as if you enjoyed the Italian sunshine. That's quite a tan."

"Vera fussed incessantly, but I managed to slip away from her. Let's go into the den. How about some wine? I have some of that Pinot Grigio you always liked."

"How nice of you to remember." She was going to say it was too early, but instead she nodded. "Yes, that would be lovely."

The den had the comforting appeal of leather furnishings, family pictures, and an impressive collection of first editions. Annie unbuttoned her suit jacket and sat in a Windsor rather than on the couch. Couches were for relaxing, and this definitely wasn't going to be a relaxing visit.

James returned with her wine and a scotch on the rocks for himself. "Vera's on the phone with Betsy. She'll be right out. So what have you been up to? Business doing well?"

"Yes, very well." She sipped the wine. Icy and crisp just the way she liked it.

"And what about Annie Hunter? An interesting social life, I hope. Something besides working?"

"I play some tennis when I can. Redecorated the guest room. Gardening, of course. A college friend was here for a week in June and we did some bar hopping at a few of the old haunts. Nothing like running into old college friends to make you wonder what you ever saw in them." He smiled and she paused, thinking for a moment just how bereft her life had been.

Apart from work and a few stray social activities, she

had very little going on. Until Cullen had appeared on her back porch. Until Linc. Ah, she thought, no wonder he was so appealing. He'd given her something to think about besides her business and walking Rocky. Maybe it had nothing to do with an attraction to him and everything to do with a too-dull life. "Oh, and Betsy and I have gotten together a few times," she finished, then, not wanting James to think their friendship was an afterthought, she added, "But we don't get together as much as I'd like." And that was absolutely true despite the disagreement about Cullen.

"I'm glad to hear that you two have remained friends." He leaned forward. "No men in any of those pictures," James commented softly as though he were disappointed.

"Are you asking me if I'm dating?" Annie asked, amused. Because Vera too often could be abrasive and cool in manner and words, Annie had stayed away. However, in so doing, she'd deprived herself of James's company. These few moments made her glad she'd come.

He sipped his scotch, obviously liking that she wasn't huffy. "Of course I'm asking. And if there isn't a man in your life, there should be. You're too young and pretty to sleep in an empty bed."

"James!" Vera Hunter, slim in powder-blue slacks and a tailored blouse, stood straight, regal, and outraged in the doorway.

"Phone call finished?" he asked, unruffled by her disapproval. "Betsy and everyone okay? Sure did enjoy seeing the kids this past weekend."

"Never mind that. How many of those scotches have you had?"

"Two," he said with no apology. Which should have been followed by Vera chastising him again, but James added, "Annie *should* have a man in her life and in her bed."

"My God, James, are you listening to yourself?"

"Now, Vera, settle down. It's okay to point out that she spent too many years having sex for other reasons."

It was a poignant observation. During those years of trying to get pregnant, lovemaking had become a necessity, like cutting the lawn. You had to do it whether you were in the mood or not. Again, maybe she was afflicted with aches and eagerness for Linc because nothing was at stake but pleasure.

Vera was still sputtering. "James, I swear you can be the most uncouth man at times."

"Uncouth? There's a word I haven't heard in awhile. Let's look at the bright side. You wouldn't like it if I didn't surprise you once in awhile. Like that afternoon in the villa—"

She flushed and Annie was amazed. She'd never, not one time, ever seen Vera embarrassed.

"Can we please get to the point of Annie's visit?" Then, not quite able to let James get the last word, she said, "If you'd asked me, I could have told you Annie isn't dating anyone."

"A pity."

"Enough, James."

Annie glanced over at James, who was seated beneath all those framed childhood drawings of Richard's. In what had to be the least important thought she'd had all day, she wondered if Cullen had any of his early childhood drawings.

Vera was perched on a damask-green cushioned side chair, knees together, hands folded in her lap as though she were waiting for an opera to begin. The chair looked out of place against the leather decor, but then, given the past few moments, Vera looked a little out-of-place beside the blunt-talking James.

They both were waiting, poised as if to begin another round of back-and-forthing if the silence lasted much longer.

Annie cleared her throat, speaking slowly and softly. "I really appreciate both of you thinking about me, but that's not what I came to talk about. I came to talk about someone else." She took a another sip of wine, remembering suddenly she hadn't had anything to eat since the rye toast at breakfast. She set the glass down on the marble-topped table and pushed it away.

How to get into this? Annie thought. There was no easy way, so she took the shortest. "While you were away, a thirteen-year-old boy came to see me." She paused. "His name is Cullen Gallagher." She paused again. "He thought I was his birth mother."

Vera glanced over at James, who instead of saying anything, lifted his glass and took a long swallow.

"Why how strange, Annie," Vera said. "You must have thought he was crazy. Obviously he'd made a mistake."

"About me being his mother, yes." She looked over at James, who seemed to be barely listening. She continued, "Cullen's mistake, however, originated from something else. He says he's Richard's son. He assumed I was his birth mother."

Pins dropping couldn't have described the silence. Annie felt as if she'd stepped into a tomb. From James, who wouldn't look at her, to Vera, who had lost all the color in her cheeks. Neither of them spoke, sitting transfixed as if the words she'd just spoken needed to be translated.

Finally, with only the distant ticking of a clock and three adults breathing, Annie couldn't stand it any longer. "Please say something. Ask me questions. Tell me you don't believe it, tell me you do believe it. Tell me it's impossible. Tell me I must be wrong."

Even as Annie tried to relieve the tension, she realized that at some level she, too, wished it wasn't true; not because of Cullen or even because Richard had betrayed her, but because of the Hunters. They looked numb. Whoever said a life can be irrevocably changed in a moment could have used this scene as an example. Instant grandparents. Instant grandson. Instant questions. Except no one was asking them.

Finally James stood. "Excuse me."

"You're not leaving," Vera said horrified. Annie watched in bewilderment as James rose to his feet and picked up his glass. "How can you walk out after what she just said?" When he didn't immediately answer, she warned, "Don't you get another drink, James Hunter."

With raised eyebrows, he said, "I would say this news calls for many drinks." And he left the room, leaving Annie with Vera.

"I don't understand him, I simply don't." Then, as though she had nothing more to say about her husband, she said, "Obviously this boy is as mistaken about Richard as he was about you." She looked almost pleadingly at Annie for her nod of agreement.

"I don't think so. Cullen has information from his adoptive mother that indicates it's true."

"What kind of information?"

"He overheard a conversation between his parents, and Richard was referred to as his father."

"That's all? That isn't proof. It's probably someone else. There are probably a dozen Richard Hunter's in Rhode Island alone."

"Cullen looks like Richard."

"And I always thought James looked like Cary Grant. That doesn't mean anything."

"He has a birthmark on his neck in the exact same shape and in the same place that Richard had one."

"Meaningless. That's not proof, that's just a coincidence."

"Vera, tests can be done, but I'm positive they will prove he's Richard's son. Look, I'm not trying to force anything or anyone upon you and James, but Cullen is here in Bedford and other people know. I didn't want you to hear from someone else."

With her face as tight as her posture, she said in a cold voice, "Have you called this mother who wants to soil Richard's good name?"

"She's dead."

"How very convenient."

"His adoptive father didn't want him anymore after his wife was killed."

"So he decided to shop around for someone who did."

"That's unfair to Cullen and to me. I would not have come here if Cullen were some hustler. He lived in a few foster homes, not very successfully, and ended up on the street. Currently he's living at Noah House—"

"Noah House!" Vera was on her feet. "Now I know this is all a mistake. If he were Richard's son, he would not be housed in a place for bad boys."

Annie blinked at the absurdity of her reasoning. She wished James would come back. She didn't want to argue with Vera, but this wasn't making any sense.

"Have you ever been there?"

"Oh, I've been there. Once a few years ago when my bridge club donated food. It was run by a man who looked as if he'd grown up there."

"Linc McCoy."

"Perhaps. He was very gruff, more than a little rude, and acted as if we were all trespassing. Where is James?" She went to the doorway, then took a step back and to the side when her daughter appeared. "Oh, Betsy, I'm so glad you're here. Maybe you can talk some sense into her. You are not going to believe what Annie just told us. It's the most outrageous story about Richard having a son—"

"Goddammit, Annie, what did I tell you? How dare you come here and tell those lies!" A very rushed and disheveled Betsy steamed into the room. She wore a denim dress splattered with rain drops, her feet were in wet sandals, and her hair was damp and scraggly. She was breathing like Annie did after a hard tennis match.

"It's not a lie," she said softly, still as puzzled today by Betsy's volcanic fury as she'd been the week before. Even the Hunters weren't this overwrought.

"You knew about this boy?" Vera asked, pure befuddlement in her expression. "Why on earth didn't you say anything?"

Betsy's voice softened. "I didn't say anything because there's nothing to any of this. If I'd known Annie was going to break her promise to me—" She turned. "How could you do this to them? To me? We were friends and—" She swiped a hand across her eyes, and Annie felt her own fill. This was all wrong. This shouldn't be happening.

"Betsy, we *are* friends and you know I didn't do this to hurt anyone."

But the mist of tears was gone and Betsy loomed, hands planted on her hips, her anger so visceral, Annie saw her temples throb. "No *friend* would do this. You had no right to peddle this—this outrageous fabrication. What is wrong with you?"

"You know me," Annie pleaded, a hollow emptiness opening up inside her. "You know I wouldn't have done this if I didn't believe it was absolutely necessary. They had to know. Cullen has been telling people. He's so proud of Richard."

"You're insane. You are totally insane. I warned you, and you promised you wouldn't do this—"

"I did not promise. I said I'd think about it. I did and I made the decision."

"You'd think about it? You'd make the decision? What are you, some self-proclaimed town crier? When mother told me on the phone you were coming for a visit, I just knew."

"So you rushed over to swear at me and call me names. That's real useful," Annie snapped, giving up on trying to reason with her.

"This is about my brother, who can't defend himself from an outrageous lie."

"No Betsy, this outrage is about you. Even your parents aren't fulminating the way you are. Richard would have never acted like this."

Betsy folded her arms. "Oh really. And what would he have done? Opened his arms and said welcome to the family?"

"Yes, I think he would have. I don't believe Richard would have turned his back on Cullen." Although this was the first time she'd put it into words, she knew it was true. Richard would not have denied him.

Betsy's face was red, and her eyes were narrowed to near slits. She came closer to Annie, gritting out the words. "That kid is not Richard's son. We will prove it."

"Fine. You do that." Annie stepped around her, her own fury simmering just below boil. That Betsy, who she'd considered such a loyal friend, would turn on her with such venom made her sick to her stomach.

Vera, the grizzly bear before Betsy had arrived, had deflated into a confused teddy bear and slumped back down in the chair, looking more than a little glassy-eyed. "I simply don't know what to do . . . Perhaps if I saw the boy . . ."

"No!" Betsy shouted. "You can't do that, you can't."

Annie ignored her. "Vera, you don't have to make any decision today."

"For Christ's sake, will you keep out of this?"

Again she spoke to Vera. "If you want to see Cullen, call me. You and James decide what you want to do."

"Where is James?" Vera asked as if just noticing that he hadn't returned. "Oh, I don't know. Richard and a son, I don't know. I guess—"

Betsy interrupted by taking her mother by the shoulders and turning her so that her back was to Annie. "Mom, look at me." Betsy shook her to get her attention. "You can't just fold up and let her have her way. We need to get a lawyer." She looked around. "Where is Dad? Why isn't he in here?"

Annie wondered the same thing.

Betsy said to Annie, "Why don't you leave."

She touched Vera's arm. "I'll call you."

"Get out. Just get out."

Annie shouldered her bag and left the den with the sound of Betsy telling her mother once again that it was all a lie.

Slamming out the front door appealed to her, but what would that accomplish? Grabbing Betsy by the shoulders and shaking some sense into her had even greater appeal. She felt drained and exhausted and deeply disappointed. Nothing had been accomplished by this farce. Betsy's invective had probably soured and forever damaged Cullen's story. It wasn't a matter of who had the facts, but who could make the most viciously untrue accusations.

James had left the room for a reason, and not for a moment did Annie think it was because he feared discussing Cullen. James was too steady and too practical for such a mental retreat.

She glanced back into the den where Betsy was seated on the couch next to her mother. She was speaking softly, holding tight to her mother's hands as though Vera had escaped from reality. The contrast between the Vera who'd grilled her with legitimate questions and a natural defensiveness and this pathetic soul was breathtaking.

Opening the front door, she stood for a few moments, and then, whether it was anger or concern or just the smidgen of a possibility that she could save this visit from total disaster, she went looking for James.

She found him in a small office off the kitchen. He

was seated with his back to the door, staring out the window, where the rain had begun again.

"James?" Annie walked in, moving around the chair so she could face him. "I'm so sorry this was such a shock. I didn't come to hurt or upset you with the news of Cullen."

"You got a full dose of Hunter logic—shoot the messenger when the news is messy. Is Betsy still here?"

"She's with Vera." She didn't mention the confrontation. Obviously James had heard his daughter yelling. No doubt a few neighbors had heard her, too. "I'm worried about you. Why did you walk out?"

"I didn't want to hear any more."

"James, Cullen doesn't want to hurt anyone. I understand that this is startling and discomforting and yes, embarrassing." She thought he'd at least nod, but he remained stoic. Annie sat down on the footstool and took his hands. Could he be in emotional shock? She would never have thought it of him, but then her news had been extraordinary. "James, talk to me, please."

Finally he looked at her. "I've always been very fond of you, Annie. Vera is, too, she just has a harder time admitting it. I know she blamed you for not giving Richard a child, and that was wrong. She so wanted him to give her grandchildren. Sometimes, I think she focused too much on what couldn't be than on what was."

"The grandchildren she didn't have instead of the ones she did."

"Well put, but then I've always admired you for your logic and reasoning." He stared at the raindrops dribbling down the glass, then said, "You probably don't know that Betsy is adopted."

The statement, coming out of nowhere, was so startling she thought she'd heard wrong.

"We adopted her when she was three. I'm not surprised

Richard never told you. As you've learned, the Hunters are very good at keeping secrets."

At first she wasn't sure what he meant, then realized he had to be referring to Richard's betrayal. "But why would you keep Betsy's adoption a secret? Adoption is wonderful and something to be proud of."

"Vera preferred that it not be a subject of gossip, so when we moved here to Bedford, everyone assumed the obvious and we never changed any of those opinions. There was never any reason to."

That seemed so archaic, as though there were an element of shame. Unless there was. The culture had been different thirty plus years ago, or Vera, in some misguided way, thought that not telling anyone made Betsy more their child.

"I may be stepping over the line here, but you already had Richard, so why wouldn't you have had your own second child?"

"She was afraid. She had a hard time with Richard and we almost lost him. She refused to go through another pregnancy."

"But she wanted another baby, so you adopted. That sounds wise and logical and very strong—I don't understand."

"Where we lived before, some of her friends couldn't imagine why she'd adopt when she could have her own child. She became very defensive."

"She should have told them to go to hell. It was none of their business."

James smiled. "That's what I told her. Nevertheless, she was ashamed of her own fears and weakness. Her friends had convinced her that adopting was a cop-out when she could have had her own."

"I would say she needed new friends."

"But because of that, when we moved to Bedford, she made up her mind that no one would know Betsy was adopted. Of course there were never any questions."

"Why are you telling me?"

"It might explain why Betsy is so angry at you. Richard once told me that he usually forgot she was adopted, but Betsy never has. She and her brother were close growing up, but Betsy always felt inferior."

No wonder, Annie thought. She grew up thinking her mother was ashamed of how she came into the family.

James continued. "I think, although she'd probably deny it, that she was always glad Richard and you never had children. She was afraid we would have loved his children more than hers. His would have been the grandchildren by blood whereas hers—"

"Were the grandchildren of your heart? Wouldn't they have been? Aren't they right now?"

"We adore those three grandkids, and they wouldn't have been treated any differently than Richard's."

"Of course they wouldn't," Annie said, at least to her, the obvious.

"She's terrified that what you said is true. That Cullen is Richard's son and that he will replace her kids because he would be a 'real' Hunter."

"Would he be more important?"

"No, of course not."

Annie got to her feet, urging James up also. "You have to go in and talk to her. You must reassure her. She's very angry."

"Yes, I imagine she is." Then, instead of going into the other room, he glanced at his watch. "I have to go. My chess game is in about twenty minutes."

Annie watched incredulously as he put on a jacket and a tie. "James, for godsakes, how can you just go play chess?"

"Because chess is about strategy and not emotions, and I need some time to think without the hysteria of my daughter and my wife." Then, as though the subject were closed, he said, "Richard cheated on you. That has to be hard to accept."

"I don't accept it. There's a difference between accepting it and just believing it."

"Do you know who it was?"

"No."

"And you don't want to?"

"It wouldn't change anything."

"But you're cheerleading for the boy. That's quite remarkable."

"At the risk of sounding trite, he's the innocent one in all of this, and I believe him."

"He must be very convincing." Then he kissed her forehead. "Do start dating, Annie. You need something more in your life than other people's secrets and problems. Now run along. This isn't your problem anymore."

In her car, wet from the pouring rain that she'd barely noticed, Annie concluded that of all the reactions she'd thought of coming from the Hunters, leaving here with what she knew now would never have occurred to her. Betsy adopted. She still couldn't grasp that, but if her fear was for her place and her children's in her family's affection, then her fury over Cullen made sense. However, she still thought it was a dangerous and terrible response and would have no good end.

Now a new concern arose. Where indeed would Cullen fit? Caught between a glassy-eyed Vera and a James who seemed to have disconnected or hungup like a punching bag for all Betsy's insecurities . . . No way was Annie going to let that happen. My God, she thought, with relatives like this bunch, Cullen might actually miss his adoptive father.

Chapter Fifteen

Linc looked at the clock on the wall. It was 3:45.

Cullen slumped in a chair opposite him, rolling a can of soda between his hands. He'd come into the office just as Linc was getting ready to leave for Annie's. He wanted to tell him they'd talk later, but the unease in the kid's expression changed his mind.

"Okay, what have you got?"

"I talked to a guy today who knew the woman my dad was doin'."

"You mean your birth mother."

Cullen's eyebrows closed into a frown so that they hooded his eyes, making his expression cold and defensive. Around Noah House it had become known as "the look."

"Yeah, her . . . like—there weren't no other women— except Annie." Cullen wouldn't even entertain the idea that his old man slept around. Not that Linc knew otherwise, but as his old man used to say, if a guy dicks around once, only a dumbass would trust him twice.

Of course his old man was referring to the assortment of drug dealers on his Christmas-card list, but the point was the same. Cullen had framed Richard into this superhero of sorts, and anyone who tried to say differently got one of those "looks."

Linc shrugged. "So how did you find this guy?"

"Danny said he knew my father, so I went to see him. He said he'd lived next door to her."

"And he just happened to give you a name."

"Yeah, cuz I held a knife to his throat until he squawked. How come you're always so suspicious?"

"I asked a question, Cullen. Someone has to be suspicious around here, and like it or not, I got elected when I took this job. My suspicion is because at least thirteen years have passed, and unless this guy had a big reason to remember her, he probably wouldn't. Most people can't name their present neighbors, never mind ones from years ago."

"Maybe he had a big reason."

Linc conceded. "Maybe he did."

"He said my father was there all the time."

"When was this?"

"Nineteen eighty-eight. She drew pictures, the guy said, and he'd see my dad stop to see her on his way to work."

Hunter the art critic. "Where is this?"

"Over on the west end of Godfrey."

"You mean that row of cheap cottages?"

"Yeah."

Richard had been in the house-restoration business, and Linc knew there'd been some historical sites in the Godfrey area that had been restored some years back. The kid might be on to something.

"Where's this guy live now?"

"In his car."

"Always high on the credibility meter," Linc muttered. "So did he give you a name?"

"Carolanne or Carolyn. Last name was Rooney, he thought, but he couldn't say for sure."

"Could he say for sure which cottage it was?"

"The one next to his."

"And his house number was . . . ?"

"Shit." He slumped deeper and folded his arms. "I don't know, forgot to ask. He did say the house had some rose bushes in front."

Linc sighed and got to his feet. "Look, Cullen, I can't check into this now. I have a four o'clock appointment and I'm already late."

Cullen's eyes followed Linc around the desk and then he sat up, leaning forward, his arms dangling between his spread knees. "I don't know what to do. I want Annie to be my mother. What if this woman is a bitch? What if she doesn't want me the way my mom did?"

"I think you're getting ahead of yourself. This woman might not even be your mother."

"You're doin' it again!"

"What?"

"Sayin' he did other women."

"And you're talking stupid. You don't know. You can't close off possibilities just because you don't like them." Linc got "the look" again. "You have a name, so what did you do with it?"

"I went through the phone book. She's not there."

"Doesn't mean anything. She could be married, she could have moved six states away, she could be unlisted." And then, because he knew the boy needed some reassurance, he said, "Do you want me to dig around and see what surfaces?"

"I don't know. What if you find her and what if she freaks and says she never had a kid?"

"Could happen."

"Jesus."

"Meanwhile, I want you to stop telling anyone who will listen that Richard is your father."

"He is! Why shouldn't I say what's true? If I hadn't

told Danny, I wouldn't know what I just told you."

"I understand that, but from now on I'd like you to be quiet about it. Others are in this now besides you. Annie went to see the Hunters this afternoon. This is going to be a shock to them, and if they're like most who get this kind of unexpected news, they're going to be all over her like flies in a hot morgue." Linc went to the door and opened it. "Now, I gotta get out of here. You've got kitchen clean-up plus laundry to do. I would suggest you get busy."

Cullen shuffled into the hall before turning and saying, "Do you think Annie would let me come and live with her?"

"No."

"Why not?"

"Because you live here."

"Bet she wouldn't make me clean no fuckin' kitchen."

"Stop complaining. You've skated for the past two weeks. I'm hearing complaints from the other guys, and they're right."

"I'm gonna call Annie and find out what happened."

"Not before you get the laundry done."

"Shit." He walked down the hall toward the kitchen.

Linc closed his office door and stopped in front of Vesco, who was absorbed in some space-alien comic book.

"I'll be back. Anyone calls and you don't know where I am."

"Don't know nothin'," he muttered without even looking up. "She already called lookin' for you."

"She pissed?"

"Like a dog on his first hydrant."

Linc took the truck. He was almost an hour late, but the dark afternoon skies made it seem even later. The rain had stopped, but instead of leaving the air cool and fresh, the dampness clung heavy and hot and close.

He drove too fast through the slick streets, pulling into her drive and bracing himself for her annoyance. He'd intended to be early, he'd intended this visit to be about her talk with the Hunters, and he'd intended to make sure he didn't cross into any personal stuff that could turn tense. He grimaced. Getting here late would not make for a welcome smile from her.

He liked Annie, more than he'd expected to, and more than he wanted to. Unprepared-for reactions usually rattled him, and the ones he'd had in the past few days about her were no exception. Friday had been the culmination of it all; the tension, the wanting, the sparked snap of desire had stretched between them like hot wires. And that kiss in the apartment hallway still spiraled through him like a shot of fierce energy when he gave it too much thought. He didn't like any of it; it scared him, made him angry, and worst of all he had no clue how to deal with it. Christ, when had he ever spent more than ten seconds on inner debate about sex with a woman?

When he stepped up on the back porch, Rocky bounded across the kitchen, skidding, barking and wagging his tail. Through the screen door, he saw Annie come into the kitchen wearing shorts, a sleeveless top and barefoot, looking like she'd walked off the Island for Lost Souls. In her hand was a glass of wine.

"Can I help you?" she asked as if he were a pest selling magazine subscriptions.

When she didn't come forward, he pulled on the screen. Locked. Rocky raced around and then into the other room and back again. "I thought you never locked the door."

"When I don't want someone to come in, I do."

Linc wiggled the door—a quick yank would have taken care of it. "You call this a lock? A four-year-old could open it with a Popsicle stick."

"I'm mad at you."

"And you're whacked."

"I've only had two glasses, and if I want to have five more I will."

Ah, defiance. "Sweetheart, I'm not the wine police. Come on, open the door." But she didn't move forward. She held the glass as if it were her only friend. Linc shoved his hands in his pockets. "I'm sorry I'm late. Cullen came in and wanted to talk."

It was these words that moved her. With a bit of a wobble, she poured what remained of the wine into Rocky's empty water dish. He happily lapped it up. Then she set the glass aside, pressed her hands against her mouth, her eyes rings of distress; she wasn't quite sobbing, but clearly on the verge. "Cullen . . . that poor boy is going to wish he'd never learned that Richard was his father." She looked at Linc, a kind of virgin shock in her expression. "It was horrible, Linc. Betsy came and she called me names and swore at me like I was her enemy . . . and—and she was my friend . . . a best friend—I just don't understand why—"

Linc yanked the door, the lock sprang loose, and the door opened. Rocky swayed a bit, then went to sniff where Linc had walked before laying down on the floor to sober up.

As he went toward her, he said, "Betsy's an idiot."

"She was my friend—my friend . . ."

"Then she's a disloyal idiot. And you're gonna fall down if you don't sit down." He put his arm around her, trying not to notice how much of her wasn't covered by clothes. And those bare feet with purple-polished toenails. This was a very bad idea.

He got her to the arch that led into the living room, but she shook her head and directed him into another room. "How many rooms you got in this place?"

She scowled, as though trying to count through the haze of wine. "Nine . . . I think." They were in the den.

"This is where Richard spent his time. He loved this room."

Just what he'd come for. To talk about Richard.

"Annie, tell me about the Hunters," he said, trying to redirect her attention. "What did they say?"

"You want some wine?"

"No."

"Beer?" And just as he was about to say no, she added, "I bought some for you. I didn't know what kind so I asked the guy and he told me two brands that were favorites in his store, so I got both."

Considerate to a fault. He sighed. "You sit down. I'll get the beer."

Back in the kitchen he opened the refrigerator and took out a can of Coors. Popping the top and taking a long drink, he said to Rocky, "I'm in a helluva mess, buddy, any advice?" For an answer Rocky smiled. Linc wasn't sure that meant he was a sucker or sucked in. Probably both.

Back in the den, Annie was on the couch and patted the place next to her.

Linc sat in a chair. She looked as if he'd slapped her. He set the can of beer down, moved over to the couch where he put his arm around her. "Come on, tell me what happened."

And she did, in a halting, sometimes choked voice. "Betsy makes me so furious. I wanted to punch her in the mouth."

Linc raised his eyebrows and tried not to smile. Wine notwithstanding, Annie punching anyone was ludicrous. "You're telling me you got nowhere with the Hunters."

But Annie wasn't about to be diverted. "She deserves to be slapped for sticking her nose in. I wish I'd done it, dammit. Poor Vera. She looked so stunned, and every time I tried to talk to her, Betsy interfered. James just left the room. He didn't ask any questions either. Most of his worry was about Vera and Betsy. I tell them they very well might have a grandson, and they hardly reacted. Well, Vera did before Betsy came and turned her into a withering flower. It was awful."

Linc squeezed her shoulder. "This is a shock for them, Annie, they probably don't know how to react."

"Betsy sure does."

"She's trying to protect her parents."

Then, as if he'd just admitted he was part of some plot with Betsy, she pulled away, scrambling to the other end of the couch. "You're taking her side?"

"Of course not, I'm just telling you what might have been her reasoning."

"There was nothing reasoned about the way she acted. And anyway, the other day you were saying I should ignore her and go see them. You thought they should hear this directly, not by gossip."

"Maybe I was wrong."

"Wrong? Oh, that's just fine. I've lost a friend and hurt the Hunters and all you can say is you fucked up?" She got to her feet and walked across the room, turning and glaring at him. "Is this how you run Noah House? Give an order and when it fails you just say, 'oh well, guess I was wrong'?"

Linc hadn't moved, watching her as she paced around the room as if standing still were impossible.

"Don't you have anything to say?" she asked.

"About how I'm a fuck-up? Nope, already know that." He got to his feet. "Cullen has the name of a woman who could be his birth mother. I have to do some checking, make some calls. When I have something solid, I'll let you know."

He stepped around her, walking toward the open doorway.

"No, you can't leave . . . you can't . . ." He turned just in time to see her ashen face and stricken eyes. Then, as though that weren't enough to stop him, she ran to him, her hands going around his waist and locking like clamps. At first he simply stood still, then her sob sealed his fate. He slid his arms around her and she practically climbed into his clothes.

"You're making this tough, Annie," he whispered as the holding tightened.

"I'm sorry, I'm sorry. I shouldn't have said that. It's not your fault that I let Betsy steamroll me. I just don't want her to do this to Cullen."

"Cullen is a survivor—he's been through much worse—"

"So that makes it okay?"

"I didn't say that."

"He shouldn't have to go through any more," she snapped, reminding him of a cat he had as a kid who scratched whenever anyone went near her kittens. She backed away, resuming her pacing. "I understand the Hunters will want some proof beyond what Cullen claims. But she's poisoning the relationship before it ever has a chance to happen. Protecting her parents? That's just cover for her own dysfunctional thinking. She's afraid of him and instead of admitting it, she's trying to destroy him."

A bit dramatic, Linc thought, but this wasn't the time to point that out. Her outrage, however, was a mighty sight to behold. "Why don't you call her tomorrow and talk to her? If you've been as good friends as you say, some of that is still there."

"Call her? Me call her? I'd probably get arrested for making an obscene phone call." She folded her arms. "I don't want to talk to her. Ever. I'd like to—"

"Yeah, I know, punch her out." He refrained from any more defense of Betsy.

"She called him a hustler, and just when Vera was on

the verge of agreeing to see him, Betsy acted as if I'd suggested bringing in a box of cobras."

Linc folded his arms.

"How can you be so calm? Cullen is going to be rejected and you stand there as if that's nothing."

"I didn't say it was nothing, but there's not a helluva lot you can do that you haven't already done. You had to know that the Hunters weren't going to be delirious with joy. From their perspective, this came out of nowhere. Their son is dead and here comes this kid who's being promoted by their daughter-in-law. First rule of a hustler is to make himself appear nonthreatening. What better way for a kid trying to shake down some rich people than to use their dead son's widow."

This time instead of denying or attacking him, she just stared, her eyes filling with a pained realization. "Goddamn Richard for doing this to me."

And then he knew. Her anger at Richard for his affair was at the heart of her fury. Poor Betsy, whatever her motives, had been tossed in by Annie because Richard, fortunately for him, was dead. "Betrayal is nasty and almost never happens in a vacuum. You just had the misfortune of not only learning that he cheated, but that he had a kid. He got the lucky break. He's dead." When she didn't disagree, he asked, "So besides Richard and Betsy, what else is pissing you off?"

She turned away. "Nothing. They're more than enough." And then as though he'd pricked a very new sore, she whirled back. "No, that's wrong, there is something else. It's you. You piss me off." And then instead of launching some list of his faults, of which there were numerous and he expected to hear about a couple of dozen, she caught him totally off guard. "It's because of you that I'm miserable. I don't want to do any of the things I used to love. I think about you all the time and it's stupid and I feel like a jerk and even telling you this . . . It's like I'm throwing myself at you like some whore—"

"Annie, stop it!" Linc was reeling. "I don't want to hear that kind of talk."

But she went on as though not hearing him.

"I don't know what to do anymore . . . I can't seem to stop thinking about you—oh God . . ." She'd wrapped her arms around herself as if trying to hold her feelings in check. She sank down on an upholstered stool, knees tight together, arms hugging herself, the picture of misery. She looked as if she were dissolving into herself.

Absorbing this made Linc feel like the worst kind of bastard. How in God's name could he have allowed this to happen? For her to want him this way came from somewhere. He'd kept his distance; yeah, sure, he liked her and there was Cullen, but no way had he intended that she'd fall for him. A little fun, a little sexy talk, teasing, a kiss . . . Well, hell, the kiss had twisted *him* in knots so why hadn't he figured it had done something to her?

You misfired on this one, pal. You figured she was some sophisticated socialite like Brooke who took flirting with the same stride as she did her work and her wealth. No big deal. Instead she'd taken it seriously. She'd taken *him* seriously.

Linc couldn't leave her. Not like this. He knelt down in front of her, curling his hands around her balled fists. She sniffled and curled in against him like a wounded animal seeking surcease.

"I didn't want any of this to happen, Annie. This was always about Cullen and his search for his father. You and me . . . this is my fault that we're in this mess."

She looked up at him. "It doesn't have to be a mess." Then as if she realized what she was proposing and what his answer might be, she shook her head. "You don't have to say anything."

"I don't want to hurt you—"

"I hurt right now." She shook her head when he started to speak. "No, don't say anymore. You must think I'm some whacked-out widow in starved hormonal overload and looking for anyone to make me feel wanted, or maybe sexy, or maybe it's just making me feel something—"

"Annie, stop."

"You don't understand. Oh my God. You don't understand." Tears streamed down her face. She rubbed them away, her voice somewhere between sadness and anger. "You think I want this? You think I like this empty, twisty pain that tells me what a fool I am? I know you're not interested in me. I know—"

And because he couldn't listen to any more of her self-chastisement, he pulled her to him, off the stool, tumbling to the floor, cradling her to him and then he kissed her. Kissed her hard and hot and deep, sliding her along his body and fitting her against him.

She went eagerly, pressing closer, her hands clawing at his shirt, her mouth opening and fervent and soft beneath his.

This was insane and he was too old for groping sex on the floor. "Annie . . . easy, babe . . ." but he might as well have tried to stop an already detonated bomb. She was all over him. She wiggled closer and his hands slid around her hips, lifting her so that she rested against him. She pulled her mouth away and searched his face. If he'd expected to see desire or passion or desperation, he couldn't have been more wrong. What he did see nearly took his breath away.

"You think you love me, don't you?" he asked, already knowing the answer.

"I do," she said simply.

"Sweetheart, it's sex. You know better than to confuse the two."

"Yes."

"It's not the same as being in love."

"I know."

"I can't say the words you want to hear. I don't have those emotions to give you."

She lowered her lashes, but she didn't move. "That's okay."

"Okay? It's not even close to okay. You're not some quick lay."

Then she stunned him by smiling in that misty way women have when they think they've discovered some secret path through a guy's heart. "Thank you for your chivalry. You're very sweet."

"Christ."

She kissed him again, her hands moving from his now-opened shirt to his belt and zipper. "You're not going to leave, are you?"

"No," he said gruffly. "I think I've gone nuts."

"Just for tonight," she said pressing her mouth against his chest. "Just for tonight."

Getting out of their clothes seemed remarkably easy, but then most of the details eluded him. He tucked her beneath him, thankful the carpet was the plush type. His hands brushed her breasts followed quickly by his mouth. He felt her heat and her eagerness and her impatience. He didn't even want to think about his.

Sliding into her felt better than any anticipation. She closed around him and he sighed deeply. "Ahh, Annie, this is too good . . ."

"It's better than good," she whispered back as once again their mouths came together.

Their motions were quick and slow, warm and slick, and Linc felt as if he were drowning in some deep endless bliss. He felt her climax, the soft sounds of satisfaction spreading through him like a brand new morning. She clung with such faith and resolve, Linc was awed. And then he came, spilling from so deep within him, he wondered how he'd managed this act with anyone else.

They lay quietly, bodies still gloved, breathing slowing with the easy sounds of contentment. She kissed his cheek and his chin and his mouth. "I've never had sex on the floor," she whispered, as if it were a proud acknowledgment of what she clearly viewed as decadent.

"I have and it was always lousy." Then he grinned. "Until now."

She hugged him as though he'd given her some great gift. Then almost shyly, she said, "I have a nice comfy bed upstairs."

"I can't stay, Annie."

"Oh."

"It's not because I don't want to," he said when her face fell in disappointment. "I have to get back to the house. Vesco is the only one there and well, he's not enough."

She nodded, moving away and standing up. "You're beautiful," he said. The trite word wasn't enough, but Linc's mind was so fried he couldn't think.

"So are you," she said softly, then, "No, we were beautiful. What we did, how you made me feel . . ."

He rose and walked toward her. They stood naked and just barely touching before he cupped her face in his hands. "An hour," he murmured. "Let me stay an hour."

They kissed quickly and then gathered up their clothes. Annie took his hand and pulled him out of the room, around the corner and into a center entrance hall with a Palladian window, a vase of roses on a side table and a long mirror framed in dark wood. The staircase was carpeted and plush and very blue. Upstairs he followed her into a huge master-bedroom suite.

It was decidedly unruffled, but had a soft decor that looked both luxurious and comfortable. She let go of his hand, tossing his clothes and hers into a clump on a side chair. She pulled the covers back and urged him into the king-sized bed. He'd just settled into the soft sheets with her snuggling in next to him when a voice called from downstairs.

"Annie, are you here? Are you okay?"

Annie leaped out of the bed as though she'd been shot. "Oh God, Linc, it's James Hunter." She scrambled for her clothes as she rushed to the door. "I'll be right down, James."

"You know your door was open and you got a strange truck in your drive?"

"Uh, yes, a friend left it here."

Linc chuckled. "You treat your friends well, babe."

She stuck her tongue out at him. "I'll be right down, James," she repeated.

He stretched out, stacking his hands behind his head. "So you have friends who leave vehicles in your driveway?"

"Of course not, but I can hardly say it belongs to my lover for the night." She dashed to the dresser where she ran a brush with lightning speed through her hair.

"Sweetheart, it's not going to work unless the Hunters are totally stupid and naïve."

Buttoning her top, she said, "If you hadn't broken my lock, then they wouldn't have just come in. Poor James, he probably thought I was being robbed."

"At the risk of sounding like a know-it-all, this is why good locks can be helpful."

"You broke it."

"The lock you never lock?"

"Oh shut up."

He grinned, crossing the room and pulling on his own clothes while she searched around for a pair of shoes. "You stay here. Who would have thought they would come tonight?" she muttered as she shoved her feet into leather sandals.

"Maybe they're having second thoughts."

"Oh, I hope so." She was almost out the door when he

caught her arm and pulled her back, turning her so she could see in the mirror. "Oh God."

"Hmmm, the ravages of rug sex."

"Well, I don't care. I'm not a child."

Linc chuckled. "Good for you. Hurry back. My hour is running out."

She threw herself into his arms, kissing him deeply. And then she was out of the room and flying down the stairs.

Chapter Sixteen

Annie stopped at the bottom of the stairs and caught her breath. Her heart was pounding as she cast a look back up the staircase. Not in a thousand years could she have envisioned this. A man secreted away in her bedroom. It was so deliciously crazy, she almost giggled. Annie Hunter, practical and organized and never, never reckless. She almost went back to kiss him again.

She wasn't the same woman who'd been married to Richard. She'd changed, evolved, grown up, grown away, grown out of all those things that had always involved her. This wasn't bad or awkward or even predictable. It was just different. She was different.

She turned into the living room where James and Vera were seated on the couch. They sat close, dressed impeccably as always—Vera all coordinated in beige from her blouse to her canvass sandals, James, daring by contrast, in red slacks and a blue-and-white shirt. But despite a perfect outward appearance, Annie thought there was something just a little off-kilter about them.

James stood when he saw her, but even that gentlemanly gesture seemed clumsy as though remembered just in time.

"We shouldn't have barged in," he said.

"You're always welcome." Although tonight would not have been her choice to play hostess.

Obviously something was going on. Vera looked distraught, sitting motionless and rigid as though she might fall apart if she relaxed. James, however, seemed composed and resolved. "Your back-door lock is broken," he said. "I was concerned so I just came in."

"It's okay."

"I'd be glad to come and fix it for you," he said quickly, reminding her of how he'd come after Richard died when the basement flooded and she couldn't get the sump pump to work. She'd called because the guy who'd installed it had been out of town. James had arrived within ten minutes and when he'd left, the pump had been working. "You know, I'm kinda handy with that kind of thing."

"I know you are. Thank you." *But why are you here?* she wondered. Curiosity bloomed inside of her, yet neither was saying anything. "Can I get you a drink? Some wine?"

"I would like wine," Vera said, sighing and taking a picture of Richard from a side table as if to look at it more closely. *What* was going on?

"Nothing for me," James said, settling back beside Vera.

Annie went into the kitchen. Rocky came to attention when she poured wine into the two glasses. "No more for you," she whispered sternly. He whined, laying down looking disappointed. "You're supposed to bark when someone comes into the house. You need to brush up on what you learned in guard-dog school." He looked properly chastised. She reached down and ruffled him behind his ears. "Want a cookie?" At his soft woof, she reached into the cupboard and took out two Oreos that he chomped down with a smile. Oreos and wine. No wonder he was so healthy.

She returned to the living room with the two glasses. She gave one to Vera and then sat down on a chair opposite them.

And the three of them sat silently. The watch on her left wrist felt heavy. James seemed to be studying the cover of *House Beautiful* on the coffee table. Vera, who usually took an entire evening to drink a single glass of wine, had drained a third of the goblet. Annie wondered if Linc had fallen asleep, if he was posted in the shadows listening at the top of the stairs, if he was impatient for her to return.

Finally, when she could stand the quiet no longer, she said, "What did you want to tell me?"

Vera glanced at James, trying not to cry.

He patted her knees. "It's going to be okay, honey." Then he leaned forward, his hands lining up the five magazines on the table. "I'm going to take a lesson from you, Annie, and get straight to the point."

Annie's pulse began to race. "All right."

"We know Cullen is Richard's son."

Annie set her glass down before she dropped it. "You know? You know for sure?"

"Actually Vera didn't until I told her a few hours ago. It's been a shock and she's not herself."

Annie nodded automatically.

He lowered his head as though he didn't want to see her face when he spoke. "I've known for years. I knew about the other woman, and I've known that a child existed. Richard came to me when the woman was pregnant."

Annie sat back, overwhelmed by his revelation. "You've known everything? All these years?"

"I've known." Then, as if anticipating her question, he said, "I didn't tell you earlier this afternoon because I wanted to break it to Vera and Betsy."

Annie tried to get her mind around this. Realistically,

she couldn't have expected James to tell her something that Richard had kept secret, but that didn't change the fact that she felt disappointed and betrayed all over again.

James continued. "Richard ended the affair some months before the baby was born. He came to me because they'd decided to put the boy up for adoption and he wanted the name of a private adoption attorney. We used one when we adopted Betsy, so I made some calls and Richard contacted an attorney in Massachusetts where the baby was born. The woman was agreeable and willingly signed all the papers, giving up all her rights . . ."

The words flowed over her in a surreal cascade. Richard was living a whole other life apart from her, and James had been party to it. But how could she have not known? Were James and Richard that good at their mutual deception? Had she been so preoccupied with her own need for a child that she'd blinded out what was going on under her nose?

". . . quite wealthy and apparently they had plans for her that would have been thwarted if she were to keep the child."

"Who was wealthy?" she said, trying to stay focused.

"Her parents."

"Oh." Then as James started to speak again, she said, "Wait a minute. Her parents were involved? How old was she?"

"I'm not really sure."

"Please, James, don't do that."

"I wish I didn't have to tell you any of this."

"I wish my husband had seen the necessity in being faithful."

Vera gasped, but no one paid any attention.

"She was in her early twenties," James said softly.

For no reason that was even close to sane, Annie was relieved. God, talk about settling for crumbs, but eighteen or nineteen would have been too bitter. She rose and crossed the room, catching her breath. She shivered; she wanted Linc to suddenly appear, put his arms around her, and tell her it was okay to cry.

"You okay? If you'd rather I didn't say anymore—"

"No, please finish." She returned to the chair, sitting in an unrelaxed perch at the edge.

James continued. "Richard told me they threatened to disown her and they wanted nothing to do with her 'bastard child.' The boy went to a college professor—"

She interrupted. "You said the affair ended months before the baby came. What happened between them besides the adoption?"

"I don't know."

"So he got her pregnant, ended the affair, and except for hiring a lawyer, he just walked away?"

"I'm sure he kept in some kind of contact through the attorney. I'm puzzled that you'd be concerned about her."

She scowled. "So am I." But whether it was the image of this woman or the very recent reality of Tiffany with no parents, no money, and a baby she wasn't sure what she would do with, Annie felt a kind of sorrow that she wondered if she would have had it not been for having met Tiffany.

Twenty-two, pregnant, an ended affair, abandoned and threatened by her parents . . . all combined had to be pretty frightening. She pressed her fingers to her temples. Was she crazy? Feeling sorry for the woman Richard had betrayed her with. But she did. Sorry for her and furious with Richard that he'd created this mess that had hurt so many people.

"I'm okay, James. Go ahead."

"As I was saying, the boy went to a college professor and his young wife. I told Richard he should tell you, because adoptions don't stay secret the way they did years ago. To hold this secret could be dangerous, for it could come back and take a huge chunk out of his future."

Ah yes, Annie thought in disgust, *protect Richard's future.*

"He'd said he would think about it, but I knew he was wary, fearful it would be disastrous for your marriage."

"He should have thought about that before he slept with her."

"Consequences are usually murky when secrets are involved."

"Well, he got one thing right," she said flatly. "I would have left him." But it was a retaliatory comment, a hindsight remark. She had no idea what she would have done if Richard had confessed. Probably either allowed him to charm and apologize his way back into her heart, or blame herself.

Vera scowled, speaking for the first time since she'd asked for the wine. "You would have left him without letting him explain?"

"Explain? Explain what? He cheated on me. No explanation can change that."

"He must have had a reason," Vera said looking imploringly at James. "He must have."

Yes, one as old as time. She was young and made him horny. But she didn't say it aloud. What was the point? Hurling nasty comments and denigrating their son wasn't the salve for Richard having hurt her.

James squeezed Vera's hands. "Honey please. None of that matters now. Annie, I know this has been too much all at once. Richard did love you very much. By remaining silent, he didn't want to hurt you. You and he couldn't have children, and this would have been mortal for you to know. He was playing the odds that the adoption and the woman were in the past and wouldn't ever surface. If the boy later decided to look, he assumed the boy would search for his mother, not him."

"Richard had it all figured out, didn't he?"

"He knew this would be hurtful for you."

"And he wanted to avoid that?"

"Of course. He loved you."

Annie had had enough. "That is just so much—so much bullshit." James didn't flinch but Vera did. She didn't care. She was going to say this because it needed to be said. "He said nothing because he believed he could get away with it. This was about Richard having it all— an affair for God knows how long, and his naïve wife to whom he came home every night and pretended to be a husband and a lover and a friend. We were trying to have a child, and he's having one with someone else. Not only did he betray me, but another woman had his child. How do I know there weren't other women? Maybe he learned that getting one pregnant was too complicated so he made sure that didn't happen again. And what of the others? The woman who gave up her son to please her family, and no doubt Richard. And Cullen. A boy who's had so much upheaval in his life that I'm amazed he's not a druggie. All of this is a sorry mess, and excuse me while I don't have a lot of sympathy and understanding for Richard."

James and Vera were somber. Sad and sorry expressions that Annie wished she'd felt. If possible, she was even more disillusioned about Richard and her marriage and the seamless life she'd thought was so happy than she'd been those first hours after she'd learned of Cullen.

In defense of his son, James said, "Annie, he thought he was doing the right thing. Telling you there'd been an affair would have been hard, but confessing a son by another woman would have been impossible."

"So he did nothing. Keeping it a secret was to save him, not me. How convenient that he's dead and doesn't have to deal with any of this."

All the color drained out of Vera's face. "What an awful, horrible thing to say."

"Oh, pardon me for being angry."

Vera rose. "James, let's go."

Annie said nothing.

"Why don't you go on out to the car. Let me talk to Annie."

"Don't try to comfort her, James," Vera warned. "After that remark, she doesn't deserve anything from us. We come here in good faith and this is what we get. Attacks on our poor dead son." Then she marched out of the room.

James came over and took her hands. "I'm sorry, Annie. First the boy and now this."

"Who was the woman?"

"Annie—"

"Her name, James."

He sighed, clearly not wanting to tell her. "Caroline Rooney. Her family lived in Brookline at the time, and she was estranged from them. Richard had told me she'd wanted to be an artist and they wanted her to follow in the family tradition of going into the medical field. She'd come to Bedford as a kind of 'I'm going to live my own life' rebellion."

"Which included my husband," she said sourly. "How rebelliously kind of her."

He shoved his hands into his slacks pockets. "I know this has hurt you, but I wanted to reassure you that we are very interested in Cullen. You could arrange a meeting, couldn't you? We'd like to meet him, get to know him. He is our grandson. Maybe we can make up a little for what happened."

Annie was hurt, disappointed, angry, and resentful. She wanted to let go of all of this, let it slide away, and yet here it was again, coiled around her like sticky sap. "How did you know about the affair?" she asked.

"I'd rather not go into that."

"Oh no you don't. No waffling. What could possibly be worse than what I know already?" When he continued to hesitate, she wanted to stamp her feet and scream.

He must have sensed her mood, for he said, "All right. I saw them together in a bar." He paused, and if ever a pause was bloated, this one was. Finally, when she continued staring at him, he said, "It was obvious it wasn't a business drink. I'm not saying any more. The place wasn't around here. It was north of Providence. Richard didn't see me—"

"He didn't see you because he was too busy with her," she muttered.

"I called him the next day and asked him what the hell was going on. After a number of attempts to duck, he finally told me. Where are you going?"

But she was already out of the room and into the den, pulling the box out of the closet. From behind her, James said, "What are you doing?"

On her knees, she went through the carton, tossing papers aside, coming finally to the round tin container. She opened it and rifled through Richard's collection of matchbooks. She picked up one. "Duke's Place. That was the bar, wasn't it?"

"Annie, this isn't going to solve anything."

"Answer me. It was Duke's Place."

He sighed. "Yes."

And now that she knew, the knowledge took on Herculean meaning. She'd puzzled over the odd matchbook that first weekend, but she'd assumed it was just one he'd never mentioned. A bar he'd been in with some guys and automatically picked up the matchbook. Nothing sneaky or nefarious, just a place he'd forgotten to mention. Now it was clear *why* he'd never said anything. And his girlfriend or the place was important enough for him to add the matchbook to his collection. This was a slap of lies that deeply hurt. This tin, with its dented cover, had been special because it had been full of their memories—most of the matchbooks had a story that connected the two of them. This one, as far as she was concerned, tainted the entire collection.

James took her arm and helped her to her feet. "Can I call someone to come and stay with you?'

"Someone is already here," she said, more numb than she thought possible.

"The truck?" he asked.

"Yes, he owns the truck."

He drew her to her feet and then, as if not knowing quite what to do, he squeezed her shoulder. "Then I'll leave you with your friend. Can I call you? We really do want to meet Cullen."

"I don't want Cullen hurt. I won't let him be hurt," she said, as vigorous in her words as she felt in her heart. There was no way she'd allow him to be examined and judged by the Hunters.

"Still his cheerleader, aren't you?"

"Always. He deserves none of this."

He kissed her forehead. "Goodnight. I'll let myself out. By the way, I'll stop by and fix that lock tomorrow."

She barely nodded, standing in the middle of the room as his footsteps crossed the kitchen and the door closed behind him. How long could Richard continue to hurt her? She thought she'd moved on, put it all, including a mysterious affair, into perspective. But now with a name and a place and a matchbook, it washed over her like new news.

Then he was behind her, his hands on her shoulders, turning her. He was dressed but his shirt was open and untucked. He looked rumpled and tired and welcoming. Tears filled her eyes and he drew her close. "I heard most of it."

"I feel so violated. I wanted to think it was a one- or two-time thing, but he went to bars with her and they probably necked in a booth." She shuddered. "It's all so seedy and horrible."

"Come on. Let me put you to bed."

"You can leave. It's okay. I'm probably not very good company anyway."

"Do you want me to stay?"

"You can't—"

"I called somebody to cover for me."

"You did?"

"Just for you."

Then the tears came. "Oh, Linc, what would I do without you?"

"You'd have to sleep alone and we can't have that." He grinned. "Come on, babe. Tomorrow will be here to shake all of this out."

"I know her name."

"Yes, I heard that, too."

"Can you find her?"

"Probably."

"Maybe I'll go see her."

"All right."

And she hugged him. "Thank you for not asking questions that I don't know how to answer."

Then she picked up the box of matchbooks and went to the fireplace. Linc said, "Sure you want to do that tonight?"

"Oh, I should wait until I'm calm and reasonable?"

"I just don't want you to regret it later."

"He's lucky I'm not burning our wedding pictures."

She emptied the fifty-plus matchbooks into the fireplace. Lighting a newspaper, she set the collection on fire. Watching it until it had all burned, she got to her feet.

"Feel better?"

"No. Before tonight I was angry and hurt, now I'm totally disgusted."

"The wrath of a woman scorned. Good thing I'm not in love with you."

"You wouldn't cheat on me if you were."

"Sweetheart, I wouldn't cheat on you period."

For the next few days, Annie threw herself into her work. She was backed up on both pending projects and phone calls. By the end of the week, she concluded that there was nothing like work and ordinary events to make the uncomfortable stuff fade into a back-of-the-mind closet.

James had come and fixed the back-door lock, and the unease between them was heavy. Neither brought up Cullen or Richard. And while Annie sensed he wanted to ask again about a meeting, she deliberately ignored his signals and remained silent. Linc offered to set up a meeting, but she spurned that idea. She knew she was being pissy and ornery and unfair, but that's the way she felt.

There was a baby shop near Design and Details, and yesterday afternoon on a whim, she'd gone in and picked out a dozen outfits for Tiffany's baby. With her hands full and anticipating Tiffany's happy reaction, she was all the way to the sales counter when she realized she'd chosen little-girl items and had no idea what the baby's sex was. She put them all back. Besides, Tiffany would need practical things like diapers and formula, even a washer and dryer. Maybe she'd do that. She could well afford it and it would be fun spoiling Tiffany. She doubted anyone ever had.

Today, she'd had an appointment with a client a block from her mother's, so when she finished, she decided to stop by.

"What a lovely surprise." They hugged with Marge Dawson ushering Annie into her bright kitchen. "I just made fresh coffee, would you like some?"

"Love it," Annie said, glancing around. The kitchen table held packages of shelf paper, cut pieces, scissors, and a yard stick. Stacked on the floor across the room was the contents of the cupboards. "Looks like you're busy."

"I've been meaning to do this for months," she said, pulling a stool over and preparing to climb.

"Mom, let me do those high shelves."

"Why, thank you, dear."

They worked together with her mother measuring and cutting and Annie doing the lining. While working, they chatted about the church bazaar and that her mother's table had been the biggest moneymaker. Then, in a moment of candor, Annie told her mother about the Hunters' visit and Linc.

"I don't think he's the marrying kind, Annie Jean. Evelyn told me he don't stay with one woman for long. Never has."

"We're just seeing each other. It's not serious as in marriage serious."

"What kind of serious is it?"

Annie didn't say anything.

Her mother nodded, opening a new roll of paper. "I hope you know what you're doing."

"Probably not, but you know what? I thought I knew what I was doing for all the years I was married to Richard, and look where that got me." Her mother scowled, and Annie knew she was headed into an argument by saying anything against Richard. Trying to temper that, she said, "I know you don't want to hear anything bad about him, and I'm not just angry for what he did. I'm annoyed with myself for being so clueless."

"He was always kind and generous to me. I can't forget that and I don't want to," she said with her classic stubbornness.

"You're not the one he betrayed, Mom. Not just once, but over and over."

"If it wasn't for Cullen—"

"I'd still be clueless?"

"And happier. Sometimes knowing the truth is a door opened that was better left closed."

"I like 'the truth will out' better."

"It did, and I don't see a lot of dancing in the street," she said, measuring and cutting the next piece.

Annie couldn't argue with that, and she was more than a little curious about this philosophical side to her mother. "You're smarter than you want people to think."

"Yep."

Annie grinned, watching her take the cut piece, pull off the backing, and smooth it on a lower shelf. "Maybe I'll take that advice about Linc. I'm happy with him and not much else matters."

"Funny, I said that to my mother about your father. About being happy and not caring about anything else. Tuck that end into the corner, will you?"

Annie blinked, sure she'd heard wrong. Her mother actually bringing up her father? She tucked in the sticky-backed paper without looking at what she was doing. "Gramma warned you before you were married? Why?"

"She didn't like him, said he was selfish and couldn't be trusted. She would shake her finger at me and say, remember my words, for the day will come when you'll wish you heeded them."

Her mother's mother had always predicted family troubles and their dire consequences, or so Annie had been told. She'd died when Annie had been four.

"Did Gramma know something? I mean besides the fact she didn't like him and didn't trust him?"

"She never liked or trusted anyone I liked. So to me this was just her running her mouth. I always hated that she'd been right. Now, enough of that." She took a few steps away and admired the freshly laid paper. It was yellow with blue bachelor's buttons and a thin white stripe. "Been meaning to do this since last spring. Don't know where the time goes. As for your Linc—"

"Mom, I want to know when you knew Gramma was right."

"I don't talk about your father, you know that. The man is dead, no point in saying things now that make him small."

"But don't you see that by staying silent, you raise questions?"

"Questions? I don't have no questions and the answers are no one's business. They just feed the gossips. I married him, lived with him, had his child, told him to leave, and never asked anyone for anything. I'd say that gives me the right to not answer questions—even yours."

And that was that. Annie had learned nothing more in the way of facts about Nathan Dawson, but she'd discovered a lot about her mother and it resonated. Her mother knew things, the truth, if you will, about Annie's father . . . things that would make him look bad. Very bad. She could have bashed and blamed and spewed hatred, but she'd chosen silence. Not for a moment had Annie suspected that this was not just about her father, but about her mother's pride, too.

"Well, Mom, I have a new opinion, late-coming that it is. You don't want to talk about what happened between you and my father because then others will know and feel sorry for you. And you would hate that."

She stiffened, waving away Annie's words. "I would, and I won't talk about him." She turned from Annie and went about putting her dishes back on the new shelf paper.

"Are you afraid Linc is like my father? Selfish and unreliable? Is that why you said you hope I know what I'm doing?"

"I think Linc's a good man. Evelyn has told me a lot about him. From what she said, he's had some problems, but he's okay now."

Her mother's vague but simple response warmed her. Annie waited for her to say more, but she didn't.

"I thought you were going to warn me against him."

"Nothing to warn about except Evelyn tells me he's not one to stay with one woman for long. She said he's wary of stuff he can't control. Seeing his brother killed and then his dad going to prison—guess it showed him how little control he had." She shrugged. "But since you say you're not that kind of serious, it don't matter."

Annie blinked, trying to absorb what her mother had just said about Linc. She quickly tucked it away to mull over later. Right now, she wanted to know something else. "Why did you bring up my father now? I didn't even ask about him."

"I thought it fit what you said. You said you were happy with Linc and you didn't care about anything else. Just wanted you to know I felt that way, too, a long time ago. Would telling you about your father have made you happy? You wouldn't have paid attention because you were determined to see him as some cast-out, misunderstood victim and I was his bossy, nagging wife."

That was certainly true. "But Mom, you made him look good by refusing to tell your side."

"You wouldn't have believed me. Just like I never believed my mother. You're stubborn, Annie Jean, and you wanted your father to be your hero. You wanted Richard to be your hero—"

"I don't want to talk about Richard."

Her mother looked at her.

"Oh God, I sound just like you."

"Broken heroes always hurt more than false ones. And that's all I'm gonna say about it."

This was truly amazing—all these years she'd carried this resentment of her mother because of her silence, now she was still refusing to talk but somehow it didn't matter anymore. And like her mother's affection for Richard, Annie's feelings about her father were unshakable. Perhaps it was misguided, perhaps if her mother told her all she knew about Nathan Dawson, Annie would grow to resent and hate him too. Annie sighed. It was a profound conclusion to realize that Marge Dawson was allowing the flourishing of Annie's love for an absent father by her silence. But there it was.

"You're a wise lady, you know that," Annie said softly.

Marge shrugged and went about cleaning up the scraps of leftover paper. "What I'd like to know is when I can meet this young Cullen."

"I'd like you to meet him, too. I wish Richard could have."

"Keep that thought. It will make the bad side less bitter."

Chapter Seventeen

Three nights of great sex, she decided, definitely made a woman feel special, plus there was that added bonus of rampant anticipation. Something she hadn't felt about anything for a very long time.

That morning, she'd found Linc in the kitchen making coffee and toasting bagels.

"Why didn't you wake me?" she asked when she came in and slipped her arms around him.

He kissed the top of her head. "You needed the sleep."

"I need you." She slid her hand into his jeans.

He chuckled. "You're wearing me out."

"Doesn't feel like it."

He looked down at her, his smile lazy. "How about some coffee?"

"You're no fun."

"You have an appointment at nine. And I have to get over to Noah House before they fire me." He put a toasted bagel on a plate, buttered it, and then placed it on the counter for her.

She slid onto one of the counter stools and opened the blackberry jam. "They wouldn't do that."

"Monthly review comes in today." He set down a

steaming mug of coffee for her, then leaned against the counter and sipped from his own cup. "The board of directors will be taking a look. Anything could happen."

She bit into her bagel. "Don't worry. If they fire you, you can come here and live and be my love slave."

"How much do you pay?"

"I would definitely make it worth your while."

"*You* would make it worth my while," he said so easily and so naturally, her throat went dry. He looked at her, something confident and intriguing in his eyes.

I love you almost tumbled from her lips, but she lifted her mug and sipped instead.

Linc said, "I also have to make a decision on a kid today. The people who had him want him back and I'm not convinced that's wise for them."

"He's a really bad kid?"

"When he's sober and not using he's okay. He's been in rehab and outpatient treatment centers but he always goes back to his old life."

"But if the couple want to take him—"

"Why should I object? Because Penny is convinced she can save him. She and her husband Nick are good friends and far too idealistic for a punk like Eddie. I can't see them going through the hell this kid has already put them through once before." Linc told her of Penny's frantic call and the taking of Eddie to Noah House. "That's why I was late getting to the police station when Cullen called me. Anyway, Penny felt guilty that she hadn't done enough. The truth is she did too goddamn much."

"Can you do a temporary stay? Say a month."

He was quiet while he refilled their mugs. "That could work. Maybe Eddie will wise up if he knows he'll be yanked if he doesn't."

"It's hard, isn't it? I mean if the kids were all like Cullen or Tim and Tiffany, it would be easy."

"Tim grew up, and Tiffany—she's a wiseass, but she's

good for him. As for Cullen. I think for him it's because he has a purpose. He had some real problems after his father threw him out. Drinking mostly, but some drugs, too. Then when he got on this quest to find Richard, it was as if he turned on a dime."

"Thanks to you."

"Hey, I only make suggestions. The kids make them work. He checked out the other Richard Hunters in the Bedford area. To be honest neither Cullen nor I considered that the one we wanted might be dead."

"So how did he finally settle on my house?"

"We were pretty sure, but I didn't want Cullen making any mistakes so I went to see his old man."

Being in control, just like his mother had told her mother, Annie thought. "You went to Parker Gallagher?"

"Yeah."

"Cullen asked you to?"

"No."

She pushed the remaining pieces of bagel aside and looked at him closely. "My but we're talkative. You went on your own?"

"All by myself. I was even allowed to go out of town all by myself."

"Come on, Linc. You know what I mean."

"Cullen was getting frustrated and I decided to hurry things along."

"And Parker Gallagher just gave you what you wanted."

"Slick as grease."

Annie sighed. "Okay, what did you ask for?"

"Birth parents. Unfortunately all he had was Richard's name and address and that was because Richard had given it to them. He didn't know or didn't remember the birth mother's name."

"He just told you this? I'm dumbfounded."

"Why? He doesn't give two shits about Cullen."

"Still, I'm amazed."

He shrugged. "Hey, you want an answer you go to the source."

"It seems too simple." She studied him, getting only a bland expression in return. "Linc?"

"Don't get your panties in a wad. It's okay, it's taken care of. Old man Gallagher is still the same miserable bastard he was when he tossed Cullen. The kid's happy, I'm happy, the Hunters will be happy, and you're beautiful." He winked at her, then drained his coffee mug before glancing at the wall clock. "I gotta go."

He came around the counter and she swung around when he ran his hand into her hair.

"You didn't do anything illegal, did you?" she asked, hating that such a question would pop into her mind. That it did troubled her.

"Like what? Break into sealed adoption records? No."

Relieved, she asked, "And you got the information from Parker Gallagher? For real?"

"That's what I said."

She took another breath. "Did you threaten him?"

"Christ, you're worse than getting hosed by a cop in an interrogation room. No, I didn't threaten him." Then he kissed her to stop any more questions and promptly changed the subject. "I don't know when I can see you. I'm backlogged with paperwork, and the boys have a basketball game tonight."

She nodded, her worried frown not going away, but he said nothing more. "All right," she said vaguely. "I have things to catch up with, too."

"One of them being?"

She gave him a blank look, then, "Oh, yes, set up the meeting with the Hunters."

"Good." He kissed her, lingering, deepening, drawing her mouth against his, tangling their tongues, then easing her tighter against him, holding her as though he couldn't let her go.

When he finally drew back they both were breathing heavy.

"I'll see you later," he murmured, his voice so husky the words seemed like a caress.

"Yes, later."

And as she watched him walk out the door, then heard the truck start, she slid off the stool, letting Rocky into the house. Maybe she was being a tad paranoid. However Linc had gotten the information, it wasn't illegal and she knew Parker Gallagher was okay—she'd seen his name a few days ago in one of the Boston newspapers. He'd been listed in a news account with some other professors in calling for the ouster of a colleague involved in a messy affair. Gallagher had even been quoted in the piece.

She wiped the counter down and put the dishes in the dishwasher, recalling the things Betsy had said about Linc when Annie had told her that he was going with her to talk to the Hunters.

He made bad boys look like saints . . . father a drug dealer in prison for murder . . . he'd bummed around . . . parties and drugs and connections . . .

"Hardly a garden-variety nice guy by most standards," she muttered. But she'd defended him to Betsy and nothing he'd done had shaken that until this. Well, maybe not shaken, but raised some—some what? Questions about his integrity? Questions to make her doubt him? Questions to make her think twice about her involvement with him? Maybe.

Or was that his point? To make her not trust him and break off the relationship. That possibility made her feel empty, not uneasy.

* * *

A few days later, Annie had set up the meeting with the Hunters. They were coming to her house later that afternoon and she'd called Linc at Noah House to tell him to make sure Cullen was there.

Coming home from work, she got out of her car and walked into the back yard to find Cullen and Rocky tossing a ball back and forth. Standing on the porch was her mother, smiling and cheering the boy and the dog as if she were at a Fourth of July parade. The scene could have passed Norman Rockwell muster for back-porch Americana. Annie waved. And her mother waved back.

"Linc dropped me off," Cullen said, coming over to her and throwing the ball to Rocky. "I figured I'd play with Rocky while I was waitin' on you. That okay?" He was jittery and she saw an anxiousness in his eyes that he was trying not to show.

She gave him a reassuring smile and ruffled his hair. "You're welcome any time."

"Really? Like I could come and live with you?"

That caught her speechless. "I don't know about that. You live at Noah House and I know you like being with Linc."

"Yeah, but this is where my dad lived." His face was open and vulnerable and Annie had all she could do not to hug him.

"There are other considerations, Cullen. Your grandparents and maybe even your birth mother."

"But they aren't like you."

Her heart caught at his sweetness. "That's one of the nicest things any one ever said to me." She swallowed the lump in her throat. "You know what? I think you're going to have an abundance of choices very soon."

But there was no nod of agreement. His worry spilled, outflanking her reasonableness. "What if they hate me? What if they say they don't want a bastard for a grandson? And her? I don't even know where she is or what she's like. Is she dead, too? Who knows? Maybe she won't see me. Maybe she'll say I ain't hers. Maybe she'll tell me to get the fuck out."

"Cullen, stop it." She took him by the shoulders and shook him gently. "I won't let those things happen. Do you hear me?"

He looked down, scrubbing his fist across his eyes, then muttered, in a very low voice, "I'm sick of nobody wanting me."

Annie drew him close. "Oh, Cullen . . ." And she couldn't say any more; she had no right to make promises or give hope, for to do so and not be able to follow through would be the worst kind of cruelty. However, she knew one thing very clearly: she would not allow this young boy to be abandoned again.

At that point, Rocky came over with the ball in his mouth and nosed Cullen's leg.

"I think your friend wants to play," Annie said, turning her attention to Rocky to give Cullen a moment. Like most kids he got his emotions under control quickly. Then she said, "I guess you know my mother."

He sniffled again, and then brightened. "She's cool. We talked and talked, like she told me all kinds of stuff about my dad. Like he'd always been so nice to her, buyin' her a car and callin' her every week to see how she was. That's kinda neat, doncha think?"

"Neat."

"So how come you never told me you had a mother?"

"Uh, well, I don't know. I guess it never came up."

"She'd be like my grandmother, wouldn't she?"

"Well—"

"Oh, I know not for real, but she could be a fake one, couldn't she? She said I could come to her house and stay, you know like if I don't have no place to go. She lives near the Skateboard Roll, so I figured next time I go, I could stop and see her."

Annie's head was reeling. Her emotions were teetering, and she couldn't help but be awed by Cullen's resilience.

Searching around for something to say, she commented, "You didn't overdose Rocky on cookies, did you?"

"Nah, I don't need that stuff anymore. He's just glad to see me. Hey Rocky, see if you get this one!" In an aside to Annie, he said, "He thinks he's a retriever. I don't wanna tell him any different." Cullen raced across the yard, throwing the ball high so that Rocky leapt into the air.

Annie walked up onto the porch, and when her mother stood up, Annie hugged her. Not a quick airy hug, but a warm embrace. "What a nice surprise. I'm glad you're here."

"Why Annie Jean, I don't think you've ever said that to me."

"Well, I should have. This seems to be a day for surprises," she said. "Cullen certainly likes you."

"He's a nice young man. Richard would be proud."

"Yes, he would."

"He should have been your son."

How right that sounded. Annie watched him roll on the grass with Rocky. "Yes, he should have."

Then her mother opened her tote bag and took out an envelope. "I want you to have this."

Annie pulled her gaze from the boy and the dog and frowned at the envelope. "What is it?" she asked as she opened the seal.

"Just something."

The something was a plain gold band. Annie carefully lifted it out, sliding it onto her thumb.

"It was his wedding ring," her mother said. "He didn't take it with him. I came across it this morning and, well, I don't have no need for it."

Annie ran her fingers around the band. Her father had small hands, artist's hands.

"Why did you keep it?" Annie asked. "You could have sold it." Considering her mother's animosity toward Annie's father, she would have thought her mother would have taken pleasure in getting rid of anything that reminded her of him. But instead, she said, "We could have used the money, we were kind of poor as I recall."

"Sell the wedding ring that I bought him? I couldn't do that," she said as if Annie had suggested she sell her mother's collection of cameos. Here was the woman who refused to even say Nathan Dawson's name, yet she'd kept his wedding ring. Annie didn't understand that, but she was grateful for it.

"I'm glad you didn't," she said, kissing her cheek. "And thank you for giving it to me."

Her mother flushed. "I best be going. Cullen said the Hunters are coming to 'check him out' as he put it."

"Yes."

"I think he's scared."

"I know."

"They won't be nasty to him, will they? I never did take to that Vera—all dolled up to go out to get her mail. She don't strike me as the kind who'd take to a messy little boy."

"James is excited about Cullen and Vera—well, we'll see. I won't let anything happen to Cullen. Actually, I think they are really anxious to get to know him."

Her mother picked up her tote bag and slipped it over her shoulder. "Evelyn is meeting me for supper, so I better be going."

"Thanks again, Mom." Annie kissed her cheek.

She nodded and went out into the yard. "Cullen, don't forget I want you to come and visit."

"I will."

Her mother left, and Cullen came up on the porch.

"Rocky's whipped," he said. And indeed, the husky had stretched out on the grass under the shade of a maple tree.

Annie opened the door. "Come on, let's get a Coke before the Hunters get here."

Six blocks away, Caroline stood in the empty living room of a two-story post-and-beam colonial with a recently added flagstone patio in the back and a wraparound porch in the front. There was a flagpole in the front yard, a brick chimney, and flower beds looking sad and dying in the late summer dryness. Tomorrow the furniture would come, but today she had driven down with Gordon and the kids to see the house for the first time.

She had no interest in it; she didn't want to live in Bedford and Gordon knew it.

Nevertheless, she had to give him credit for taking on the finding and renting of the house.

On the few occasions when they'd moved in the past, she'd handled all the moving, but this time she'd simply been too distracted and unfocused. Bedford memories—Richard was dead and his wife still lived here. She felt a kind of twisting tension that had settled so deep within her that only the vodka made it bearable. Her drinking, of late, scared her, for it had become a refuge for her despair.

She had everything that was right and perfect—a family, a comfortable life, a future of promise. And yet, in the past few weeks, most of her thinking had revolved around when she could sneak away and have a drink.

She'd done a good job of hiding it from the kids, making sure she was totally sober when they came home from school. Gordon had been tolerant, but she feared he was growing weary, which only added to her own inner tension.

From upstairs came the whoop of Johnny and Rose;

she knew Rose was in the bedroom with the flowered wallpaper and the window seat, while Johnny would choose the oddly shaped room with the built-in book-shelves. She should be up looking at the big master bed-room and marveling over the adjoining room with its exceptional northern light. It was an artist's dream, and the reason, Gordon told her, he'd taken this house.

"So what do you think?" Gordon asked as he came in from a walk through the two-car garage.

"It's lovely."

"You haven't moved since I went outside."

"I was just thinking about where the furniture would go. The couch opposite the fireplace, don't you think?"

"Uh, sure, whatever. The kids upstairs?"

She nodded. He started past her and she grabbed his sleeve. "We're not staying here tonight, are we?"

"With no furniture? I don't think so." He looked at her closely and she could see the worry in his eyes. "Caroline, this self-imposed despair has gone on too long. You've got to get it together."

"I know. It's just that being here is so hard."

"It's hard because you insist upon making it so. He can't hurt you or expose you. It's over. It was over years ago. He's dead and you're cowering about as if some spook is going to leap out of the past with photos and incriminating love letters."

"I'm sorry, there're just so many memories, and it hurts me that you've made me come here when you know it makes me unhappy." Oh God, did she really sound that whiny and self-obsessed?

"What was I supposed to do? Tell the company I couldn't come here because my wife had a lover who lived in Bedford?"

"The kids and I could have stayed in Wellesley—"

"Enough. We've walked this path into a ditch." He crossed the room, looking out a bowed window into the front yard. He stood for a long time, then slowly turned. His face had lost the brittle edge of moments before. "Moving here isn't the end of the world, sweetheart. Your past doesn't matter. It's long ago. I don't understand why you're so obsessed with it."

"It just hurts to be here."

"It hurts me to watch you self-destruct. It doesn't make sense. This obsession you have with memories of Hunter came out of nowhere."

"I loved him," Caroline said, defending herself despite knowing it would hurt Gordon. "I thought he'd leave his wife and we'd be married. He loved me. I know he did. My memories didn't come out of nowhere, but before, they were just pieces of my past put away. But then they all rushed forward when you said we were moving to Bedford."

His face had washed out of color and she knew that she'd crossed the line—said too much, looked too impassioned, belittled by contrast any passion their marriage had harvested.

In a low voice, he asked, "Do you want a divorce?"

Caroline knew her eyes were wide with horror. "No!"

"Then what? You've wedded yourself to the past. You want me to shelter you while you down a couple of bottles of vodka a week? You want me to watch you deteriorate over a dead man? You want me to continue to cover your ass with the kids when they ask me why Mom has weirded out?" Her hands covered her mouth in a new grief of realization. Gordon shook his head at her reaction. "You think they don't know about the drinking? Then you're more deluded than I thought."

"Oh God." She buried her face in her hands.

But he gripped her wrists and pulled, making her look at him. "I've seen your tears and your regret. What I haven't seen is you doing anything about it. Your sorrow, whatever the hell you've based it on, has become tiresome, and I for one, don't want to deal with it anymore."

And with those words, he went upstairs. She could hear him talking to the kids, hearing their laughter and then his. It sounded a long way away, as if it were from her past, a haunting of how it used to be.

Three hours later they were back in Wellesley. They'd had dinner at a restaurant north of Providence, passing Duke's Place, which once again flooded Caroline with too many memories.

At home the kids went to their rooms and Gordon went to the study to make a few phone calls. Caroline opened the bottle of vodka, started to pour, and then stopped. Instead she dumped it down the drain. Her hands shook as she watched it go. She had to get herself together. She had to, or lose everything.

Chapter Eighteen

"Well, well, this must be Cullen." James Hunter extended his hand to Cullen and Annie noted that this usually very easygoing man was a little nervous. That warmed her.

He and Vera had just arrived, and they were standing in the kitchen. Rocky sat outside the screen door as though there to make sure no one ran out the door. Cullen, wearing jeans and a Yankees shirt, had been watching out the windows for the past hour. Now he gave James a guarded smile that indicated clearly to Annie that this meeting was as much about Cullen liking them as the Hunters accepting him.

Annie was glad to see they were dressed very casually, even Vera had abandoned her too-put-together air, which could be intimidating. Today she wore a brown skirt and a lemon-yellow flowery pullover.

James rocked a bit back on his heels trying to look nonchalant. Vera said, "Cullen, we're anxious to hear all about you and what you've been doing—" She stopped suddenly, glancing over at James in panic. "I mean, we're excited about a new grandson—uh, no I don't mean new, not new, but not expected—I mean, not by us and uh . . ."

Cullen tipped his head to the side, looking confused by Vera's tortured sentences.

Her gaze darted from James to Annie in a "bail me out" plea. But it was Cullen who said, "Hey, I'm cool with it. Sure he, my dad, uh, you know, screwed around, but he tried to do good for me."

Vera looked as if she were going to faint. After a slight hesitation, James said, "Well, yes, that does get to the heart of the issue."

Cullen looked at Annie. "Huh?"

Annie leaned down and whispered, "Easy on the language."

"What'd I say?"

"Screwed is—"

"Bad?"

"A little rough."

That seemed to amaze him. "Linc just told me not to say fuck or shit."

Annie drew a deep breath. "Yes, let's try to avoid those."

"I was," he said, looking offended that she'd reconfirmed the obvious.

She urged Cullen forward. "Why don't we go into the den?"

Cullen and James went ahead. Vera clutched at Annie's arm. "Oh my God, I don't know if I can deal with this."

Annie patted her hand. "You're doing just fine. It's awkward for Cullen, too."

"But he's so—so indelicate," she said, still looking a little dazed.

"Vera, he's thirteen. And like most kids his age, carefully crafted and sensitive sentences aren't a parameter of their lives."

"You don't think it's because no one taught him any better?"

Annie shook her head. "Some know better than to be

so blunt in front of their grandparents, but that doesn't mean they use Miss Manners—speak with their friends." Like Betsy's boys, Annie thought. Two wonderful kids who threw four-letter words around with hip-hop enthusiasm when they thought no adult was listening.

"Yes, I suppose you're right," she said after some thought. "But what are we going to say to him, Annie? I don't want to talk about my son and another woman."

"Neither does Cullen. What he wants is to know about his father. He wants you both to brag about Richard. He's immensely proud, and I think he wants that pride validated by you and James."

Vera beamed. "Oh my, I never thought of that. I guess I was afraid he'd try to push himself upon us. I just need to take this slow. It's been very hard believing that Richard would have done such a thing."

"I understand. It's been hard for me, too."

They started toward the den, when Vera said, "Betsy is coming over as soon as Ron gets home from work to stay with Lydia."

Annie flinched. "She's coming here?"

"Is that a problem?"

"I'm just surprised. I didn't know she was speaking to me."

"Oh that," Vera said dismissingly. "That was before we knew the truth."

"Vera, I told you the truth and you believed me until Betsy arrived shrieking in hysteria."

"She was very upset."

"So was I."

Vera sighed heavily. "I do hope you aren't going to carry a grudge."

"Why is she coming?"

"She wants to meet Cullen."

"Why?"

"Because he's Richard's son. What other reason would there be?"

"I don't know. She hasn't called me, so this is the first I've heard. I guess it's okay, but I will say this: I will not permit Cullen to be either a target or a punching bag for Betsy's delusions." Her insides clenched as fiercely as a mother protecting her child.

Vera looked down at the floor. "I wouldn't want that either. I'm sure that boy has gone through enough."

"Believe me, he has."

In the den, Cullen had straddled a leather stool and Jim sat in a nearby chair. They were talking about the Yankees and their perennial rivalry with the Red Sox, with Cullen telling how Linc had taken all the guys to Fenway to see the Yankees play the Sox.

"How many boys are there?" James asked as Vera and Annie sat down on the couch.

"Right now, twenty I guess. But one of them, Eddie, wasn't there back then, and Linc took him, too. Then there's Tim, a guy who used to live there. He's kinda cool and a big Sox fan. Tim and me, we argue about who's got the best pitching."

"This Linc sounds like quite a guy."

"He's the best."

"The man at Noah House?" Vera asked.

Cullen turned. "He's the *boss* at Noah House. I been livin' there for awhile. Linc helped me find my dad."

"How did he do that?" Vera asked.

"Well, I had the name but I didn't know where he was. Didn't know he was dead, and that's pretty lousy. I didn't like findin' out he'd croaked."

Vera stiffened just a bit at the word "croaked," but she continued. "So what did this Linc do?"

"He talked to the bas—uh, the—the jerk who'd adopted me."

James sat forward, a real concern on his face. "Wait a

minute, the man who adopted you? It was my understanding that it was a couple. What happened? Why aren't you with your adoptive family?"

"Cuz he threw me out."

James scowled. "How old were you?"

"Ten."

"How could he have thrown out a ten-year-old?" Vera asked looking amazed and troubled at the same time.

Cullen related how Parker Gallagher wanted him to be some perfect kid and Cullen could never measure up no matter how hard he tried. He told of his adoptive mother who'd always protected him and how she'd been killed by a drunk driver, and how afterward Parker didn't want him anymore.

Vera sputtered, "That's outrageous. The man is a—"

"Goddamn bastard," James injected, his voice trembling. "So what happened then?"

"I ended up with Linc."

Annie said, "In between, he was in foster care and then fended for himself on the streets before he was placed in Noah House."

Cullen shook his head. "That ain't exactly the way it happened."

Annie frowned—she was sure that was what Linc had told her.

"My guess is that it wasn't that simple, right Cullen?" James asked.

"Mostly it ain't nice." He paused a long, long time.

Finally, Vera said, "You don't have to say."

"I don't want you to think it's like killin' or dealin', it's just that it's hard to go back." He paused again.

Vera and James looked at one another.

Annie braced herself, caught between knowing that the Hunters wanted to know—perhaps legitimately—and wanting Cullen to be free to keep something unpleasant to himself.

"I guess it don't matter." And then as if he were re- citing the factual images of someone else's life, he laid it out. "I was in two foster places. In one I had to steal food to eat, and in the other I got beat a couple times a week. I ran away, lived in a fridge box, started drinking, did some drugs. Linc caught me trying to break into a store. He took me to Noah House."

Annie heard the stark, succinct words that made her want to choke those who had mistreated him. James was red-faced with fury. But it was Vera who rose, walked toward Cullen, and then stopped, kneeling down in front of him. "Cullen, look at me."

Very slowly, he raised his eyes, the wariness still ap- parent.

"I'm so glad you found us," Vera said with a warmth in her voice that Annie had only heard a few times in the fifteen-plus years that she'd known Vera. "Your father would have been horrified if he'd known what had hap- pened to you. Your grandfather and I are horrified for him, and I promise—we'll do everything we can to make up for what you've experienced." Without taking her eyes off Cullen, she said, "Won't we, James?"

"Absolutely."

Cullen looked at both of them and then over to Annie, who nodded, saying in effect that the Hunters could be trusted.

"I'd kinda like to know some things about my dad," Cullen said, finally smiling just a little.

Vera stood. "Well, he loved chocolate-chip cookies."

"And the Yankees," James chimed in. And with that they began telling childhood details, growing-up dreams, and that his father had given him up for adoption because he and his birth mother believed it was the best for Cullen.

"He would never have wanted what happened to you," James said with fierceness. "If he'd known he would have found some way to help you."

Annie recalled her conversation with Linc about his getting their address from Parker. Had Linc said how Parker had gotten it? She couldn't remember, for she'd been too focused on whether Linc had done something questionable. She'd have to ask him, for like the Hunters, she knew Richard would have acted if he'd known of the horror the boy had been subjected to.

Later, as she was seeing the Hunters out, James was talking about Cullen coming over and seeing his woodworking shop. When he told Cullen he had a lot of his father's tools, Cullen grinned with enthusiasm. The two of them walked out to the yard, where Rocky was running around with the ball.

Vera said, "Oh, Annie . . ." And then she hugged Annie, drawing her close, her voice breaking just a little. "How can I thank you."

"Vera, you don't—"

"Yes. Not just that you came and told us but that you've befriended Cullen and stood by him even after Betsy and I were so terrible. I am so sorry."

It was then that Annie realized Betsy had never shown up. "Vera, what counts is that you and James and Cullen have found each other. He's a fine boy and I can't think of anything that would make him happier than to be part of the Hunter family."

"Richard's son," she said as if awed in a wonderful way by the revelation. Then, as she walked away, Annie heard her say, "I still can't believe it."

Annie waved as the Hunters walked on to their car with Cullen getting a handshake from James and a kiss from Vera.

He came back to the porch. "Now I have a family."

"You certainly do."

Then, with a sudden sheen of tears that he tried to hide, he said, "Thanks."

She squeezed his arm, wanting to hug him, to hold

him, to keep reassuring him that this new family loved him, but instead she settled for the simplest of gestures. She combed his hair back with her fingers and said, "I wish you were my son."

His eyes widened, and he looked at her so imploringly that she should have guessed what was coming. "If I was then I'd be living here."

"You certainly would."

And with that, he hugged her. It was tight, quick, and over in a nanosecond, but Annie cherished it. The son of her husband's mistress was the son of her heart if not of her flesh.

On Wednesday, as Annie had promised, she arrived at Tiffany's to find the door open, the apartment looking as though it had been turned upside down, and the young expectant mother lying on the floor.

"Tiffany!" Annie tossed aside her purse and the bag of baby necessities that she'd bought on her way there.

The young girl groaned, and Annie grabbed the phone to call 911, immensely relieved she wasn't dead.

"No, can't pay for that. I'm okay."

Annie ignored that. "You're hurt and you're going to be looked at." She gave 911 the particulars, then went back to Tiffany. "They're on their way. What happened?"

She winced and cried out in pain when Annie touched her arm.

"I was at the store and when I came back two kids were tossing the place. I tried to stop them and they hit me and knocked me down. I didn't want them to hurt the baby so I pretended I was hurt bad."

Annie felt her own rage erupt and made herself calm down. Now was not the time to indulge her fury. "You were very brave."

"Jesus, it hurts," she said delicately touching her swelling cheek. To Annie, it looked as if she'd been punched, not just hit.

Annie also noted red marks on her arms that already showed bruising. "I hear the siren. You're going to be okay."

The EMTs were in the room in seconds. Annie moved back to let them work on Tiffany. After doing a routine preliminary check, they gently put her on the stretcher. Annie followed them out where they slid her into the rescue wagon.

"I'll follow you to the hospital," she assured Tiffany.

At the emergency room, Annie went through the side doors just as Tiffany was wheeled in. Annie was right there to hold her hand as the nurse took her vitals. Tiffany clutched her hand when the nurse checked the baby. She listened while Tiffany, with her head slightly raised, tried to read the nurse's face. Annie, too, watched intently.

The nurse glanced up. "Heartbeat is strong."

"Thank God."

"The doctor will be in in a few minutes." Then she looked at Annie. "Are you her mother?"

"No. We're friends. I was the one who called nine-one-one."

Tiffany held Annie's hand as tight as a clamp. "I want her to stay."

"She can stay."

After she left, Annie said, "Is Tim at work? I think we should call him."

"Wait until the doctor says I'm okay."

"You seem pretty confident," Annie said, smiling for the first time since she'd found Tiffany.

"This hurts, but it ain't that bad cuz I faked them out. My old man useta beat me worse than those punks. I figured out I could get him to stop by makin' believe I was hurtin' real bad. He'd get super pissed if I was fightin' him."

Annie absorbed this with a prolonged silence. She simply didn't know what to say. Tiffany's survival savvy had Annie looking at her own problems as astonishingly irrelevant.

The doctor, a tall reed-thin man with a long bland face and a gray comb-over, appeared. "I'm Dr. Morris. What happened?" he asked, reading the notes the nurse had made and then looking closely at her bruises. Tiffany told him.

Gently, he touched her cheek where she'd been hit. She winced. He felt some more, then checked the bruises especially around her face. After the examination, he said, "Nothing appears to be broken. You're going to have some swelling, but I think the discoloration will be minor. You told the EMTs you're three months pregnant?"

She nodded.

He felt and pressed and then listened with his stethoscope. Straightening, he asked, "Are you having any cramps or abdominal pain?" At her frown, he clarified, "Stomach pain."

She shook her head. "Is the baby okay?"

"Seems to be. Heartbeat is steady, but your doctor will want to check you. Who's your doctor?"

"I don't have one."

"What about a clinic doctor?"

She shook her head, biting her lip as though she'd failed an important test.

"Tiffany, let me call Dr. Rouse," Annie offered, waving away her objections. "You need a doctor for yourself and the baby. He took care of my sister-in-law when she had her children and he's wonderful."

"Excellent idea," Dr. Morris said. "In the meantime, I'm going to admit you overnight for observation."

"What does that mean?" Tiffany asked. "I thought you said I was okay."

"Tiffany, it's only to make sure," Annie said, calming

her. "It's best for you and for the baby. I'll get in touch with Tim—"

"We can't pay for me to be here," she whispered to Annie.

"Shhh. I'll go and call Dr. Rouse's office. And then I'll call Tim."

Getting Dr. Rouse's office and making those arrangements was simple compared to finding Tim. After three calls to the trailer office at the construction site, she finally got someone who knew where he was. Once she gave him the news, she went back to the front desk, got Tiffany's room number, then rode up in the elevator.

The nurse was just coming out of her room when Annie arrived.

"She's a spunky kid," the nurse said.

"Yes, she is."

Tiffany lay in the hospital bed, her face turned away from the door. "Tiffany?"

She turned her head, and Annie knew she'd been crying. "Did you talk to Tim?"

"He's on his way."

New tears formed in her eyes. "I didn't want this to happen."

"I know you didn't."

"Tim is going to be pissed—spendin' money for me to lay here when I could be doin' this at home."

"I told you not to worry about it."

"Easy for you to say."

Annie squeezed her hand. "I'm going to go and let you rest. I spoke with Dr. Rouse's office. He'll be in later this afternoon."

"We can't pay him, neither," she mumbled.

"I'll come in this evening and you can fill me in on what he said."

"You ain't listenin' to what I'm sayin'."

"I'll see you later."

"Annie!"

But she was out of the room and walking down the hall with a new kind of energy. She had lots to do, and she couldn't wait to get started. Something inside of her had blossomed or rebloomed, or maybe just found its way out of the morass of the ordinary. Certainly before Cullen and Linc had come into her life, it had been conventionally mediocre.

And boring.

And shallow.

While her own inner realizations were secondary, they were also profound.

Her denial, transformed into belief in Cullen, had pulled her out of that morass of the superficial and insignificant. She began to see that life around her was more than a successful business and propped-up anger at her mother for past neglects. Cullen and Linc and Noah House, the Hunters and now Tiffany and her baby.

Indeed, they had changed her life.

Chapter Nineteen

"So tell me, Linc, what do you think?" Annie asked.

"About what?"

"The new place for Tim and Tiffany?" When Linc didn't answer immediately, Annie found herself wavering between worry and irritation. Ever since she'd called him after Tiffany had been beaten up, Annie sensed he'd begun slowly pulling away from her. Nothing overt or easily pinpointed, just a general feeling of distance. From that first time of intimacy, he'd made it clear he didn't love her; now this new less-than-interested attitude added credence to her fear that their relationship was slipping away.

Given that reality, for her to even think about a future together would be foolish. Stupidly, perhaps, she'd accepted the parameters he'd set, but what other choice was there? He was not a man who was going to fall into some neat little true-love-forever mindset, however much she would have welcomed it.

Yet in all honesty, *she* hadn't been giving any serious thought to a future together either. But abruptly now, in the midst of this distancing he seemed to be laying out between them, she became overly aware of the tenuous cords that held them together. Truth revealed gave no hiding place for hopeful yearnings.

Now he rose from the glider on her back porch, where they'd been seated to catch some of the evening breeze. The day had been hot, and Linc had insisted they have dinner in town; she'd asked him to come back to the house for a glass of wine. She'd told him about what she'd worked out for Tim and Tiffany, and she wanted his opinion and any suggestions, plus there was Cullen . . . She couldn't wait to tell him what she and Cullen wanted to do.

She sipped her wine, unexpectedly chilled by the simple absence of him sitting next to her. "Linc, what's the matter?"

"Just a lot of stuff on my mind." The man was a master at vague nonanswers.

"Noah House?"

"And other things." He stood in profile, watching Rocky take a bead on a courageous squirrel working his way down the trunk of the maple tree. Annie could only wish that Linc's interest in her would be as intense. She debated on bluntness, she even rethought where speaking her mind would get her. Nowhere, she concluded, but she plunged anyway.

"Other things? Like telling me we're finished?" She held her breath, too aware that her heart was hammering so hard it hurt.

He swung back, looking a bit startled, and she was struck once again by the dimension of the man. He was attractive, but not handsome. Sexy, but without the need to show it off. There was no innocence, too much cynicism, and not enough light in his dark eyes. She knew more about him than he knew she knew. And that was okay. She hated all those laundry-list conversations of past flaws and distinctions that either brought pity or pride or prejudice. It wasn't the Linc she didn't know that mattered. It was the Linc she did know, the one she loved and yet couldn't quite grasp.

"How can you ask me something like that?" He seemed guarded and puzzled in the early evening shadows.

"Because I want to know. You've been acting very distant the past few weeks. I'm all grown up and I won't get hysterical. You've never lied to me about where we're going. I just want you to tell me the truth. Do you want to end our relationship?"

He swore.

She set her wine glass down, then stood and walked over to him. "That's not an answer."

"I don't have an answer," he snapped. She felt suddenly emboldened, glad she'd chosen bluntness. He, however, simply glared at her.

"Linc, a nonanswer either means you're trying to spare my feelings or that you want to continue seeing me and you don't want to admit it."

"What the hell are you, a pop-psych analyst? Don't try to drag me into some sensitivity whirlpool of gutless personal meaning." He bit the words out, then as if he had to dig deep into a territory of his soul that he rarely traveled, he said, "You want the real deal? Well here it is. My nonanswer means this: I don't want to let you go. Not yet."

"Oh, Linc . . ." She wrapped her arms around him and spontaneously kissed him.

He, however, broke away, holding her back. "That wasn't supposed to give you comfort. Bastards don't do that. And don't give me that doe-eyed understanding crap."

But the more he talked the more she found her footing. "Okay, no doe-eyed understanding. How about if I say what I really think?"

"And you haven't already?"

"There's more."

He held his hands up. "No. I don't want to hear it."

"You know, don't you?"

"Annie, I'm warning you—"

"I love you."

"So she says it anyway," he muttered, as if he were a drowning man who'd just lost his last lifeline. Then as though reciting the mantra of his nature, he said, "It's sex, Annie. S-E-X."

"That, too." She grinned and hugged him again. There was something reassuring about him when he was at his wit's end. Fighting those better angels, she supposed.

"Shut up."

She grinned.

He didn't. He kissed her instead. Deeply, angling their mouths, tightening her against him as though to imprint the feel of her against him. His hands slipped down the folds of her dress, molding it to her body, slipping his hands over her bottom and lifting her against him. Then he rested his hips against the railing, tugging her between his legs.

"What am I going to do about you," he whispered, biting lightly on her lower lip, then kissing her, then drawing her close so that her head rested on his upper chest just below his jaw. His steady heartbeat warmed her, and his even breathing brought solace.

His comment wasn't a question, and she guessed that a flip sexy answer or a serious one would have canceled the pleasant mood between them. It was strange how she could read him. There was this intensity, this cusp of passion, almost like a musical prelude. Yet instead of the obvious coupling that could easily follow, there had been many times in these past nights when being together, cradling close, had been enough. For her it was a testimony to the discipline of the man that he could find surcease in this very mutual and basic holding and feeling and thinking and wanting.

"Linc, I don't want to push you where you don't want to go."

"I appreciate that," he said and she thought she felt his body relax. There was truly a time to talk and explain and a time to savor the silence.

He released her and she stepped away.

"I could use a beer. Do you want one?"

"Sure." She went back to the glider and sat down, amazed at how calm and resolved she felt. It was all going to be okay. Tim and Tiffany and Cullen, too.

He opened the screen door, bringing Rocky to attention. The squirrel had escaped, so he was up on his feet loping inside to get the cookie he knew Linc would give him. Annie leaned back in the glider, closing her eyes. It had indeed been a busy few weeks, personally fulfilling and satisfying despite Linc's reticence.

After she'd left Tiffany at the hospital, she'd returned to their apartment to get some overnight things for Tiffany. Between the location, the dismal condition, the cheesy locks, and finding Tiffany beat up and robbed, Annie shuddered at the thought of her returning here and being vulnerable to more risk.

Finding another place seemed like the obvious answer, but where and at what cost? And was it even her business? Getting involved, something she'd done albeit reluctantly with the couple at first, suddenly became very important.

There was a sweetness to Tiffany, and a vulnerability, but most surprising was that under her hard-assed attitude were common needs and wants. A man who loved her, cherished her; wanting her baby; needing friends; and unwilling to fall victim to her circumstances. Annie wanted to help because she could.

A better neighborhood meant much higher rent, and while Annie could easily afford to cover their rent, she knew both of them would balk at that. Tim had already insisted on paying the hospital bill and no amount of arguing by Annie would budge him. If he wouldn't accept her offer for a hospital bill, helping them pay their rent on a month-to-month basis would never happen.

Actually she respected Tim for his independence, and she did understand. Although she didn't think of it as charity but more as sharing her own abundance, she knew that Tim was proud and something even more basic. He didn't want to be beholden to some "rich" woman as he called her.

Then she remembered Grace's cottage. Grace Tooley had a rambling house on three acres of land with lawns that cascaded into forever. On the property, not far from the main house, was a pretty cottage that had been used for spillover summer guests back when Grace and her late husband had entertained. In the past years, the resident gardener had lived there until his death the previous April. The cottage had been empty since.

To Annie's knowledge Grace hadn't changed her mind about not renting. Why would she? She certainly didn't need the money. But at the same time, Grace had been looking to hire a handyman and had asked Annie if she knew of anyone.

Annie had promised to ask around, but in the chaos of recent events, she'd forgotten all about it.

So why not combine her idea with Grace's?

She'd gone to see Grace and presented her with the idea of Tim and Tiffany living in the cottage and instead of rent money, Tim could be the handyman, a simple barter arrangement. Annie made sure Grace understood that these two kids weren't well-versed in social graces, but they were honest and hard-working and wouldn't disappoint her. The older woman seemed a bit skeptical, but the idea of a handyman right on the property held great appeal.

"Does your friend Mr. McCoy have anything to do with this?"

Uh oh. Her question was obviously based on that visit Grace had made to Noah House to seek it out as a potential charity. "Not directly. Tim was at Noah House until he reached eighteen and moved out on his own. Linc still checks up on him every few weeks to see how he's doing."

"Then he'd be coming here?" Grace stepped back as if she definitely couldn't abide that.

"Actually, it was more of a visit than checking up. I would imagine Linc would come and see them just as their friend. Part of his reason for keeping an eye on them was because of where they lived. He worried about them." She paused. "They live on Godfrey Street."

Grace pressed her hand to her chest. "Oh my."

"Yes."

"Does Mr. McCoy have a say in where they move?"

"No."

"Doesn't mean he won't have something to say when he finds out about me." Grace folded her arms, her nostrils flaring. "I got the distinct impression your Mr. McCoy doesn't approve of money from people like me, although I can't fathom why. Where does he think charities get it if not from the wealthy? While this isn't cash, I'd still be doing something. Why wouldn't he get all huffy about this, too?"

Annie had no idea how to respond to that. She knew Linc had been burned in the past by big check writers who then turned around and expected him to either do their bidding or wanted to dictate how Noah House should spend their money. Yet, she, too, had found his attitude toward Grace and her generosity appalling. Linc, of course, didn't give a rip what either of them thought. Nevertheless, she said, "Truthfully, you'll be doing something Linc really admires."

"I will?"

"Directly helping some kids who need a fresh start."

For sure, Annie knew Linc wouldn't balk at that. Action, not talk, was always his preference.

Grace looked a little confused, venturing in carefully by saying, "All right, Annie, tell me about them."

And Annie did. From meeting Tiffany, the pregnancy, her own realization of how determined they were, then forming a real friendship with the young woman and finally finding her beaten up by burglars.

When she finished, Grace sat down, her usually pink cheeks pale. "That's frightening. Why are they living in such a dangerous place?"

"Because it's all that they can afford."

"Well, something should be done," she said firmly, her eyes bright as though presented with a cause she could support. Then she grinned. "And I can do something, Annie, can't I?"

"Absolutely."

She pressed her lips together, tapping her finger to her cheek. "Now I understand him," she mused. "Your Mr. McCoy."

"You do?"

"It's very simple, Annie," she said as if she'd acquired instant clarifying insight. "Your Mr. McCoy thinks I should have volunteered to do something, not just write a check."

Since she knew Linc so well, this sounded obvious, but this was a breathtaking conclusion from a woman who rarely thought deeply about other people's motives. Blandly, Annie replied, "Linc does believe in involvement."

She was thoughtful for a moment. "And I'd be doing that with the cottage. I'd be involved and I wouldn't even have to write a check."

Annie grinned at the ever-pragmatic Grace. "You're a gem."

"You be sure and tell your Mr. McCoy."

"As soon as I tell Tim and Tiffany. I didn't want to say anything until I'd spoken with you."

At their apartment, Annie described the cottage and the arrangement of Tim working as a handyman for Grace.

Tiffany's eyes were as big as saucers, her delight and excitement obvious, but Tim was leery, and he wanted the details.

"What does she want this handyman to do?"

"Minor fix-up and repairs on the main house, maybe some lawn care in the summer—although Grace has a landscaping service—shoveling snow in the winter—that sort of thing."

"Doin' her? Is that part of the deal?"

At first, his words didn't register. Then they did. Linc had told her that day at their apartment that Tim had once been a sex toy for rich older women.

Without flinching, she looked directly at Tim. "No. I can absolutely guarantee that. Grace is more apt to nag you and fuss and worry about whether you're wearing warm enough clothes or if Tiffany is taking her vitamins for the baby—now, if you can deal with those . . ."

He absorbed that, then straightened. "What do you think I'm some kind of wussie?" Then he narrowed his eyes, suspicion always on the surface. "How come you're doin' all this? I mean I know Cullen thinks you're cool, but how come to us? We ain't nothin' to you."

"Do I have to have a reason beyond I want to do it?"

"I don't know. I ain't never knew anyone but Linc who just does stuff."

"Let's put it this way, Tim. I've spent a lot of time doing things for just me, and I decided that the time had come to change that."

"I guess," he said, still looking a tad skeptical.

Tiffany looked around the small hot apartment. "A cottage," she said breathing out the word as if it were a synonym for heaven. "I ain't never lived in a house or a cottage. Windows and a yard and a door that opens outside. . . ."

Annie treasured the look of happiness on her face. "Grace wants to meet both of you and, of course, you'll want to see the cottage. You know, I bet we can get Linc to bring his truck to move your things."

Tiffany laughed. "He could bring his motorcycle. We ain't got much. . . ."

That had been a few days before. Grace had since met them, decided Tiffany needed fattening up, and when she asked Tim to fix a loose leg on a patio table, he did it easily and quickly, impressing her. For Annie, the entire episode had filled her with a tremendous sense of accomplishment and satisfaction that she couldn't name. But she was positive that the benefits for Grace and two struggling teenagers would be long lasting. Deep in her heart and soul she knew this to be true.

Now as Linc came back out to the porch with the two beers, she asked, "What took so long?"

"Had to make a phone call." He handed her one of the beers.

She raised her eyebrows as Rocky crept off the porch and down the steps.

"Rocky Hunter, how many Oreos did you eat?"

He cocked his head and looked at Linc. "Looks like we didn't fool her, buddy."

"Not when he's got crumbs around his mouth." Amusement danced in her eyes. She liked this easiness with Linc, this naturalness, this feeling that life was lazy and normal and definitely good.

"Couldn't find the Oreos. He had three from that package on the top shelf," Linc said.

Annie blinked. "The chocolate macadamia cookies?"

"Uh oh."

"No wonder he looks so guilty. He knows he's not

supposed to have those." Rocky looked suitably guilty and Linc suitably chastised.

Linc ruffled Rocky behind the ears. "Next time we'll stick to Oreos." To wit, Rocky woofed.

Linc sat down beside her, stretched his legs out, rested one hand on her knee and tipped the beer can to his mouth with the other.

"So Tim and Tiffany are going to move into a cottage and out of that grim apartment. I think it's a great idea."

And suddenly here was his opinion as easy as melting ice cream on a summer day.

Her smile was broad with pleasure. "I just knew you'd like this."

"Why wouldn't I? Two young kids with a future that isn't stuck on Godfrey. I just hope they appreciate the break they got."

"I think they do." She told him about Tim's initial fear.

"Good. He's thinking and he's aware. So what else did you want to tell me?"

"Cullen is going to move in with me." She carried the momentum of her pleasure into this announcement and she glanced at him to get his reaction. What she saw was not reassuring. That wonderful lift of enthusiasm she'd experienced about Tim and Tiffany now plummeted her back to earth.

"You don't want to let him do that," Linc said quietly.

"Why not?"

"It's a bad idea."

"Just like that?"

"Since the alternative—it being a good idea—isn't what I think, I figured I'd save us a lot of time. Good intentions, sweetheart, but trust me, you don't want to do this." He glanced at his watch, then set the beer can down. "Gotta run. I promised Penny and Nick I'd stop by. So far things seem to be going okay with Eddie, thanks to your suggestion of a test period. I think the punk finally got the message that life was not created just for his pleasure."

He started to get up and she pulled him back. "Wait a minute. Don't hit and run like that. Why is it a bad idea? Save us a lot of time from what?"

"The argument that just arrived."

"I don't want to argue."

"Good."

She took a breath, feeling her annoyance bubble up. "Okay, tell me why you think it's a bad idea."

"Because what's going to eventually happen with him is still a question."

"Maybe I'd like to have something to say in what happens to him. Maybe *he'd* like to have a say. He's not a baby incapable of making a decision."

"Annie, you're too smart to believe Cullen's situation is as simple as you making a decision on where he lives. What about when the Hunters decide they want him to live with them?"

"He can visit his grandparents. I wouldn't stop that."

"You're not listening. I said live, not visit. Or what about when Cullen decides he wants to search for his birth mother? And when and if he finds her or she finds him, what about if he wants to go live with her? What if she wants him back?"

"What if, what if, what if? None of that has happened yet, and meanwhile he's at Noah House when he could be in a real home." Regret immediately swamped her.

He simply looked at her. "You've got my answer. End of discussion."

"Linc, wait. I didn't mean that the way it sounded."

"Really? Then put it in context for me."

"Okay, that was unfair. But come on, even you have to admit that Cullen living here would be better than with twenty other kids."

"Better for who? Him or you?"

She stiffened. "Are you accusing me of doing this to benefit myself? Better yet, you should question your own motives for not wanting him here."

He rose, walked a few steps away, turned, crossed his arms, and asked, "And what do you think my motives are?"

Again, she'd spoken without thinking. "I don't know."

He lowered his head and shook it slowly. "Let it go, Annie."

"I can't. This means everything to me, Linc. More even than getting the cottage for Tim and Tiffany." She looked at him pleadingly. Not because she wanted his permission, but she did want his goodwill, and she didn't understand why he refused to give it.

"As I said before, the issues are the Hunters and his birth mother—neither of those have been sorted out, and when they are . . ." He paused, glancing out across the darkening yard, and suddenly Annie felt as if she were speeding toward a wreck she couldn't divert. She wanted to jump up, cover her ears, and run into the house. "Cullen will make his choice between those two. You're not in this picture any more than I am."

She knew her eyes were wide with the same pain that just twisted through her heart. "You don't know that. I want him here and Cullen wants to be here. Why is that wrong? A few weeks ago you were pounding on me to accept that he's Richard's son. I've done that and more. I love Cullen as if he were my own son and you're acting like there's some nefarious motive on my part."

He spoke very softly, no temper, no rising cadence. "I gave you my opinion. Do I think you can get your way? Sure I do. Right now Cullen is awed by you, and probably loves you as much as he loved his stepmother. He's going to get pulled in a lot of different directions. You have money, a certain amount of influence, no doubt more than a few connections. You'll use them and get what you want and what you think Cullen wants. I'll say what I said before. It's a bad idea. It's bad for Cullen and it's bad for you."

"Stop saying that! You don't know anything about how I feel." She knew her voice was too raw, too loud, too angry, but his words hurt and jarred her and all her defenses came rushing forth. "And where the hell do you get off to accuse me of wanting Cullen because of some sort of selfish need that I can make happen?" She stopped, took a few breaths, and glared at him. "I'm very disappointed in you, Mr. McCoy. I thought the purpose of a place like Noah House was to provide a home for troubled boys when they had no place else that would take them. Well, my house is a place, and my heart is an even bigger place, and I want to take Cullen, and all you can do is accuse me of using influence and money and pulling strings. That insults me and offends me and makes me furious."

"So be it."

"You are a coldhearted bastard."

"Why, because I'm stating facts and not wallowing in the emotion of this?" He dumped the remaining beer over the railing and tossed the can in the nearby trash. "As my old man used to say, ride in on your heart and you'll go out with it busted. That's what you're doing, riding your heart. But hey, what do I know? You're going to do what you want just like you did with Tim and Tiffany. Just because that worked has no bearing on Cullen's situation. I can't stop you. I just hope you don't regret it."

And with that, he stepped off the porch, ruffled Rocky's ears, walked across the yard and out the gate. A few moments later, she heard his truck start and back out of the drive.

Annie sat without moving, realizing with an eerie chilliness, that her fury over his misguided opinion about Cullen went much further. So much for wondering when their relationship would end. It just had.

Chapter Twenty

Two weeks later, Caroline parked her car at the edge of the road. She'd done her homework and now she walked quickly as the rumble of thunder in the distance accompanied her.

The caretaker, loading a mower into a pickup truck, told her it was on the north side, a modest gray monument three rows in. "There's a rose bush next to the stone. His wife planted it last summer. Better hurry," he cautioned, eyeing the darkening sky. "Rain's a comin'."

Caroline thanked him and made her way between the headstones, approaching the gravestone with a catch in her throat.

Then she was there. The wind whipped around her, pulling at her hair, causing her blouse and slacks to billow and flatten. She kneeled in front of the granite, quickly crossing herself, then drew her fingers across the engraved letters. She bowed her head, squeezing back the tears. Getting to her feet, she pressed her hand against his name on the stone. "Goodbye, Richard. Rest well. Rest peacefully."

She turned and hurried back to her car just as the rain began. At least her other secret was safe.

* * *

Cullen moved into Annie's house with little fanfare.

No one objected, and in fact the Hunters were thrilled. It never occurred to Annie that their response was anything less than reenforcing her own belief that Cullen living with her was the best decision for all of them. Emboldened by this, she'd called Linc, and to her surprise he'd already started the process. He'd contacted Social Services to make sure the state had been notified, and then, to her wonder, he went a step further and pushed the paperwork through the grindingly slow system so quickly Annie was amazed. His focus and determination couldn't be ignored, for she'd expected either a stall or a wall.

"You truly do the unexpected."

"By cutting through the bureaucracy? Why would you think I'd stall? You'll offer Cullen a good home. Even this coldhearted bastard knows that. My objection was and is personal, not professional."

Annie knew there was more here, something he believed that he wasn't telling her. No doubt to avoid another fight. What did it matter—everything was working out perfectly. "Thank you for making this work so quickly," she said, keeping her voice even.

Sadly, he gave no indication he wanted to see her, and for the few moments she saw him when she went to Noah House to pick up Cullen's things, he was polite but remote. She would have preferred sarcasm or anger or even an argument she knew she'd lose. But this sanitized disinterest punched at her, proving his insistent claim that what they'd had together was indeed only sex. If she'd had any doubts they were finished, she no longer did. It was over—yesterday's intimacy shredded and thrown away like old newspapers.

By the time she drove away, her throat was raw from

swallowing her heartache. It wasn't supposed to be like this. It wasn't supposed to end and be so soon forgotten by him. Time to move on. Next woman, next relationship, next span of temporary tension.

Determined not to pout or spend any more time wondering how she could have been so utterly foolish, she threw herself into making Cullen welcome. She redecorated one of the bedrooms in a sports theme, and enmeshed herself in the utter joy of learning and preparing what he liked to eat—cheeseburgers and chocolate milk and pizza—answering his questions about Richard, and settling happily into the role of being his mother.

School was starting in a week, and Annie wanted to take him shopping for his clothes.

"My stuff's okay," Cullen told Annie when she suggested going to the mall.

"They're fine, but don't you think we should fill in a bit with some shirts, pants, new sneakers?"

"Like Nike?" His grin was huge.

"Nike it is."

"Okay!"

She ruffled his hair. "Your grandmother wants to go with us."

"Grandmother . . ." He rolled the word around as if testing it. "Sounds funny, but kinda cool."

The shopping trip was fun, and Annie loved watching while Cullen picked out the clothes he wanted, and those Nikes. Afterward, they stopped for pizza.

Back home, Annie made tea for herself and Vera while Cullen hauled the bags of new clothes up to his room. He bounded back down the stairs for chocolate milk and a handful of cookies. In a few moments she heard the FM music. How normal it all sounded. How normal she felt. She was a mother. For real. It simply made her heart overflow.

Annie poured tea, and she and Vera sipped while they

discussed their shopping trip. Never had her relationship with her mother-in-law been so easygoing. The woman positively glowed whenever Cullen was mentioned.

So perhaps that very relaxed atmosphere added to her not quite getting the impact when Vera casually said, "We want Cullen to legally have the Hunter name. In fact, James and I are looking into adopting Cullen."

"I was thinking the same thing," Annie said.

"Oh, I'm so glad you agree, Annie. James and I want to fix Richard's old room up for him—"

"Wait a minute. I meant I wanted to adopt him."

Puzzlement lined Vera's face, followed by, "You want to adopt him? Why would you want to do that?"

Annie blinked, setting her cup down before she spilled the tea. The question seemed absurd, the answer obvious. "I love him as if he were my son."

"But my dear, he's not. Oh, I think it's wonderful that you feel such a closeness to him, and we're thrilled that he's staying here for the time being. It's obvious Cullen feels very relaxed with you. It was so very evident today at the mall. James and I felt you would be a wonderful transition."

"Transition?" The word sounded like the Hunters viewed her as fleeting temporary nanny until the "real" relatives came along. Them. "Surely, you're not serious. Cullen is here because he wants to be, because I love him and I think he's beginning to feel the same way. This is Richard's son, and now he's mine."

"Oh my," Vera said in a distressed voice. "Wherever did you get the idea that boy would live here permanently?"

"Wherever did you get the idea that he wouldn't?" Annie felt like she'd just been exposed as naïve and silly.

But Vera continued on as though Annie hadn't spoken. "It will be best for Cullen, my dear. Really it will. You will no doubt marry again someday. James told me you were close friends with that Linc McCoy. Perhaps . . ."

"My relationship with him is over." Annie realized this was the first time she'd ever said this aloud, and it hurt all over again.

"Oh, well," she said, dismissing Annie's words as though they were throwaways. "Frankly, I think he would have been a poor choice after Richard, but James told me that wasn't my business. But apart from any new close friends or relationships in your life, you also have a full-time business. That does take a lot of your time. Whenever would you have any time for Cullen?"

"Vera, that's a ridiculous question. Cullen is the most important thing in my life."

"James and I are his grandparents, Annie. We're blood relatives. You're not."

The words were bad enough, but the taut steel in her tone was so tight, Annie could only stare. Why oh why had she ever assumed this would be straightforward?

"Of course," Vera said, "you can see him, and he can come here to visit. . . ."

"He told me he wants to stay here," she said, knowing instantly that although his words to her meant everything to Annie, they probably weren't that relevant to someone bent on having her own way. Fleetingly, she remembered Linc pointing out that she would do whatever she could to get *her* way. What he hadn't said was that the Hunters would obviously do the same.

"Now, Annie, surely you understand our position."

"I think Richard would want me to adopt him. If he were alive this wouldn't be an issue."

"Of course not. But he's not." Her voice softened and she patted Annie's hand. "Now don't you worry. We want you to be part of Cullen's life." She glanced at her watch. "I have to run. I have a lot to do. Shopping for him was fun. Thank you so much for including me." She kissed

Annie's cheek and in a few moments, unaware of the havoc she'd just wrought, she was gone.

So typical of Vera. This is the way it is so just adjust, my dear, and of course you can see Cullen. Here are the crumbs so be happy. End of discussion. End of story.

From upstairs came the pound of FM. She sat for a long time staring at her still-full teacup.

Linc had said it was a bad idea for Cullen to live here, but for Annie, the bad idea was trusting that this would all work out in some nicely tied happy ending for everyone.

First she'd lost Linc and now Cullen was slipping away. She felt defeated and sucker-punched and unbearably sad.

Days later, she was at Design and Details, trying to track down thirty yards of toile drapery fabric that was supposed to have been delivered two weeks before. Her client was justifiably frantic; between Annie trying to keep her own temper in check with a supplier who had little regard for deadlines, and reassuring her tearful client, it had been an exhausting week.

"Jock, either find it today or reship. We're already behind schedule. Yes. All right. I know it's not your fault, but you've got to make it right. I appreciate it. When will it be delivered? No later, Jock. Thursday is it."

She hung up, poured a glass of water, and downed three aspirin. It was days like this when she wondered why she didn't simply close the doors and retire. It had not escaped her that at one time she had rolled easily through all these glitches, and now they were annoyingly tiresome.

There was a soft knock and when she looked up, Betsy stood in the doorway. God, just what she needed.

"Can I come in?"

Why? But she bit that back. "Sure."

She eased in like a cautious cat expecting to see a shoe hurling at her. In a long navy dress with red accessories and a new haircut—a spiky frosted-tip style that seemed to narrow her face—and was quite attractive. A roomy bag hung from her shoulder. She eased the door closed. "I'm doing a column on Noah House."

"Congratulations." She knew she sounded snippy and short, but she had no patience for another round with Betsy. "What does your column have to do with me?"

"I wanted some quotes from you. Your impressions, what you think of the work that is being done?"

"The work is laudable and Linc should be commended for setting so many boys on the right path. Now, if you don't mind, I've got a headache, too many phone calls to make, and I have plans later with Cullen."

"Annie, look, I know you're angry with me."

She should have just waved her off, but something inside blew apart. She came around the desk, taking note that Betsy had taken a step back. Her reaction reminded Annie of when she'd told Linc she'd wanted to punch Betsy. Maybe Betsy knew that, too.

Annie no longer wanted to hit her, but since Betsy brought all of this up, she wasn't going to wimp out. "Don't try and make *my* anger *my* fault. You're the one who attacked me and accused me of trying to hustle your parents by forcing Cullen on them. And you know what? I should have taken that first advice you gave me and never said a word. Then I wouldn't be in any of this mess. I'd have a wonderful boy who would be mine and instead—never mind. It's not your problem."

Looking alarmed, and seemingly anxious to make amends, Betsy slid the bag from her shoulder and set it on a chair. "May I sit down?"

"Whatever." Annie indicated the chair. She herself remained standing.

"I didn't come to your house that night my parents came because I—well, I was just too embarrassed. Look, I know I'm asking a lot for you to forgive me. I acted like the bitch from hell." When Annie didn't say anything, she said, "You were right about Cullen. He's a wonderful boy. My boys think he's about the neatest kid they've ever met and Lydia adores him."

"I'm happy for you and your family." And she was. She really was. "Cullen needs a family, people who care about him and want to be with him."

"Annie, it's the right words, but what happened to that softness you used to have?"

"You mean all that gushy emotion that breaks your heart? Been there too many times and it's too painful." She turned away, hating that she was on the verge of crying.

Then she felt Betsy's hand on her shoulder. "Annie, I want to be your friend again. I know I don't deserve to be. . . . I was so wrong about everything. I guess I saw Cullen as some threat to my kids. He's much more street savvy, even more mature, but he's also Richard's son. And you know how much Mom and Dad wanted you and Richard to have kids." At Annie's concentrated look, Betsy said, "I know they weren't being fair, but sometimes when you want something too much you only see your own view. That's what I was doing—seeing Cullen only as a kid who would take attention from my kids. I feared my parents would be so taken with this gift of Richard's son that they would forget my kids."

Annie sighed, pressing her hand to Betsy's. Suddenly she was too tired to hold onto what felt to her now like stale resentment. And Betsy's reasons, as misguided as they were, made perfect sense when viewed through the eyes of a mother protecting her kids. Given her own worries about keeping Cullen, Betsy's confession softened Annie. "You're not the only one with fears, Betsy."

"Let me guess. My parents wanting to adopt Cullen?"

She turned around. "He's like my own son, Betsy." And then the tears filled her eyes. "No, dammit, he *is* my son."

"This is going to be hard. Look, they don't want to hurt you, and I know they don't want a fight, but they aren't going to give up. They really believe that Cullen should be with them."

"What do you think?" Annie asked, searching Betsy's face.

"God, Annie, don't make me answer that."

"You agree with them."

"Yes," she said simply. Annie folded her arms and turned away. "Annie, I know this hard, but you have to think about Cullen—"

"Think about Cullen?" She was astonished Betsy could suggest she wasn't. "Cullen is all I think about."

"But to get into a huge fight with my parents—"

The phone rang.

"Excuse me." She answered. "Hello."

"Hi."

"Hi yourself." It was Linc, and she turned slightly away.

"You got a few minutes?" he asked.

"Sure. Is this about Cullen?" There was no other reason that he would call her.

"Yeah."

Betsy picked up her shoulder bag and whispered, "I'll call you later."

"I'll be in touch," she said to Betsy.

"Annie, you want me to call you back?"

"No. Betsy was here, but she just left."

"With no swollen mouth, I trust."

"We've buried a few hatchets."

"Who blinked?"

She smiled although it wasn't anything to grin about.

Maybe it was just because Linc was saying it. "She came here."

She heard his soft chuckle. "Good. She made the first dumb move, only right she should make the first smart one."

Annie leaned back, relaxing for the first time in weeks. She'd missed him. She'd missed his sharpness and his black-and-white approach when she thought she dithered too much. With Linc she always knew just where she stood. Not always in a good place as far as she was concerned, but she knew. "So tell me about Cullen. He's doing great by the way."

"Annie, what I'm going to tell you could be a problem."

She sat up, her pulse racing and her heart following. Her relaxation vanished like spinning smoke. "What?"

"I've located his birth mother."

She closed her eyes. God, was there some sort of black spell on her life? "Where is she?"

"She's here in Bedford."

"She's here?" She wasn't sure why, but this stunned her. Perhaps because she'd wanted to hear that the woman was in some far western state living in a town that hadn't made a listing on the latest map. "She's come to get Cullen, hasn't she? No, she can't—"

"Take it easy. From what I've been told she doesn't know Cullen is here. Her husband is an on-site executive for the new Maguires that is going up over on Ledyard. They've moved here from Wellesley. They have two kids enrolled for the new school year in St. Mark's. Her name is Caroline Sheplin and she lives at eight forty-two Colonial Drive." He waited for a few moments. "Annie?"

"How do you know all this?" she asked, wondering why it even mattered, but nevertheless awed at how he could find out things with utter ease.

"I made some phone calls."

"Who did you call?"

"The information is good, Annie."

"But—"

"You're going to have to trust me. I can't tell you where or how I got it."

"Connections."

He remained silent.

"Okay, no questions about where. And you're sure she doesn't know about Cullen?"

"Not yet."

"Meaning?"

"Meaning that it's only a matter of time. I'm sure it's occurred to her that she's now living in the same town where she was involved with Richard. Unless she's a total dimwit, which I doubt. A lot of people know Cullen is Richard's son, and at some point she could learn it, too. This is just to let you know she's out there, probably innocently, but out there."

"So you're leaving me with a choice of telling Cullen now or telling him later." Or she could go see the woman herself.

Linc continued. "I'm simply giving you some information. Better to be informed than caught unprepared."

"Advice?"

"Annie, you haven't been too receptive to my advice in the past, so I'm not venturing into that land mine again."

"Terrific," she muttered. "You could make an exception."

"To be honest, I'm not sure if there is a right or wrong answer here. I know what I'd do."

"Tell me."

"I wouldn't go myself."

Does the man read minds? "Okay, but what would you do?"

"I'd tell Cullen and let it play out. But you probably

won't want to do that. Anyway, once you make your decision, I'm here if you need me."

Somehow in the midst of this bomb-dropping news, she took comfort from his words. *I'm here if you need me.*

Chapter
Twenty-one

Three days later, Annie was curled up in the den,
no closer to a decision than she'd been right after Linc's
phone call. Three days of mental wrangling, of indecision,
of fear, of wishing she had a crystal ball to gaze into the
future.

She'd considered almost every scenario: Telling Cullen
and not objecting if he chose to pursue seeing his birth
mother. Uh huh. Like she had any right to object. Not
telling him and just waiting until Cullen chose to ask or
search on his own.

Or she could go with her original thought: Go and tell
Caroline herself, who no doubt would be either terrified,
shocked, outraged, furious, or all four. And Annie
couldn't blame her for that. Some stranger shows up and
throws this explosive news into her life when years ago,
she'd done what she'd believed was the best thing for her
baby. Now that turns out to be a disaster for her. Even
with only a minimal amount of empathy, Annie would be
hard-pressed to be critical of her.

Then again, perhaps Caroline has been looking for Cullen. Perhaps she even wants him back. Selfishly, Annie
didn't want this last scenario. She had no doubt that if

Caroline decided she wanted Cullen . . . Annie didn't want to think about that possibility.

Then, of course, there was the ostrich way. Ignore the entire issue. Pretend that Caroline didn't live a few blocks away. Pretend to Cullen that she knew nothing about his birth mother. While she supposed that might work for awhile, realistically it would not last forever.

She rose to her feet. Her brain was tired and she'd been circling this for so many hours she was more confused than ever. She knew what she wanted. She wanted a happy ending for everyone. She wanted to keep Cullen. She wanted his birth mother to be a Carol Brady type— sweet, considerate, and full of seasoned wisdom, a woman who would love him but not want him. Already, she'd anticipated a protracted go-around with the Hunters over Cullen. Now, adding his birth mother and whatever she wanted was a complication with an ominous outcome.

She glanced out the window. Some leaves scattered across the yard, a harbinger of fall. In a few weeks the colors of autumn would festoon the trees with a spectacular brilliance. The color of death; dying leaves, the dying summer, all necessary for the turn of seasons. The cycles of nature always led to spring, and she desperately wanted to believe there was a spring in all of this, but in these past days she felt as if the she were mired in the adversity of winter.

Her own life had taken multiple turns in these past weeks. Some had turned out happy, but not before she'd experienced sadness and betrayal and disappointment. She would have gladly relinquished those, but like most turning points, they sometimes come with pain or calamity, and revealed a new wisdom. She wanted desperately to believe that this wavering dilemma, too, would cement into something good, something that a year from now she could look back and say, "Now, why was I so worried? All is well."

Linc always assured her Cullen was a tough kid, a survivor. Annie had certainly seen that, and she was both encouraged and amazed by his resiliency.

Caroline Sheplin was the wild card. Should she be told about Cullen, she could open her arms to him, reject him flat out, perhaps even flatly deny he was her son. . . .

"Hey, Annie, Gramps is here," Cullen said, loping into the room from the hall wearing old shorts and a "Yankees Rock" tee shirt. He frowned at her. "Hey, you okay? You look kinda bummed out."

"Just doing some heavy thinking. Tell James I'm in the den. Where are you off to?"

"I'm gonna take Jimmy and Ronnie over to Noah House. Aunt Betsy said it was okay. They want to see where I used to live."

Gramps. Aunt Betsy. How easily and happily he'd adopted those lovely family terms. "Does Linc know you're coming?"

"Nah. It's okay. He told me I could come anytime. That's what's so cool about him. You ain't ever a visitor or a stranger. See ya."

"Wait." She crossed the room and touched his shoulder. Then, before he could object, she gave him a quick kiss on the cheek.

"What was that for?" His embarrassment was the same reaction Betsy got from her boys whenever she was the least bit affectionate.

"Just because I wanted to."

"Oh." He sort of smiled, rubbing his wrist across his nose. "Can I go now?"

"Supper's at six."

"Got it." She heard the back door slam. And a few moments later, James stopped in the doorway, looked at her, and then came into the room. "You look worse than you sounded when you called."

"It has not been an easy few days."

"Cullen? He sure didn't look as if he was having a problem."

"Not that kind of problem. I wish it were as simple as some minor bit of teenage rebellion. I don't even know if I should have called you."

"Annie, you know you can always call. Vera and I are your family. Just because Richard is gone doesn't change that."

"Thank you," she said softly. "I need your advice and I know you'll be honest with me . . . and since you know the details around Cullen's birth . . ." Her voice trailed off.

"You know I'll help if I can."

And so she began, telling James what Linc had learned and then tossing out all the scenarios she'd considered and reconsidered about Cullen and his birth mother.

"Mr. McCoy must know who to call. That's very precise information."

"He wouldn't tell me the details."

"No doubt that's why he got it so quickly. Sounds as if Linc is a man who knows how to get things done." Annie didn't miss the admiration in James's voice. "Did Linc have any advice for what you should do with this?"

"He said I should give Cullen the information and then let it play out in its own time."

"And you don't agree, obviously, otherwise you wouldn't have conjured up all these possibilities."

"I don't want Cullen hurt, and since I don't know anything about this birth mother, I don't want to plunge Cullen into her life when it could be a disaster."

"So you're thinking about contacting her yourself . . . ?"

"Yes."

"To do what?"

"Just to get a sense of what she's like—"

"So you can prepare Cullen."

"I don't want him hurt, and I sure as hell don't want

her making some emotional promise that only lasts a week."

He nodded, sliding his hands into his pockets and walking the length of the room and back. "Annie, you're not trusting the history you have."

She scowled. "I don't know what you mean."

"Cullen came here to find his father without having any idea what he would find. And what did he find? He learned that the father he'd been so anxious to meet was dead. Sound familiar?"

For a long moment she didn't know what he meant, and then suddenly she did. "Oh James . . . I never thought of that," she whispered, pressing her hand to her mouth. "That's what happened to me."

He nodded. "You dealt with that. Not easy, I know, but you did, and I think it made you a stronger person. Cullen, too. He came through that just fine. And there's this. You took a huge risk when you decided to bring Cullen into our lives. That could have been a disaster. We could have demanded tests, denied and rejected him, accused you of being conned by a couple of slick strangers."

"But you knew it was true because you knew about the adoption."

"But you didn't know that at the time, Annie. You took a great risk, stepping off a cliff you might say, and doing so without having any idea whether there was a net beneath you."

"I admit to being scared of how it would turn out."

"Like you are now."

"But this . . . this, there's more at stake."

"For who?"

She looked at him for a long time, then turned away. "Now, you sound like Linc," she muttered. "But honest, this isn't about me."

"Sure it is," he said with no animosity. "You love Cullen as if he were your son, and you're terrified he'll want to go with his birth mother and that she'll want him. You know that even if we can adopt Cullen, that he will always be a major part of your life. Neither Vera nor I want that to change. But if he goes with his birth mother, you fear you'll lose him completely."

"So would you."

"We're his grandparents, and I trust that Cullen wouldn't forget that, because I trust him." He crossed to her and touched her cheek. "Annie, I didn't say Cullen would forget you. I said you're afraid he will. He worked too hard to find Richard to simply toss the woman he believed was his mother from his mind. You need to trust him. He won't stop loving you or caring about you whether he lives here in Bedford or across the country."

She searched James's face and saw the wisdom and the insight that were his hallmarks. She put her arms around him while he patted her lightly on the back. "What would I do without you?"

"Well, I certainly hope you'll never have to find out."

She hugged him and then drew back. "I should have called you three days ago and then I would have gotten some sleep."

He chuckled. "Sometimes we need to massage and worry something to a conclusion. Part of the process of figuring out the best answer."

"Linc was right. And you simply reenforced what he said. I'll tell Cullen and let him decide."

"Sounds like a plan."

That night after supper, while Cullen was having a second dish of ice cream, she told him about his birth mother.

"For real? She's, like, living here in Bedford?"

"Yes."

"Does she know about me?"

"That you're here? No."

Annie watched him closely, waiting for some indication of what he wanted to do. But he kept eating albeit a little more slowly.

"Do I have to go see her?"

"Absolutely not."

"What if she's been looking for me?"

Annie wanted to say that wasn't likely, but she honestly didn't know. "I suppose that's possible, but she is married with a family and I think she probably assumes you are with the Gallaghers."

"Bet if she knew what a scum face old man Gallagher was, she'd want me back. Bet she'd be sorry she gave me away."

"I'm sure she'd be unhappy to know how you were treated." Annie was treading very carefully. She certainly didn't want to give Cullen ideas that might be misguided.

He scooped out the last of his ice cream. "Okay. Maybe I'll ask Linc what he thinks I should do. He and I talked a lot about her."

"All right."

He slid off the stool and started out of the kitchen when suddenly he swung around. "So, like, you know, what do *you* want me to do?"

It was a different question, and it touched some deep and soft place within her. "I want you to live here with me and be my son, but more importantly I want you to be happy and content and know that a lot of people love you."

He grinned. "Yeah, I knew you'd say that." And then he ambled out of the kitchen leaving Annie with shivers down her spine. Cullen knew that whatever decision he made, she would always be there for him.

Two weeks passed and school started.

And another week.

Annie was determined not to ask questions or probe around to learn what he'd decided to do about his birth mother.

And as the summer days waned into the autumn crispness of late September, Annie became so caught up in work that she almost forgot about Caroline Sheplin.

Cullen, however, had not.

He found her house the day following his talk with Annie. He wasn't sure if he was anxious, scared, or curious. But no way was he going to bust in like he did when he went to Annie's. Now he was smarter, better prepared in his gut, wiser with how to act. No more hoping for the best; this time he expected the worst.

She had two kids who liked to yell and screech at each other, and they had a father who drove a black convertible. The mother, *his mother*, looked okay. Pretty from what he could see, nice from the way her kids kinda hung with her. Then one day when she was alone in the yard, he was sure he saw her crying.

He almost decided to keep himself a secret when he saw her cry. Almost.

He waited until one warm afternoon—Annie called it an Indian summer day—when she was there alone. She was outside watering some big pots of orange and gold flowers.

"Hi," he said, and she swung around, splashing water on her shoes.

"Oh, you scared me." She smiled, glancing over him as though he might look familiar. Her voice was soft, and a little shaky, but he liked it. He'd worn some of the clothes Annie had bought him for school, and his new Nikes. He didn't want her to think he was a dreg.

"Sorry, ma'am. You Caroline Sheplin?"

"Why yes. If you're looking for Johnny or Rose, they just went off with some friends."

"Uh, no, I wanted to talk to you."

"Well, all right." She had a nice smile and she wasn't dorky looking. She put down the watering can, giving him that patient waiting-for-the-shoe-to-drop look. Despite telling himself that it was stupid, he felt like a sack of rotting flies. She smiled again. "Shy, I see. All right. Let me guess. You're collecting for a school project? I'll have to get my purse—"

"No, ma'am, you don't need no money." And because there was no way to break this, he just said it. "I'm Cullen. Richard Hunter's son." When she looked momentarily off-balance as though she was trying to absorb his words, he added, "Your son."

Her face pinched up like the air had all been sucked out. Yeah, well, his words probably shocked, but he didn't know how to not make it so. Her earlier warm smile thinned into frost as she tried to gather herself. "Surely you're not serious. How ridiculous. You've obviously made a mistake."

"No, ma'am."

She stiffened. "I'd like you to get off my property or I'll call the police." Then she picked up the can and started toward the house.

Cullen walked behind her. "I don't want to make no trouble for you—"

"No trouble!" She swung around, the can sailing to her right to land in a bush. Hands fisted, she snapped, "You come here and say something this outrageous and then say you don't want to cause trouble?" She looked at him sternly. "I don't know who you are, young man, but you should be ashamed of yourself playing such a horrid prank. I've a good notion to get your parents' names and call them."

Her denial seemed so real that Cullen wondered if Linc and Annie had messed up. Did they get it wrong? Had he screwed up and was he gonna be on his way to another visit with the cops? But he knew that couldn't be true.

He knew—in his gut he knew—Annie and Linc would never have been wrong about this—no way would they have tossed him into a pile of crap—they wouldn't do that. This woman was who Linc and Annie said she was.

"Yes, ma'am. Her name is Annie Hunter. My grandparents are James and Vera Hunter. I can give you their phone numbers if you want." She looked more than a little frantic, and he felt bad for her. This wasn't what he wanted; he didn't want to hurt her or scare her or make her hate him. He shoved his hands into his pockets. "This ain't nothin' to prank about, ma'am," he said, bracing himself for a drench of new denials.

"I certainly agree with that," she said, as if she hoped he was going to go away. She made a shooing motion like he was a stray dog. When he simply looked at her, he expected *her* to march off in a huff, but she didn't. She kept staring at him and then she'd glance away. Finally, she said, softer now, "Go on now. I have things to do."

Cullen sighed. How much stuff did she need to know? All of it, he decided.

"The people who adopted me were Sandy and Parker Gallagher."

She stared. She didn't move.

"I was born on November tenth and I'll be fourteen."

She turned away, but not before Cullen saw the full recognition in her eyes. She knew he was telling the truth; she knew and she didn't want to know. She staggered a little and he hurried to take her arm so she didn't fall. He let her go before she could shake him off. Slowly she sat down on the porch steps. She wouldn't look at him. "How did you find me?"

"I been lookin' for awhile," he said easily, not wanting to spook her. "I got a friend who helped me. I knew who you were and where you lived for a few weeks."

"Oh God."

"Think I was sorta scared, so I was waitin' till I wasn't. But today I decided I wouldn't quit being scared 'til I met you."

She looked confused. Well, he was too.

"What do you want?" she asked, her tone hot, her voice hard. For Cullen, it cut into a ragged core of cold anger deep inside him. She didn't care about him; didn't even sound as if she was a little scared. He knew about scared. He wouldn't have been pissed if she was just scared. Hers was an ass-to-the-wall question; she thought he wanted to jam up her life.

He wanted her to say . . . something, anything about her being glad he'd found her, or even that she was glad to know he was okay.

"I asked you what you wanted," she snapped.

He shoved his hands in his pockets and said, "I been trying to figure that out. Guess I needed to see who you were and what kind of mother would give her first kid to strangers."

She sat back as if he'd slapped her. Cullen didn't waver; he figured he'd earned his anger. Maybe he would've been different if she hadn't tried to hide. If she hadn't wanted him to go away. He hated that.

When she continued to stare slack-jawed as if she expected him to take it back, to cower, to say he didn't mean it, he asked, "So how come you did?"

"What?" She seemed amazed that he was still asking. "I have a family and a life and this isn't what I want."

Like a fierce drumbeat, he said, "I wanna *know* how come you gave me away."

"It's not simple."

"Yeah it is. Either you wanted me or you didn't."

"I couldn't keep you!" Then she twisted her hands together, blurting out her words. "He was married and my parents were going to disown me for shaming the family. I didn't have any money or anyone to help me."

He looked down at his new Nikes. He thought of Linc and his brand-new grandparents and his cousins and Rocky and Annie. "I found people that helped me. How come you couldn't have looked a little harder?"

Tears filled her eyes. "I don't know."

And then his anger collapsed, leaving him only sad and disappointed. He took a step away, his feet feeling heavy.

"What are you going to do?" she asked, clearly worried.

"I'm going home."

"You're not going to tell anyone about me. You can't. You can't."

He shrugged. "I bet you're a lousy mother. I don't wanna be your kid."

She grabbed his arm. "Look, you're angry and upset, but—"

"Yeah, I'm pissed, but mostly I'm just feeling low and wormy and wishin' I'd never found you."

And with that, he pulled loose from her, turned his back, and walked across the perfectly cut grass and onto the sidewalk. He didn't turn back, he kept walking, looking forward until he was around the corner and it was safe to cry.

Annie knew the moment he walked into the kitchen that something was wrong.

"Cullen?"

He looked up, and although there were no tears, she knew he'd been crying. "I saw her. I told her."

Annie wanted to sweep him up and hold him. This was what she'd feared; this was what she'd wanted to prevent. "You should have told me. I would have gone with you."

"Nah, I had to go by myself. Just like I had to come here by myself."

And in those crystalline moments, Annie was immensely grateful that she hadn't rejected Cullen. That she hadn't allowed Richard's betrayal to chill her heart. That she hadn't embraced her ego over a young boy's hunger for a family. She was most grateful for wherever she'd found that scrap of intuitive insight.

"Cullen," she said softly. "You want to tell me what happened?"

"Maybe tomorrow or in a few days. It's kinda raw and shitty and I don't want to be babblin' like a baby."

She understood; she knew the need to absorb and make some sense of what wasn't easy to understand. She drew him into her arms and held him. "I love you very much. I want you to always know that, okay?"

He nodded, his arms creeping around her, and they simply stood silently and tight together. Then she heard him sniffle as he pulled away and turned his back. How Cullen reminded her of Linc. So careful of his emotions, so aware of not showing any vulnerability. And yet, she was as sure of Cullen's love as she was of anything. She knew without the words; she knew because she knew the boy. She touched him gently. "Tacos for supper, and your grandfather called to say he got tickets for a Yankees game this weekend." She paused to draw out the news. "At Yankee Stadium."

"We're gonna go to New York just to see a ball game?" He was so obviously awed, Annie couldn't help but grin.

"That's what he said. Your Uncle Ron and the boys are going, too."

"Really?"

"Really."

"Wow."

They stood for a moment, then Rocky ambled over and stuck his nose into Cullen's hand. He stooped down and wrapped his arms around the dog, who clearly reveled in the attention. Her heart melted, for it was truly a lovely and comforting moment, and there in the ease of her own kitchen, knowing he was safe and happy and wanting him to always know that the people who loved him would always be there for him. There in that fullness of heart she knew she wanted no more tension or sadness for Cullen that she could prevent. She knew what she had to do. She would tell James and Vera that she wouldn't fight them in their desire to adopt Cullen.

Chapter
Twenty-two

With Cullen away in New York for the baseball game, Annie wandered into his bedroom. It was boyishly messy—the bed made haphazardly, a few drawers not quite closed. On a bookshelf were pictures of Richard, and amidst a collection of baseball cards were a bunch of the state quarters he was collecting.

She looked at all the signs of teenage life and energy and told herself she was doing the right thing. Maybe it wasn't best for her, but it was best for him. Cullen was what mattered, not her need for a child. And yes, she knew that was still a need unfulfilled, and Cullen had become so much a part of her life . . . But this was about Cullen and what was best for him.

James, she realized, had pretty much focused her decision. Not trusting history was one thing, but to step in and create chaos when none existed besides her own desires—no, that wasn't right. Not for a moment had she ever thought that Cullen going to James and Vera was a bad idea; she'd never intended to fight the adoption on those grounds.

No, all her reasons were personal and about what she

wanted. She took a deep breath and one more long look at the not-quite-neat bedroom. He'd be here for plenty of nights—she knew he'd come and stay. Maybe it wasn't all that she wanted, but it was more than nothing.

She went downstairs to lock the doors. Rocky was outside, and she went to let him in when she saw a shadow to her left. She jumped, only to have Rocky cock his head to the side as if puzzled by her jitteriness.

"Good evening."

She turned quickly and the shadow moved. "Linc! How long have you been here?"

"About a half an hour."

"You should have let me know. You didn't have to sit out here."

"Courage at moments like this tends to desert me." He came full into the light. "Cullen told me about his visit to 'Caroline Sheplin' as he calls her. It was pretty rough. He wants to tell you, but I think he's afraid he'll cry because you'll cry. He told me he cares too much about you to make you cry."

Annie swallowed hard. "Just like him to worry about me, when he's the one who's been hurt. Tell me about the visit." He did and Annie was stunned at Cullen's bluntness. "He really asked her why she gave him away to strangers?"

"Yeah, a pretty lethal question. I don't think anyone needs to worry about Caroline Sheplin being a problem." He leaned back against the railing. "Sadly, this is her loss."

"It would be hard. She'd put that part of her life into the past and to suddenly be faced with it had to be pretty rattling."

"Your husband cared more than she did," Linc said, the admiration evident in his voice.

"What do you mean?"

"Remember when I told you about going to Parker Gallagher for Richard's name, and he gave me the name and address?"

"Vaguely."

"At the time I was just glad to have that for Cullen, but after he told me how the Sheplin woman acted, I realized that Richard left that information with the Gallaghers in case he was needed. To me, at least, it shows that he wasn't trying to hide. Oh sure, he wasn't running TV ads that he'd had a kid by another woman, but he wouldn't have denied it if Cullen had needed him. If he'd been alive when Cullen showed up on your porch, he wouldn't have denied him."

"I know he wouldn't have."

"He would be as proud of Cullen as his son is of him."

Annie absorbed that, finding it immensely rewarding despite his betrayal. He had cared about Cullen and what happened to him. That knowledge gave her satisfaction. "Things have worked for the best, haven't they? And just so you know, I've decided not to fight the Hunters about adopting Cullen. You were right. It was more about me than it should have been."

"Ahh."

And again silence fell between them.

Linc folded his arms.

Annie petted Rocky.

"Annie—"

"Linc—"

They both spoke at the same time, chuckled self-consciously, and then again fell silent.

"You go first," she said.

"I should say ladies first but if I don't say this, I might chicken out." He looked at her as if hoping she might run into the house and escape. "I want to start seeing you again. I've missed you and—ah, hell . . ."

She took a step closer to him. "Is there the smallest possibility that you might want to tell me that what's between us might be more than sex?"

"I can't say I love you because I don't know," he muttered, clearly uncomfortable. Rather than causing Annie anxiety, it made her love him even more. "All I know is that I don't like being away from you. I don't like laying awake at night and wondering if you'll find someone else. I don't like getting lectured by Cullen that if I hurt you he'll fry my ass."

She grinned, trying to keep her soaring heart from leaping from her chest. "Yes, well, I agree I wouldn't want to be on Cullen's bad side." She gave him a deliberately puzzled look. "So tell me, does this mean that we might have a future together?"

"Let's put it this way: I don't want to think of one without you."

"Oh, Linc . . ." She practically leaped into his arms with him catching her and holding her with a fierce tightness.

"I don't know if this will work, Annie. I want it to. God, I want it to more than I've ever wanted anything."

"Then how can we fail?"

"We can't."

It wasn't "I love you." It wasn't bouquets of love words and wedding plans or even some forever-after promise. And that was okay. It was more than okay. Linc and she were together, and she knew in her heart it would be for always. She knew, too, that he knew it too.

He kissed her deeply, drawing her close, and she reveled in his touch and in all that he was.

"Can you stay tonight?" she whispered.

"I thought you'd never ask."

He held the door while she went inside, followed by

Rocky. Then he closed it and locked it and turned out the light.

Her life had turned once again, a deeply contented turning. She knew that whatever came her way, Linc would be beside her. What more could she want?